Chancer's Almanac

R. P. Poe

Vox Stellarum

or

Voice of the Stars

An Almanac

Containing many useful facts on the life and times of
one Chancer Wylls, student, during the eventful year of
1971, 971st year of the 2nd millennium

The almanac being characteristic of a certain style is
peculiarly adapted to the delightful and ingenious practice
of Mathematics as it pertains to the study of Astronomy
and the Physical Universe

Astronomical Events and Esoterica

Calendar

28 January: Mercury is a good evening sky object

February: Venus brilliant in evening sky all month in Pisces; magnitude -4.6

April: Lyrid meteor shower peaks; radiant near Vega

13 June: Mars in Opposition - 20.79"; magnitude -2.3

August: Perseid meteor shower peaks

18 September: Mercury is a good evening sky object

October: Orionid meteor shower; prolific meteor shower associated with Halley's Comet

03 November: Taurid meteor shower peaks. (Comet Encke debris)

November: Leonids meteor shower; Comet Temple-Tuttle debris; orbital period = 33 years

03 December: Saturn at opposition in Taurus; magnitude -0.4

December: Geminid meteor shower peaks; radiant near Castor; Asteroid Phaethon visible

Formulae

Saros is a period of 223 synodic months (approximately 6585.3211 days, or 18 years and 11⅓ days), that can be used to predict eclipses of the sun and moon

The astronomical unit of time is a time interval of one day (D) of 86400 seconds

Speed of light: $c = 299\ 792\ 458\ ms-1$

Ratio of mass of Sun to that of the Earth: $(GS)/(GE) = S/E = 332\ 946\cdot0$

Heliocentric gravitational constant: $A3k2/D2 = GS = 1\cdot327\ 124\ 38 \times 1020\ m3\ s-2$

Winter

/ˈwintər/: the coldest season of the year, in the
northern hemisphere from December to February and in the
southern hemisphere from June to August

Old English, of Germanic origin; related to Dutch
winter, German *wintar*, Swedish *vinter,* and possibly to *wet*
or *'the wet season'*.

the period from the winter solstice to the vernal equinox

Who knows what intimacies our eyes may shout,
What evident secrets daily foreheads flaunt,
What panes of glass conceal our beating hearts?

-Emily Dickinson

Chapter One

On the eve of the new millennium, fate visited
Chancer Wylls and I was once again orphaned to the
world, twenty-nine years from the day I was born. The year
predicted to begin in disaster instead ended that way. The
dice-thrown odds of my father's life had finally come up
snake eyes.

I knew nothing of that as I followed the mist-touched
streets toward my dank apartment. I had just left an over-
warm room crowded with smiling people all celebrating
the coming New Year. All, that is, except for me. I had
nothing to celebrate. Instead, I found myself pressed
against the living room wall while my ex-fiancé and his
new love stepped through the door. I turned to leave and a
stab of pain shot through the bruised rib he had left me.
Giving a quick nod to the host, I slipped unseen out the
back.

Pulling onto the dark stretch of road, I tried to put the
scene I had just left out of my mind. On the last night of
the year I wanted to forget my mistakes. Captured in the
car headlights, the roadside trees vibrated before a chill
wind.

All at once a figure appeared before me, his form
draped by a hooded poncho. I swerved, slamming my foot
on the brake pedal and stopping only feet away. He pointed
his gnarled cane into the sky, his free hand raised in
blessing, his voice song-like. I could just make out his
words above the wind.

> The darkness it nears, the fire it comes,
> Fire and darkness, darkness and fire,
> Follow your path or the land will burn!

He disappeared into the night. I blinked, unsure of
what I'd seen or if I'd seen anything at all. Gripping the
steering wheel, I angled back onto the street.

Moments later I pulled into the parking lot outside my apartment. I sat puzzling over the strange encounter when I spotted my grandparent's car parked at the curbside. A wave of dread passed through me. What possible reason could they have for visiting so late, especially on New Year's Eve? Did they somehow sense the shame of my breakup? Had my grandfather's cancer returned? My mind raced with possible explanations.

My grandparents had mostly raised me after my father decided he was not up to rearing a child alone. Having already done their time as parents, Beatrice and Penton signed on again when my dad took a position in the physics department of the local university. That was after he had spent a month trekking across Australia in search of the mother I never knew. He said he did it for me but I knew better. He could never face up to losing her.

Knowing my grandmother, Beetie, had a spare key, I hurried up the stairs before pausing at the doorway, afraid to turn the knob. Whatever the reason for their appearance, the last thing I wanted was for them to feel sorry for me. I'd seen enough of that already. I took a breath and swung open the door. There they stood in the hallway, their faces drawn, my grandmother with her purse pressed to her chest. At the sight of me she burst into tears and my heart sank. My grandfather sighed and put an arm around her, waving me toward them.

I knew that instant something had happened to Chancer. The look on their faces told it all. I stood still, my mind filling with him, his wrinkled clothes, his forgetfulness and, most of all, his mathematics obsession, endearing but exasperating. At a young age his gift for mathematics had become obvious and he'd had no trouble getting into college. That's where he met my mother, his first true love. She ended up leaving him but he never spoke so much as a single unkind word against her that I can remember, although Beetie said he had plenty of reason.

2

That first year at college something happened to him, something he would never talk about. The world of ideas became his refuge, physics his vocation. After I arrived, he did his best to be a father but it seemed I took care of him as much as he did me. So, I started calling him by his first name. I would find him in his study at all hours, grappling with this equation or that theorem. I'm not a math person so I understood little of what he said the few times he bothered to explain. My job was to make sure he ate the occasional meal and left for work on time. Even then I sensed his obsession would someday be his undoing.

So I looked at Beetie and Pen for a moment, letting the memory linger before I walked to where they stood, putting my arms around them both. Beetie sniffed and took a breath before pulling away. She was always the strong one. Seeing her cry was so out of the ordinary I braced myself for what was to come. As usual, Pen stepped aside to let her speak.

Tegan, sweetheart, I don't know how to…
-I interrupted.
It's about Chancer, isn't it? Something's happened.
The roads were slick with all this mist and fog and he…
-She stopped, unable to finish. I guessed at her meaning.
He had an accident?
-She nodded.
But he's alright, isn't he?
-Pen gave his head a slight shake and looked away, his eyes glistening.
He's in a hospital, then.
-Beetie stepped toward me.
Tegan, you have to understand…
Where is he, Beetie?
-She took hold of my hand.
Oh, sweetie, it was a very bad wreck and…

3

-I held up my hand.

No, wait, Beetie! What hospital is it? Why won't you tell me?

-Her voice dropped to a whisper.

Tegan, sweetheart…

-I saw something in her eyes and my thoughts froze.

Chancer is gone?

-I heard my voice, my words, yet nothing about them seemed real. Beetie sensed my disbelief.

We can't believe it either, Tegan.

Oh, Beetie, Pen, he can't be, not now, not after we got things straightened out.

I know, sweetheart, it's so unfair to all of us, but especially to you.

This can't be right. There has to be some sort of mistake. Are you sure it was him?

Oh, Tegan…

How can he be gone, Beetie?

-My voice seemed not my own. He'd been away many times before. I wondered how this time could feel so different. Beetie squeezed my hand.

It's a shock for us too, sweetheart. We were so looking forward to his visit.

He was on his way here?

-I stared at them, confused by her words. Pen nodded and I took a step back, trying to find some foothold for my thoughts.

But why would he come here so late, Pen? He couldn't have been coming from a party. He hates that sort of thing.

He wanted to surprise you for your birthday, Tegan. But you know him and the clock.

-Chancer was never on time. At the thought, I let out a laugh then caught myself. They stared at me as I put a shaking hand to my mouth. A moment later their faces dissolved behind a curtain of tears.

4

A week after the funeral Beetie's voice called through my door, followed by a light knocking. The sound reached my ears but failed to register as I lay on the couch staring at the ceiling, my mind stuck in some sort of limbo. Normally, I would have been out on a Saturday morning taking a walk or running errands. Instead, the tape of my strange life ran over and over through my head like a bad movie. The knock came again but louder, more of a flat pounding. I turned my eyes toward the hallway as Beetie's voice called out, muffled by the door but still forceful.

I know you're in there, Tegan. You've had your time of moping around but enough is enough. You get yourself off that couch and answer the door this minute, you hear?

-I turned my head toward the foyer knowing she would never give up. Then I pulled myself up and shuffled across the room. She pretended to look angry as the door swung open but I could see in her eyes a mixture of hope and worry. She lifted a tattered book from her purse, offering it to me.

Go ahead and take a look.

-I cradled the fragile-looking cover in my palms.

What is it?

It belonged to your father.

But where was it? I went all through the house.

-I had insisted on going through his belongings alone, trying to make sense of what little I knew of him. Chancer had never been one to talk about himself. And as an astronomer he had often been away logging time on some huge telescope in a remote part of the world. That's one reason Beetie and Pen had become like parents to me. She squeezed my hand.

I forgot about the book, Tegan. You see, I'd hidden it away. Your father gave it to me for safe keeping when you were a baby. His life was so unpredictable back then. He wanted me to give it to you if something happened to him.

But as time slipped by and life seemed to settle down, I put the thought out of mind.

-I spoke under my breath.

And then something did happen.

-She sighed, nodding her head.

A month or so ago he asked me about it so I gave it back to him. He had it in the car the night of the accident. He planned to give you the book as a birthday gift.

A Poor Student's Almanac is an odd title. Where did he find it?

-The meaning escaped me as I stood there, still in a sort of daze. Beetie tapped the cover.

He wrote it, sweetheart.

-I held up the small book, a sign of the zodiac scrawled across the front.

Chancer wrote this? What's it about?

He made me promise not to read it so I never did. All I'm sure of is that he wanted you to have it. After you read it you can tell me about it if you want to. Right now I have to pick up Pen at the doctor's office.

-My heart sank at the thought of more bad news.

Is he sick again, Beetie?

Don't you bother about him, Tegan. He's tough as an old post. It's you that concerns me. I want you to start taking better care of yourself and stop worrying me so.

As I watched her step through the door, an image of Chancer squinting into the eyepiece of a telescope came to me. Next to him a tracking motor whirred, mixing with the bell-shake sound of chirping crickets. A sky scrubbed free of clouds stretched above us, stars and planets littering the hazy darkness. Somehow, he seemed part of it and it part of him.

Without taking his eye from the lens, he motioned toward the east where a bright point of light flickered above the horizon like a blue flame. I waited for an explanation and scanned the sky trying to guess at his thoughts, knowing how he loved to keep me in suspense. Finally, he stepped back and peered at the star.

That star is Sirius, also called the Dog Star because it's in the constellation Canis Major. Sirius is the brightest star in our sky other than the sun, Tegan, and one of the closest. That light you see is about eight years old.

How can light be as old as me when I'm looking at it right now?

It can because it's eight light years from the earth, so the light takes that long to get here.

-He swept his arm across the sky.

Some of the other stars are hundreds of light years away. The light you see from those stars happened before your great-great grandfather was even born. When you look up, you're looking into the past. Isn't that something, Tegan?

-I stared at the flashing point of light and nodded, feeling the warmth of his hand on my shoulder, hearing the excitement in his voice. He led me to the telescope, steadying me over the eyepiece as a potato-like asteroid slowly tumbled across the lens. Not long after, I wandered off to bed. He spent the rest of that night tracking the asteroid, barely making it to his class the next morning.

-I pressed the thin book between my fingers, trying to patch together those scattered memories of him, wondering about the man that was my father. He had been in and out of my life so often, available yet somehow unknowable. I hoped the book would help me understand him. Thumbing through the pages, I decided at that moment I would tell his story if I could.

Chapter Two

In the early part of the twentieth century Albert Einstein developed a theory that a body in motion alters the area around it, bending space to its image, sending forth ripples of attraction at whatever comes near. Chancer had become obsessed with Einstein's theory, familiarizing himself with the peculiarities and struggling to master the mathematics of gravity, time and space. He felt somewhere within the concept lay his future.

Equations floated before him, tormenting his thoughts as he drove his rusted-out sedan from San Antonio to Houston days after the start of the New Year. He squinted at the passing street signs. Beyond the windshield, gray clouds skimmed the ragged horizon. Heading for a modest house set along a broad boulevard lined with palms, the home of his father's mother, he tried to banish the problem long enough to consider his future. His life was about to change in ways he could scarcely imagine. Having placed out of a semester and a half of coursework, he was starting college.

On the seat next to him sat a small notebook. Tucked inside, a sheaf of papers held his scribbled attempts to master Einstein's equations. He glanced at the thin book, running his fingers across the blank cover. Days before, he had decided to start a journal in the form of an almanac chronicling his first year of college, in his case conveniently starting in January. The Romans had named the month after Janus, the god of beginnings, often pictured with two heads, one looking to the past, the other to the future. He wondered what might be in store for him in this new undertaking.

A wide tree-lined avenue appeared, pulling him from his thoughts. Surrounded by sprawling live oaks, their intertwined branches black against the afternoon haze, his grandmother's red brick home came into view on a slight rise halfway down the block. Piles of leaves smoldered at the curbside. The acrid smoke carried memories of past visits as he turned into the narrow driveway, pulling past the sidewalk and up the short slope.

Grabbing his duffle bag, he made his way up the sidewalk to a narrow set of concrete stairs leading to the front door and the broad, screened-in veranda just beyond. He paused then stepped through. Beyond the veranda, the house opened into a wide living room, its hardwood floor covered by a red and blue oriental rug. Antiques from past plantation-owning relations crowded every corner. He stood listening to the sounds of the old house and breathing in the familiar smell. Moments later his grandmother appeared across the room. Jumping at the sight of him, she scolded him in her sing-song southern drawl.

Chancer Wylls, didn't your father teach you to announce yourself when you come into someone's home? You nearly took the life right out of me.

I'm sorry Gammie. I was just enjoying being back in this house.

-She nodded and fanned herself.

Well, alright then. It's not like I wasn't expecting you, although I thought you'd be here some while ago.

I guess I lost track of the time.

I believe I've heard that before.

-She eyed him for a moment.

Lord Almighty, Chancer, did you sleep in those clothes?

What? No, I didn't sleep in them.

I've never seen so many wrinkles on one person.

They always look this way, Gammie.

If there's one thing I do before I die, I'm going to teach you how to wash and iron your own things. I'll see if we can get Sister Louise to come help.

-Chancer tried to smooth out his rumpled pants.

Is she here for a visit?

Don't you remember? She moved here after your Uncle Van Horn passed on. I suppose it's been almost a year now.

-Gammie's sister had bought a house just down the street and the two widows spent most evenings at one or the other's home, sharing cooking duties and keeping each other company.

I guess I do.

She's so looking forward to seeing you, Chancer. Are you hungry, sugar?

Not really, Gammie.

But look how thin you are. I'll bet you don't eat enough to feed a bird.

-She nodded toward the kitchen.

I just took a batch of cookies out of the oven. Go on and help yourself but don't eat too many. Sister is coming over a little later to join us for dinner.

An hour later, Chancer climbed the stairs of his grandmother's garage apartment, depositing his duffle bag in the bedroom and hurrying out the door. He wanted to see the campus before nightfall. As he followed the broken sidewalk, Einstein's theories again filled his mind. He picked through the equations step by step, hopeful that he might actually understand them.

Passing a row of stout palm trees lining the esplanade, he turned onto a side street and made his way along a shade-darkened tunnel of oaks, their black limbs stretching above the roadway. Dappled shadows rippled before him, dim beneath the winter sun. A moment later, he came upon a busy intersection.

He scurried across, the beige arches of the university appearing before him all at once, rising above a thick wall of shrubs marking the edge of campus. Slipping through a narrow opening, he stepped onto a broad lawn adjacent to the physics building. Porticos framing two sides the grass-covered mall stretched into the distance. He checked the campus map, feeling the excitement that comes with a new beginning.

As he moved across the open space, the shouts and cheers of an unseen crowd echoed between the buildings. He paused to listen, the voices growing louder. A moment later a group of students appeared to his right, rounding a corner and heading straight for him. Carrying signs and placards reading "Hell No We Won't Go" and "U. S. Out of Viet Nam Now", they chanted a steady rhythm of words that tumbled between the buildings.

Current events had rarely held his attention. He preferred the self-contained world of math and astronomy. Then the realization he might be drafted had settled into his consciousness like a cloud across the sun. The lottery determining who must join in the war effort loomed only months away.

The crowd stopped as a long-haired man carrying a bullhorn turned and shouted into the air. A dozen men stepped forward, forming a circle and pulling white cards from their shirt pockets. Chancer assumed they were draft cards. A lighter appeared and he watched as the men held the cards to the flame before dropping them into a pile. A moment later a group of women ran forward, pulling several bras from a brown paper bag, dousing them with lighter fluid and tossing them onto the fire. Cheers erupted across the crowd.

Chancer stood by, waiting for what might happen next when one of the women broke from the group, making straight for him. He froze in place, mesmerized by her intense gaze and flowing red hair. She seemed an image of Botticelli's Venus. Stopping feet from him, she nodded back toward the crowd.

Aren't you going to join us?
-His eyes grew wide.
You want me to burn… uh… to… you know?

11

-Unsure of his intent, she eyed him before tucking an auburn curl behind her ear and offering her hand.

I'm Elizabeth Byerson but everyone calls me Byes.

Why do they call you that?

I hate my real name.

-He shook her hand then glanced past her, the crowd already disappearing beneath the arches of the portico.

Aren't you going with them?

-She followed his gaze before turning back to him.

You're in favor the war?

What? No, I'm not for the war.

If you're against it, why don't you join the protest?

I didn't say I was against it.

Well, which are you, for or against?

-He stared at his hands as if they held the answer, unable to match her intense gaze.

I don't know.

How can you not know? There's nothing more important, especially when you could end up getting shot at.

I don't like to think about it.

You and about a million other guys. What will you do if you get drafted?

-He looked up at her, finally feeling he had solid ground to stand on.

Based on the cut off number for the lottery last year, the odds are zero point three four two four that my birth date will be selected.

You sound like a math text book.

-He squinted at her, wondering if she meant to insult him.

I like math if that's what you mean.

Math won't help much if your number gets picked.

I understand the odds.

One in three doesn't sound so great to me.

-He stared at the ground, lost in the grim reality of the thought.

No, it's not so good considering the potential result.

-She bent toward him, peering into his face.

You never did tell me your name.

I'm Chancer Wylls. People call me Chancer.

Do they? What a surprise.

I just meant… never mind.

Where'd you get a name like that?

I got sick after I was born, real sick. The doctors didn't think I'd make it but I did, so my Uncle Trewin decided that pure chance had beaten the odds. After that, he started calling me Chancer. The name just stuck.

Well, I'm glad lady luck was with you.

You are?

Otherwise we wouldn't be here now, would we?

-She nodded toward a nearby bench.

Will you sit with me for a moment, Chancer Wylls?

I was just on my way to…

It's only for a minute.

-She stepped up to the bench and sat, patting the space next to her. Chancer stood by, shifting from foot to foot. She looked up at him.

Aren't you going to sit?

-He stopped and stared at the bench.

Yeah, okay, sure, I can do that.

-Perching on the edge, he tried without effect to smooth the wrinkles crisscrossing his pants. She watched him for a moment.

Chancer, this is not a job interview. We're just getting to know each other a little. Are you okay with that?

-He gave up on his pants and looked up, her lapis-colored eyes filling his mind, and for a moment he felt as if a warm blue sea had washed over him. Water-soaked words floated about him in nonsensical order. He blinked, finally managing to find his voice.

I'm not much good at making conversation.

I don't care much for small talk either. I want to hear about you, what you like, what you don't like. Say whatever comes to mind.

-Her tone seemed reassuring.

I don't know what to say. I just got here. I was on my way to the physics building.

So that's why you sound like a textbook. You're a physics major.

-The ground beneath him began to feel solid again.

I'm hoping to get into the astronomy program.

I knew you were a man of mystery. You're a stargazer.

A stargazer is a fish, genus Astroscopus.

Actually, I meant it in the poetic sense, Chancer.

Oh, right, you mean gazing at the night sky. Speaking of stars, I heard there's an old iron observatory on the roof of the physics building with a sixteen inch reflecting telescope. You can reserve time to use it. That's where I was going when I saw you burning your... you know.

-She chuckled at him.

They're called bras, Chancer.

I know.

What did you mean when you said you just got here?

I'm just about to start classes here at the university.

That's why you looked a bit lost when I first saw you. You've never been to campus before?

Not until today.

Then you need someone to show you around, don't you?

I don't really know anyone.

You know me, Chancer. Let me be your guide.

You would do that for me?

If you say my name I will.

What?

Say my name, Chancer. Call me by my name. I want to hear you say it.

You'll give me a tour around campus, Byes?

I'll be your personal guide if you let me, Chancer Wylls.

Alright, but only if you'll go with me to see the telescope.

-She nodded and stood.

We have a deal. I'd better get back to my friends. They're probably wondering what happened to me. Meet me here at ten tomorrow.

-She disappeared around the corner. Chancer looked after her, the feel of her name still on his lips.

Chapter Three

I walked into my office and felt the familiar tension surround me like a fog. After all that had happened outside of work, I suppose I expected change there as well, change for the better, but the simmering resentments, the blaming, the suspicions wasted no time in reasserting themselves. I chided myself for such childish self-deception.

Wondering how much longer I would be willing to put up with it, I set my things on the desk. A single card of condolence sat near the edge, signed by our student worker, Anita, the only woman in the office besides me. Other than her, none of my fellow budget-cut survivors offered any words of welcome, sympathy or greeting, preoccupied as they were with keeping their jobs. I understood their plight and how the loss of trust poisons relationships.

Instead of dwelling on the bad situation, I vowed to focus on the students. After all, they were the reason I had stayed so long, especially the student veterans. Older and more mature than the majority of college students, their determination to succeed and their earnestness touched my heart. They worried me as well. Some of them seemed to vibrate with a barely-contained anger.

I had just begun going through evaluations of in-coming students when the new director, a college vice-president, walked into my office. Having been given the job of overseeing our program on top of his other responsibilities, he was less than interested in our plight and instead wanted to have as little to do with us as he could manage. On top of that, he had the pompous air of an academic enamored with his title and position.

Our previous director had left after an unfounded student complaint reached the office of the college president and the administration refuse to back her, instead siding with the student. The new director's main goal was to avoid any such problems by assuming our office was at fault even when a complaint had no merit. He never bothered to ask us our side of the story, kowtowing to students being the safer course. Needless to say, his attitude killed office morale. I motioned for him to sit but he remained standing, launching into what he had to say without so much as a hello.

I understand you've been approaching faculty on your own.

-The implication that I needed permission to do my job annoyed me but I kept it to myself. I smiled as if he had given me a compliment.

I talk to faculty all the time, especially if there's a question or concern about a student. It's part of the job.

I'm not talking about when they ask a question. The problem is you making unsolicited contacts with professors.

There's a problem?

I wouldn't be here if there wasn't.

-I dropped the friendly demeanor, seeing it would do no good.

I talk with anyone I need to when I believe it's in the best interest of the student.

Your job is to answer questions not set policy.

I have no interest in setting policy. I'm here to assist students the best way I can.

Then your way, as you call it, will need to change.

-I searched my memory for some clue as to what he was going on about but came up with nothing.

What specifically is this about?

I was informed that you have talked to a number of faculty about services for our student veterans.

-I was less than surprised someone in the office had fingered me as a problem, considering the sinking ship we were all on. My intent to hide my anger began to fall away.

You were informed? That's an interesting choice of words.

What do you have to say for yourself?

I consider it good practice to collaborate with my colleagues. I'm concerned about the needs of the veterans. I see no problem.

Like I said, you answer questions not set policy. Besides, the professors are not your colleagues.

What do you mean?

They're highly trained professionals.

-I hated having to defend myself but saw no alternative.

I'm licensed by two state boards. That took years of training.

A professional license means nothing in a college setting.

In the real world it means I could open a private practice if I chose to. Most of my friends have already.

Faculty members have doctorates. You don't.

-I felt a growing anger at his pompous condescension.

This is not a competition. We all have a job to do and as a professional I'm obligated to do what I judge best for the welfare of these students.

You've proved your judgment is faulty. From this point on you'll stop talking to faculty unless you have permission.

-My frustration with the rampant elitism, the treatment of my co-workers, my concern for the students all came rushing at me, sweeping me along. I spoke without thought.

I can't operate like that. I can't ask for permission for every move I make. I use my professional judgment from the time I arrive until the time I leave every day. I sign my name to reports and forms, documents that could be used in court. I analyze diagnostic evaluations, hypothesize about the cause of a student's difficulty and determine a course of action to address the issue. I determine what's best for each individual based on my judgment of the facts. No one but me is responsible for those decisions. And if I fail to uphold my professional ethics and standards, I can lose my license.

You can do all that and not talk to faculty.

These students don't exist in a bubble. What happens outside this office affects them and their chances for success in countless ways. Do you have any idea how hard it is for a student to walk into this office for the first time, to go through the testing, to ask their professors to accommodate their disability?

-He stepped toward the door.

I've wasted enough time here. From this moment on you will need written permission to talk to anyone outside this office. That permission will come from me and no one else. Do I have your word you will abide by that?

You want my word? I'll give you my word. In fact, I'll give you two. I quit!

-Grabbing my purse, I brushed past him.

An hour later, I pulled out a chair and sat across the kitchen table from Beetie. Unable to look her in the face, I took a ragged breath and stared at the floor as my mind bounced from one dark thought to the next. Was I completely incompetent? Did I deserve all the bad that had happened? I sat wondering what grim fate still awaited me when my thoughts ground to a halt, stalled by uncertainty. I had little idea what I would I do next.

Beetie tapped the tabletop with her fingers, eying me the way one opponent does another, sizing me up, figuring what I'm made of. I'd seen the look before. While I knew she would be on my side no matter what, I also knew she would take me to task if I needed it. I sat there wishing I could read her thoughts but believing I had done what I had to and would do it over again if necessary. I looked up at her. After a moment, she leaned across the table, her face inches from mine.

Tell me what you think of your decision now that you've had a chance to mull it over a bit.

Well, I… there were so many…

-She sat back and pointed at me.

Don't try to dance around it or cover it over with niceties, Tegan. Just say what you think, how you feel, right now.

-I took a breath, trying to find the right words as I peered into her eyes.

I had to quit, Beetie. I saw no choice, no other way.

-She studied me a moment then slapped her palm against the table.

Well then, you did the right thing. Leave it at that.

-I stared at her, surprised by her response.

But, Beetie, I've never up and left a job before.

Don't beat yourself up with second-guesses and what-if's, Tegan. We do what we have to when the situation calls for it and this one did. Those ivory tower nitwits can continue their adolescent shenanigans, and you know they will, so you're best off forgetting them and looking to the future.

But what will I do, Beetie?

Another job will come along.

But I have bills to pay. I don't have enough saved to live on for very long.

Your father didn't leave you anything?

Not enough to make a difference. You know how he was at managing money.

You'll come live with us then.

-The thought of moving in with my grandparents terrified me. In my view there was no greater sign of defeat. I had to think fast.

I appreciate the offer but you're right, Beetie. I'll find a job soon.

Well, you're always welcome to stay with us as long as you like, Tegan. I hope you know that.

-I heard footsteps behind me as Pen and his older brother walked into the kitchen. No two brothers could have been less alike. Patient to a fault, Pen never had a hard word for anyone or anything. Trewin, on the other hand, spoke his mind without hesitation or any hint he cared how it might sound. He should have been named Frank. Pen circled the table to face me.

What's this I hear? Are you coming to stay with us, Tegan?

-Trewin snorted as he moved next to him.

You must be hard up if you want to shack up with these two cadavers.

-Beetie glared at him.

You're older than the both of us, Trewin. At least you look the part. Besides, you don't know a thing about it. Tegan has hit on hard times.

Hard time is living with a couple of old people when you're still a girl yourself. What in God's name could justify such a drastic, not to mention depressing, decision?

She's out of a job, if you must know. And she's not depressed.

Ah, but she will be soon, Beetie, she will be soon.

-She ignored him.

And she most certainly is not a girl anymore, although she'll always be Little Tegan to me.

-I hated when they talked about me like I was nowhere in sight. I raised my hand.

I'm here in case you haven't noticed and I can speak for myself. The truth is I haven't said I'm coming to stay here. Beetie and I were just talking about my situation.

-Pen sat at the end of the table, leaning his elbows on the edge.

You remember that this house was built by my father, your great-grandfather, and that he even brought over the walnut paneling from the family homestead in Wales to make it feel more like home?

-I'd heard the story a hundred times but I nodded like I needed reminding.

The bed in your room, the room we've always kept for you, belonged to your great-grandmother. And this table came from Beetie's grandmother. You remember that too, don't you, Tegan?

I remember, Pen.

-He took my hand.

I'm saying so because I want you to know you will never be alone as long as Beetie and I are still breathing, hard times or not. This is your home too, Tegan.

-I felt the tears welling in my eyes and thought I might cry but Trewin wrestled a chair from beneath the table, bumping it across the tiles and twirling it around. He squinted at me and sat, his thin arms wrapping around the back.

We Wylls have had our share of bad luck but, damn it, we get through it. Isn't that right, Tegan?

-I managed a nod before he started in again.

The English coal company took our grandfather's home so he came here and started over. The Great Depression forced our father from the newspaper business so he got into advertising. Then he built this house. Pen and me went bust in the oilfields twice but here we are. And you'll get through this damn mess too, Tegan, you wait and see. Are you with me?

Yes, Trewin, I hear you.

In the meantime, I recommend liberal quantities of beer, just to keep your strength up, you see. Speaking of drink, all this talk has given me a mighty thirst. Beetie, while you're up, how about a round for the Wylls boys and their pretty relation. Grab one for yourself too.

-She eyed him the way a cat does a dog just before swiping a paw across its nose.

As you could see if you bothered to notice, I'm sitting down. Get your own beer.

-I sighed and went to the refrigerator, pulling out an armful of bottles and setting them on the table. At that moment, I thought my life had hit its low point. I was wrong, of course.

Chapter Four

An image of my father, young yet somehow older than his years, passed in and out of my thoughts as I stepped into the small frame house he had called home for a decade or more. I had been shocked to find he had paid off the loan, knowing how he managed the rest of his life. Only blocks from the college, the location had allowed him to ride a bicycle to work most days. He had never been much good with cars. The bike's wide tires, faded frame and rusted basket seemed a perfect match for his disheveled manner.

Surveying the spare living room, I found the easy chair and sofa still piled with boxes and folders just as I had left them. A squat table and reading lamp sat in between. A photo of me, Pen and Beetie around the dining table still hung next to the kitchen doorway. Planning to sell the house, I had boxed up most of his belongings other than the picture. That was when I still had a job. Now the two bedroom bungalow would be my home.

I moved through the kitchen, out the back door and onto the square landing that overlooked the tiny backyard. A dusty alleyway ran just beyond. Across the alley, houses of a similar make stretched into the distance along the next street. Piano music drifted on the chill breeze. I leaned against the porch rail and closed my eyes, letting the melody wash over me. Then a voice sounded to my right.

Do you like Bach or are you just sleep-deprived like me?

-I turned to find a man standing on the back steps of the house next door, a steaming cup in his hand. Short and slight, with brown hair and a thin beard, he wore paint-spattered fatigues and a tattered denim shirt. He raised the mug toward me.

It's a bit chill out. Would you like some coffee?

-I studied him a moment, wary of the neighborhood, and absently reached for my bruised side. But he seemed friendly enough so I nodded and turned toward the house. By the time I reached his front porch, he had the door open and a second mug in hand. He passed me the coffee and gestured inside.

If you're brave enough to enter this war zone, I'll show you what I'm working on. Please disregard the massive dust balls lurking beneath the couch. I'm waiting out my roommate, hoping he'll finally do his share of the cleaning. If I can stand the mess, that is.

-Deciding he was harmless, I stepped through the door, the spare notes of Bach's Goldberg Variations now louder. The layout of the place seemed a mirror image of Chancer's house but instead of furniture, it had paintings, easels and blank canvases stacked against the walls. A mound of multicolored clay pots filled one corner. Pieces of metal sculpture sat piled in another.

-I followed him down the hall and into an open room that stood empty except for a large canvas propped on a heavy, wooden easel. The face of a young girl stared out from the painting, her eyes luminous and haunting, seeing yet unseeing, as if held by some sort of inner vision. I looked about the room, finding other portraits on the walls, all equally strange and beautiful. As I turned to him, a worried look spread across his face.

I know, I know, they're too bleak, too depressing. People say I'm overly serious, that I need to lighten up.

People are wrong.

-He adjusted his glasses and looked from one canvas to the other.

Maybe I should add some flowers, or a puppy or something.

They're amazing just as they are. Don't change a thing.

By the way, I'm Vincent.

-I shook his hand, studying his elf-like face.

I'm Tegan, your new neighbor.

I was sad to hear about the man that lived there. We didn't talk often but he seemed like a good person although a bit strange. He was obsessed with Bach and would borrow an album then forget where he left it. I went to search for a lost album once and he started in on explaining the mathematical qualities of music. I was lost after the third word. Did you know him?

He was my father.

-He stared at me, his eyes growing wide.

Oh Lordy, I'm so sorry. I'm always saying the wrong thing.

You couldn't have known.

-He paced about the floor.

But I should've guessed. You look just like him.

-I was touched by his comment. It had been years since anyone had said that to me.

Do I?

Well, younger and prettier of course, and with red hair. I'm sure it must have been a shock, happening so sudden like it did. Is there anything I can do for you?

-Hoping to change the subject, I pointed to the canvases.

You can tell me about your paintings.

-He looked about the room, waving his hand toward the unframed canvases, some complete, some still in progress.

How nice of you to ask, Tegan. You'd be surprised how seldom anyone does. These are for my thesis show, if I make it that far.

What do you mean by 'if I make it that far'?

Oh, why did I say that? I shouldn't have said anything. It's just that fate can be so unkind. Now I sound like I'm fishing for sympathy, don't I?

Why would you do that?

Pity is the last thing I want. I want to be a person, just like anyone else.

I don't understand.

I want my art to be judged on its own, not on me and my problems.

I've already said what I think of your work.

-In spite of my initial reticence, I liked him and felt a kinship of sorts, as if we were tethered by our mutual misfortune.

I don't want people feeling sorry for me either, Vincent. What happened to my father just happened. I won't let it define who I am.

That's what I'm trying to say, Tegan. I'm not going to let one little problem make me into a person I'm not.

What sort of little problem?

-He grimaced and gave his head a slight shake.

Actually, it's not so little.

Okay, it's a big problem and you're just about to tell me about it.

Tegan, do you promise not to pity me?

I promise, Vincent.

Alright, then, here goes. I have something called Usher's syndrome.

That sounds serious.

It can be.

-I felt sick at the thought of someone else in my world dying. But I had to know one way or the other.

Are you going to… ?

No, it's not fatal, at least not in the literal sense.

I'm glad for that.

Oh, I shouldn't complain. I have the milder form that doesn't show up until a person is in their teens, or in my case, an adult.

Is it painful?

Not in the usual way.

In what way is it, then?

-He sighed and looked about the room again.

I'm going blind, Tegan.

-I gasped.

But you're an artist.

That's what happens with Usher's syndrome.

-His words fell into my thoughts piecemeal, as if some part of me hoped to escape their meaning. Sensing my trouble, he went on.

Over time your visual field becomes smaller and smaller until there is no more. You lose your hearing too, and sometimes your balance.

-I leaned toward him, for the first time noticing the tiny hearing aids hidden behind his ears. I tried to imagine how an artist would feel to receive such news.

You'll lose your sight *and* your hearing?

That's how I found out. I kept having to sit closer and closer in class. And I kept tripping and falling at the worst possible times. Now I use a cane whenever I leave the house.

How did you catch it?

Usher's isn't like that. It's an inherited disorder. People like me may not even know they have it until something goes wrong. The good news is the hearing aids work and probably will, more or less, for awhile longer. The thought of never hearing Bach again is almost as bad as losing my sight, so I try to focus on my work.

But how will you?

I can still see enough to paint. I'll finish my degree. At least I hope I will. I can't think past that right now. Enough talk about me. I want to hear about you. But first, I know just the thing to help.

-He waved me to follow and we made our way back down the hall to a small kitchen. Tiny blue and white octagon tiles covered the uneven floor. He pulled an unmarked clay bottle from beneath the cabinet, pouring a liberal amount into my coffee. Then he did the same for himself. I stared at my cup.

What is this?

It's homemade brandy, a gift from my French grandmother.

-Taking a sip, I felt the warm glow fill my chest. I sat back, settling into the chair as Vincent leaned his elbows on the table and stared at me, his eyebrows raised in expectation.

Okay, Tegan, your turn.

-I looked around the room, considering what to say and what to keep to myself. Then all at once I felt I could tell him whatever came to me despite having just met him. The feeling puzzled me until I realized he had no hold over me the way a close friend does. We barely knew each other. That and his disarming manner, along with the brandy, had loosened my tongue. I took another sip then leaned toward him.

You already know about my father. A week after he died, I left my job at the university. I grabbed my things and walked right out the door.

You just quit?

I've never done anything like that before.

Why did you do it?

The place had become intolerable and I felt I had had no choice but to leave. That's when I decided to move here. Money was tight even before I quit, so I needed to cut back on my expenses.

Mercy, that's a lot of bad news to deal with all at once.

Two weeks before that, my fiancé threw me against the kitchen table, nearly breaking a rib.

Good Lord, Tegan, that's terrible.

-I nodded, managing a crooked smile, the memory still bitter in my throat.

He was careful to avoid my face so nobody would know what he did unless I told them. Of course, I was too ashamed to say anything.

Maybe you need a different fiancé.

Not long after that I left him.

Fate hasn't been so kind to either of us has she, Tegan?

29

Hardly, but is it fate or luck of the draw, Vincent, destiny or chance?

Are you asking me if I believe in fate, that things are predestined?

Or is life just a roll of the dice, either you're lucky or you're not?

Oh, this is heavy stuff, Tegan. We need a philosophy major to help us. Here, have some more cognac.

-He refilled our mugs as I waved my hand around the room.

I don't see any philosophers handy, Vincent.

So right you are, Tegan. Since it's just you and me, here's what I have to say. Things do happen by chance, good things and bad. On the other hand, you can sometimes see that your world is going to go a certain way, as if it was written in some unseen book and there's not much you can do to change it. Is that luck or is it destiny? I don't know.

I wish my father was here. He'd have plenty to say about probability, although I doubt we'd understand it.

You and your father were close?

-I gave my head the slightest shake, as if wanting to believe otherwise.

He was a hard person to know and often in his lab or at the observatory studying this or that star system.

-The front door opened and closed, followed by the sound of approaching footsteps. Feeling I'd outstayed my welcome, I stood to leave. Vincent turned toward the door.

Speaking of hard to know, here comes my slob of a roommate.

-A mane of dark, curly hair appeared, a beautiful man beneath. His blue eyes surveyed the kitchen, lingering on me for a moment before turning to Vincent.

I heard you, Vincent. I'll get around to cleaning up one of these days.

I'll believe it when I see it, Claude.

30

I don't really get the point of cleaning when the house will get dirty again in no time. Besides, there are more important things in life than a clean house.

Just the sort of logic that got us here, Claude.

Like I said, I'll take care of it. Who's your friend?

-As he turned to me, I realized I'd forgotten to breathe. Instead of saying my name, I stood there gasping like a landed fish. Luckily, Vincent came to my rescue.

This is Tegan, our new neighbor.

What brings you to our little slice of student ghetto? Are you renting the dump where the mad scientist used to live?

-I managed only a nod, my thoughts wedged between his good looks and his off-putting words. I considered leaving but Vincent winked at me as he rose from his chair.

Very good, Claude, open mouth and insert foot. She is moving into that cute little house because she's his daughter.

Oh, hell, I didn't... I haven't slept... never mind. What are you studying... uh, what's your name?

Tegan, I'm Tegan. I'm not in school.

-I was annoyed he had already forgotten my name but I decided to give him another chance.

I'm between jobs at the moment.

What sort of name is Tegan?

-I gave him my best smile.

It's Welsh. It means fair one or favorite.

So, you're a daddy's girl.

-I thought of Chancer's messy and forgetful manner, endearing but aggravating, and then felt guilty at the judgment.

I suppose so.

That must've been weird.

What do you mean?

Well, the professor was a bit of a wing-nut.

-Those words were the final straw, snapping me out of my daze and reminding me how fast pretty can turn ugly. I

31

walked past him, calling over my shoulder as I stepped through the door.

Thanks for the brandy and conversation, Vincent. I'll treat next time.

A dark mood settled on me as I replayed my conversation with Vincent over and over. Why was I so quick to lay out my failures in love and work? Hearing myself say it only made it worse, the reality of my dismal life impossible to escape. Without a job to steady me, the day to day world of work had become distant and foreign, as if I had grown somehow irrelevant and worthless overnight.

On top of that, Claude's arrogant disinterest had only highlighted my poor taste in men. Not that I needed reminding. My sore ribs were quite enough. As I headed back to empty out my apartment, I wondered if I would ever again be attracted to someone who cared about me as much as himself.

Chapter Five

Chancer sat hunched over the kitchen table, scribbling in his almanac as his grandmother moved about the room preparing breakfast between occasional peeks over his shoulder. He checked a lunar table taped inside the back cover only to find the full moon less than a week away. He had hoped to show Byes the university telescope after their tour but the moon's glare would make star-gazing difficult at best.

A noise sounded at the back door and a moment later Louise appeared carrying a metal baking pan between two dish towels. A year older than Gammie, her thin frame and angular features stood in sharp contrast to her sister's stout presence, yet her blue eyes held the same no-nonsense intensity. The depression and war that followed had left their mark on them both.

She hurried across the room, dropping the pan onto the stove with a clatter. Muttering under her breath, she paced the floor as she waved her hands in the air. The smell of fresh bread filled the kitchen. She turned to Chancer and grinned, sucking the air between her teeth.

That was a close one, Chancer. I was halfway here when it dawned on me the pan was still too hot to handle with a couple of dishtowels. I would've set it down somewhere along the way but that mangy stray was following me again and I just knew he'd do something to ruin my cinnamon loaf. I've never seen a canine relieve himself at will the way that dog does. He just never quits.

-Gammie sniffed at the bread.

Are you sure he didn't sneak in a squirt while you weren't looking, Weesie?

Why on earth would you say that? You're going to make Chancer lose his appetite.

Well, if you wouldn't pay so much attention to that dog's bodily functions I wouldn't have to say it.

-Weesie sat across from Chancer.

Don't pay her any mind, sweetheart. She prefers to ignore the realities of life.

I just prefer my conversation on a higher plane, Sister.

-Weesie patted his hand.

Gammie didn't ruin breakfast for you, did she?

-Gammie slung a pitcher of orange juice on the table and sat, glaring at her sister.

You're the one that brought it up, Weesie.

-Chancer saw his opportunity to jump in.

I didn't lose my appetite but I'll have to skip breakfast if you two don't stop sparring.

-Dropping her staring contest with Gammie, Weesie turned back to him.

Why's that, sweetheart?

I'm going to meet someone over at the university.

-They both leaned in toward him, Gammie the first to speak.

Is this someone by chance of the female persuasion?

Her name is Elizabeth Byerson but she likes to be called Byes.

Byes Byerson sounds like the penname a newspaper reporter would use.

Hush up, Weesie, and let him tell us about her.

-Chancer looked from one to the other, realizing he had almost nothing to tell.

I only just met her.

How did you meet, then?

She was burning her… uh, she was watching a crowd of students protest the war.

So, you picked her out of the crowd because of her great beauty?

-Gammie snorted.

Weesie, this is not one of your sappy romance novels. What did happen, sugar?

She saw me watching the crowd and came over to say hello.

She picked you out as the handsome stranger watching from the shadows.

-Gammie slapped the table.

Weesie, will you stop that and let him talk?

I'm just helping fill in the details. Go ahead and tell us what she looks like, Chancer.

-Her image filled his mind, and for a moment he sat speechless. Weesie leaned across the table, peering into his face.

Can't you even remember what she looks like? Gammie and I need to know that much at least.

-He took a breath, searching for words to suit Byes' pale features.

She has red hair that curls around her face like a wild animal, making her eyes seem bluer than any sky I've ever seen.

-Gammie sat back in her chair.

Good Lord, Weesie, he's turned poet on us. This could be serious.

-Chancer blinked.

We just met. How can it be serious?

You never can tell, sugar.

I'm new to campus so she offered to show me around. In fact, I need to get going.

-Weesie jumped up, looking about the room in a panic, then grabbed a knife, carving a slice of cinnamon bread from the pan.

Sweetheart, at least take some breakfast with you.

-Gammie poured a glass of orange juice, thrusting it at him.

Listen to Sister and your Gammie. You want to be at your best if this one turns out serious after all, now don't you?

Azure light pierced a thin veil of clouds hugging the horizon as Chancer again slipped through the hedgerow and onto the broad lawn running between the two porticos.

A low roar, strange and unidentifiable, groaned in the distance. He paused, cocking his head to listen. The sound suddenly changed pitch, rising then falling, punctuated by a series of pops and the unmistakable echo of a bullhorn, the words beyond understanding.

He started again, angling toward the sound while scanning the benches for Byes, the roar growing steadily louder. He searched his mind for an explanation. Then a voice echoed off the far building and he turned toward it as a cloud of smoke rose over the rooftop. A wave of fear passed though him.

An instant later a man rounded the building at a full run, followed by another, and then a river of people, their arms flailing, their faces contorted with fear. Screams rose above the noise. Without thinking, Chancer hurried toward the crowd, determined to find Byes if he could. The crowd shifted, tossing him aside, throwing him beneath a narrow archway as the white smoke drifted past, the fumes burning his throat and eyes. He wiped them with the back of his hand and again peered into the chaos.

There before him, not twenty yards away, Byes appeared at the edge of the crowd. Down on her hands and knees, blinded by tear gas, she struggled to get to her feet amid the melee. Chancer leapt into the mass of people, wrestling his way toward her.

Without warning, another wave of students swarmed between the buildings, the force of the crowd launching him backwards. Jumping back onto his feet, he again thrust into the mass of bodies, finally reaching her and pulling her up. Then he turned toward the building, leading her beneath the nearest archway and into the portico. A recessed doorway sat not ten yards beyond. Byes in tow, Chancer hurried through the entry and onto a narrow staircase, descending the steps to another doorway at the end of a short hall. As soon as they stepped through, the door slammed behind them.

A dense quiet filled the darkness. Somewhere in the distance, the barely audible wail of sirens pierced the silence before fading away. Chancer searched the wall with his hand, finding a switch and flipping it. A single spotlight flashed to life. Illuminated before them sat the podium of a broad lecture hall.

He turned to Byes without a word, putting his arm across her shoulders and leading her toward the pool of light before easing her onto a low stage adjacent to the dais and sitting next to her. He bent forward to study her face. Though her blouse was smeared with blood, he could find no injury. She looked up at him, her eyes dark with emotion.

Oh, Chancer, it was awful.

Are you hurt, Byes?

-She looked down at her blouse, touching the red stain with her fingers as if only just noticing it.

There was blood everywhere. I tried to help him.

Who, Byes? Who did you help?

-Her voice shook as she imagined the scene.

I didn't know him. He was just a bystander, not part of the main group. The protest was going on as usual when something happened, something I couldn't see. The police began pushing the crowd away from a building that several students had occupied to protest the university's involvement in the war. Then they started swinging their clubs at anyone in their path. That's when I saw him go down. He was only a few yards from me so I went to him. Someone had to.

I had only just gotten to him when panic took hold and everyone started running, trying to get away from the teargas. Someone knocked me backwards and the crowd pulled me along with them. The next thing I knew I was on the ground. People kept falling over me. I thought I would be trampled. Then I felt your hand on my arm.

37

I nearly got trampled myself. We're lucky you fell where you did, otherwise I might never have found you.

You went into that madness when everyone else was running the other way?

How else was I going to find you?

You did that for me? But you barely know me, Chancer Wylls.

I know enough, Byes.

-She took his hand in hers.

I want to get cleaned up. Then you can walk me home. Will you wait here for me?

Why wouldn't I? You still owe me a tour.

The following day a crumpled page of Einstein's equations stared back at Chancer as he strained to organize his jumbled thoughts on general and special relativity. If they described the interrelated workings of space and time, of gravity's effect on the cosmos, then what comprised gravity itself? How might the equations fit with the push and pull inside every atom, between every subatomic particle? What were the odds he might understand it when science readily admitted to uncertainty even in that tiniest of realms? Frustrated, he peered through the window at a cold wind whipping the leafless treetops.

Odds seemed to have played an unnatural role in his life. He should have died in infancy yet fate had spared him. If not for a lost envelope he would have attended school elsewhere and never met Byes. His future, perhaps his life, would soon rest on the chance selection of a draft lottery number. Probability equations swirled through his mind, tormenting him, intruding on his thoughts as if they carried some hidden meaning.

A light tapping at the door pulled him back into the moment and he slammed closed the book, grateful to be free of the problems. Yet the numbers held something important, he could feel it. He tried to remind himself that any meaning would reveal itself in its own time, not his.

The knock came again and he stood, stepping around the table and reaching for the door. An instant later Bye's oval face appeared behind the rust-colored screen, her auburn hair blowing before the chill breeze. She pulled up her collar.

Chancer, let me in. It's gotten cold out.
-He glanced at the clock as she hurried through.
What's wrong? Has something happened?
-She frowned and moved toward him, a glint to her blue eyes.
Act like you're glad to see me, at least.
-He took a step back, unused to such attention.
I just thought we were meeting later, Byes.
So, you *are* glad to see me?
Of course I am.
-She again moved next to him.
It's too cold to do your tour today, don't you think?
I suppose so.
-She reached for his hand, taking it between her palms.
Maybe we could think of something else to do.
What do you mean?
-She looked around the two room apartment.
You could be the one to give a tour.
-He glanced about the place.
Oh... well... there's not much to see. I just moved in. But you know that, don't you?
-She nodded toward the bedroom door.
What do you have in there?
-Chancer let out a nervous laugh.
Lucky for me my grandmother stored her extra furniture here or I wouldn't have anything. All I brought is my clothes.
-She led him to the couch and sat, pulling him to her. He peered into her eyes, wondering if he should kiss her. Byes leaned toward him.

I never thanked you for getting me out of that awful mob, Chancer.

You don't need to thank me, Byes.

Do you know you have the most beautiful eyes?

-He felt the blood rush to his face.

No one has even said that to me before.

And you have a sensuous mouth, the sort of mouth that wants to be kissed.

-She drew near and he closed his eyes as her lips brushed against his once, twice. Then she pressed hard into him. An instant later, footsteps pounded up the stairs followed by loud knocking. Chancer jumped up, looking from Byes to the door. He took a breath and pointed toward the sound.

Knocking... there's... I'm going to see who it is.

-Tiptoeing across the room, he peeked through the window. Trewin stood outside the door stomping his feet to stay warm. Chancer stepped to the door and swung it open, puzzling over why his uncle would arrive unannounced on his doorstep. He rubbed his hands together as Chancer opened the door.

Alright, alright, are you always so slow in greeting your visitors?

Uncle Trewin, what are you doing here?

Did you forget your manners, boy? It's customary to invite a person in before giving them the third degree. On a day like this a man could freeze the family jew...

-Trewin went silent at the sight of Byes. Chancer glanced at her before waving him inside. Whipping off his hat, Trewin stepped past the threshold, smoothing back his dark hair.

I am truly sorry to be interrupting the visit of a beautiful lady.

-He gave Byes a short bow.

My name is Trewin, uncle to this one here, the one my poor brother forgot to train proper.

-Chancer moved in front of Byes, blocking his view.

Trewin, has something happened?

Well, I could hem and haw and beat about the bush but I'll get right to it instead. It's your parents that sent me. Your father is ill.

It's his heart, isn't it? Is he in the hospital? Do they need me there?

-Trewin raised his meaty hand as if to block the stream of words.

Good God, son, slow down a bit and I'll tell you.

-Byes rose from the couch, slipping on her coat as she made for the door. She stopped before Trewin.

I'm Byes and I'm glad to meet you, Trewin. I must be going.

-She turned to Chancer, taking his hand.

Call me when you can?

-He nodded as she disappeared out the door, watching after her before turning to Trewin.

How sick is he?

It's the cancer that's having its way with him and it's going to have its way with you too, I'm afraid. Not in the same way, of course.

I don't understand, Trewin. What are you saying?

I don't mean that you're sick as well but that you'll need to work to pay for your schooling. It's just that he's having the chemotherapy and it costs a sight more than any normal person can afford. Not to mention he'll have trouble working for a time. So, you'll need to pay your own way until he's up and about again.

Is he going to be alright?

Yes, yes, the doctors are as hopeful as doctors ever can be, which isn't saying much, but it does look like he has a decent chance. You must know it's a bit early to tell. But I'll put my odds on the Wylls family every time. You of all people should know that.

Sometimes, I know more about odds than I'd like to.

There's no need to worry yourself just now, Chancer. In all likelihood, the worst of it will be that your father resembles a pink bowling ball for a month or two.

Maybe I should leave school.

Good God, not on your life, son. Your mother would have my hide. Besides, that's the reason they sent me here. I have something lined up for you already.

You have a job for me?

An old friend of mine owns a civil engineering company and they need help on the survey crew. Think of it, Chancer, an opportunity to be outdoors, away from stuffy classrooms full of stuffy professors, working beneath the open sky, breathing in the fresh air. It sounds so good I'm thinking of applying myself.

No one has ever offered me a job out of the blue before.

-Trewin pulled a slip of paper from his shirt pocket.

You see, it must be a good omen, then. Call this number. You're set to start tomorrow.

Chapter Six

I took a breath, stepping through the door of the old building and into a large room filled with mismatched tables and office desks set back to back so as to share phone lines. Rows of army surplus filing cabinets covered one wall, spilling out into the open area like miniature skyscrapers, all olive green. Other than the roof and a makeshift loft splitting the far end, the place appeared made entirely of stone.

A gas heater rumbled to life overhead, sending a pile of papers onto the floor. I surveyed the room, waiting for someone to notice me. To my right a middle-aged woman in reading glasses and an orange sweater sat thumbing through a thick file. When I bent to retrieve the scattered papers she looked up and, tossing her glasses aside, she hurried around the desk to greet me. With her loosely worn hair and unstudied appearance, she reminded a bit of Chancer. I tried not to smile at the thought as she held out her hand, but when her lively eyes met mine I could see she missed nothing.

I'm so glad you've decided to join our merry band of do-gooders, Tegan. I'm Esther Schultz.

-I stared at her, unsure of her meaning.

Do you mean I'm hired?

Please say you want the job. The odds of finding a licensed counselor in the middle of the school year are dismal.

I'm in if you'll have me, Dr. Schultz.

Please call me Esther. The only time people call me doctor is when they're mad at me or they want something. You're on contract so you'll be paid by the hour. Do you want to hear about your first case?

-I nodded, feeling a little unsettled by her quick pace. She pulled a file from her desk, thrusting it at me.

43

Diego's father left when he was four so his mother has raised him on her own for the most part. The rest of the family still lives in Mexico. On top of having no support, she tends toward rough men that like to knock her around and generally make life difficult. In any event, the boy is thirteen now and angry at the world. He's more than she can handle.

-I glanced at the name on the file.

His name is Diego Rivera, like the famous mural artist? Is he related?

I doubt it. His mother never graduated high school and doesn't strike me as an art lover. On the other hand, people are often a surprise when you get to know them.

Has he gotten into much trouble?

We're brining you in because he's gotten himself crosswise with the school and the juvenile authorities. He's out of school now so you'll have to go to their home. The address is in the front of the file. They're expecting you. That is, if I haven't already scared you off.

No, I'm glad to have the work.

-She glanced at her watch.

I have a meeting now. We can take care of the details later.

-I followed her out the door and we said our goodbyes before she disappeared around the corner. I watched after her, my head spinning, and wondered what I'd gotten myself into.

An hour later, I turned off a narrow roadway at a sign reading "Siesta Acres". A brisk wind coursed through the trees. I followed a rutted gravel drive scattered with trailers and unfinished shacks, their yards littered with cast-off furniture and rusted bicycles. Over-filled trash cans lined the roadside. The path narrowed as it passed through a dense stand of cedar, dipping into a shallow wash before rising again onto a rock-strewn ridge. Before me, the street ended in an oval clearing, a trailer sitting at the far end.

44

Checking the address to be sure, I angled my car next to a small mesquite tree and climbed out. The trailer, leaning to one side and painted two shades of blue, sat perched on cinderblocks beneath a gnarled live oak. Used tires covered the tin roof. An expensive sports car parked behind and to one side of the trailer seemed out of place. I puzzled over who it might belong to as I reached through my car window for a legal pad and pen.

As I turned back toward the trailer, the screen door flew open, smashing against the outside wall as a dark-haired boy jumped out. He disappeared into the trees. An instant later, a bald man appeared in the doorway and pivoted, yelling back into the house. I guessed his accent to be from somewhere in Eastern Europe but had no way to be sure.

And you must make the tea in the correct manner! You must have it waiting when I return from the airport or you know what will happen. A man must be treated with respect!

-As soon as he stepped off the stairs, he noticed me and began walking in my direction, his expression less than friendly. I reached into my purse, slipping my fingers around a small canister of mace. Stopping a few feet away, he jutted out his chin, his dark eyes flashing with anger.

What do you want?

I'm looking for Diego Rivera. The school sent me.

For what purpose do you seek him?

The school wants me to talk with him.

Good. You find him and tell him he must have respect for his elders, he must go back to the school. You tell him that.

Is he here?

-He nodded toward the woods beyond the trailer.

He is there. You find him and teach him to respect.

-Without another word he turned and climbed into the sports car, throwing up a spray of gravel as he sped off. I mounted the trailer steps and rapped on the doorframe. The door stood wide open. Hearing nothing inside, I knocked again. Nothing.

-Despite the brilliant sunlight, the air held a chill and I had no coat so I decided to try another time. In view of the bald man's demeanor, I guessed Diego's mother had taken a back exit. As I turned to leave, the boy rounded the corner and ambled toward me as if he had not a care. He nodded toward the trailer.

She won't come out because she doesn't want you to see what the bastard did.

I'll bet it's nothing I haven't seen before.

-A hint of surprise crossed his face. He nodded and leaned on the doorframe, yelling into the trailer.

Mom, the counselor from the school is here. You said you wanted to talk to her.

You're Diego?

My street name is Yay-go.

I'm going to call you by your given name. I don't work for the school, Diego. I do what I think is best, not what the school tells me to. Do you understand what I'm saying? This is between us. We decide how we're going to do things. We'll include your mom as much as we can but we'll decide that together. Does that make sense?

I get it, lady.

My name is Tegan Wylls and you can call me Tegan, not lady.

Alright, Miss.

Not Miss either.

Alright, I get it... Tegan.

-The floor creaked behind me and I turned to find a young woman, much younger than I expected, with a beautiful mane of black hair framing her dark eyes, one of which peered out at me from a ring of yellowish-purple. A red mark in the shape of a hand stretched across her left cheek, freshly made by the look of it.

Your bald friend is right-handed, I see.

46

-She lifted a hand to her face.

How do you know?

I used to work in a women's shelter.

-She frowned at the words but stood aside and motioned me through the doorway. I was encouraged to see Diego follow. The spare living room, filled with castoff furniture and a threadbare rug, seemed tattered but clean. All the windows save one were broken, their cracked glass bending the afternoon sunlight into strange patterns. A small television held together with duct tape sat in one corner. I turned to Diego's mother.

What should I call you?

My name is Celia. I am sorry for you to come to my house and see it like this but we have not much money. Still, I am glad you are here to help us. Please sit.

-My mind was still on the bald man.

The man that left said he was going to the airport. Will he be gone long?

The lesson, it takes about three hours.

He's learning to fly? That's an expensive hobby. How do you afford it?

He has money, much money, but has little for us. And I do not make much in my job to pay the bills. So, the lesson, it belongs to him, not to us. But he is not a bad man.

-Diego snorted.

How can you say that, mom? Look at what he does to you.

He has promised to do better but he has much difficulty in his work, many things to worry him.

What work are you talking about, mom? All he ever does is talk on the phone and bring those other losers here to eat our food and trash the place. I hate you for bringing him here.

-His anger had wasted little time in showing itself. I raised my hand to get his attention.

Diego, you and I will talk soon but now I want to hear from your mother. You can leave if you like but if you stay, I want you to let her talk.

-His eyes flashed at me before he vanished through the door. Celia lowered her head, her voice just above a whisper.

I am sorry my son, he acts this way when a guest is here.

He is angry often, Celia?

-She nodded.

I know my Diego, he has reason for the way he is. His father did not want him. I have bad luck with men and he fights them. He wishes for them to leave.

He wants to protect you?

Omar is not a bad man. He…

-She raised a shaking hand to wipe her eyes. I leaned toward her, trying to see her face.

Celia, I can help you if you want to leave, if you want to be safe and away from him.

-She shook her head.

He will change. He has told me he will.

I wish I could believe that, Celia.

I must believe what he promises me is the truth.

-I absently touched my sore ribs. Then I peered into her soft eyes, their look uncertain, vulnerable. I hesitated, unsure if I should talk instead of listen, but I decided I needed her as an ally.

Celia, what's happened to you could happen to anyone, even me. But all my training says he'll continue hitting you. My experience tells me the same.

You have been treated so too, Tegan?

-I winced at the thought, the shame of my poor judgment still fresh.

I was, and not very long ago. I'm telling you so you know I won't judge you. I understand you have to make your own decisions. But I hope you will do what's best for your son. I will do what I can to help him whatever the case. That's all I'm going to say about it now or ever again. My responsibility is to Diego. Still, I need your help if you'll give it.

Diego is my only child. I will help.

-I stood and she followed me through the door and down the steps. Diego had vanished again. Rather than coax him into talking to me, I decided to return another time so we could start fresh. As I turned to tell Celia my plan, an old man carrying a gnarled cane appeared out of the trees, hurrying toward us with a sideways gait, his sand-colored face framed by a snow white beard. A multi-hued serape draped from his shoulders, flapping behind him in the brisk wind. He stopped just feet away, squinting at me with a watery eye. Celia took a step toward him.

Senor Fuego, what do you want of me? Can't you see I have a visitor?

What do I want of you? I want nothing *of* you, daughter, I want only *for* you. Do you not see I am your slave?

But I don't want a slave, senor. Why have you come here?

I desire you to be free of evil, the evil brought by that devil.

I don't know what you mean, Senor Fuego.

-He stared into the distance as if in some sort of trance, his voice a low whisper.

He is no man, mija. With him I see the sky set to fire, the street to ash. The stars, they sing, ten and one, ten and one. The virgin, she weeps. Her messenger, he brings sorrow...

-His voice trailed off and Celia turned to me.

Senor Fuego is a very spiritual man.

-He held up a bony finger and began circling us, dancing a jig and singing in his hoarse tenor.

   The spirits of trees, the spirits of stones,
   they sing a warning, to beware the bones!
   A hairless evil breaks the sky,

the evil jumps, the evil flies!

-He stopped where he started and raised his hand as if to bless me. An image of the hooded figure on New Year's Eve flashed through my mind.

The spirit of this one is far from evil, daughter. Stay close to her.

-Then he faced Celia, his face contorted, his arms outstretched. He pointed his cane to the sky.

Why must you make me your slave, daughter? Why do you torment an old man? Release me! When will you release me?

But, senor…

-With that he turned and scurried across the road, disappearing into the trees.

As I bid Celia goodbye and bumped back down the rutted roadway, Senor Fuego's words again came to me, eerie and haunting, as if in his madness there lurked a dark truth that only he could see. An idea tugged at the back of my mind, a vague connection, ethereal and unreachable. Could it have some tie to Diego, to the difficult start of his young life, to the odds that stood against him like a great wall? I thought again of my father and his struggle with probability, his search for what is through what might be. With his fate decided, I wondered at my own.

Chapter Seven

A sea of gray clouds scudded across the horizon, wavelike, undulating as Chancer peered through the side window of a white paneled truck. Serrated treetops stretched across the valley below. He and two others sat in silence while the truck bumped along a rutted logging road, the four wheel drive whining against the grade. Having received a last-minute change of plans, the reasons left unclear, the crew had been ordered to a new worksite. Chancer sensed a vague apprehension from the others.

The truck entered a dense stand of pines, their red-hued trunks clogged with undergrowth. Smoke from a nearby paper mill drifted past, dimming the pale sunlight. Around a curve the road widened, ending in a broad turnaround at the edge of a shallow swamp. Cypress trees towered above the black water, their gnarled roots rising into the air like tiny mountains. Green scum drifted between scatterings of lily pads.

Chancer climbed from the truck to survey the clearing and the wall of trees beyond. All at once the crisp fragrance of pine needles surrounded him. Wind whipped through the treetops like crashing waves, hissing as it moved into the distance, carrying with it the rich odor of rotting wood. Directly opposite the swamp a stable stood abandoned, the shattered double-door hanging off its hinges. He pulled on a pair of rubber boots and helped unload the equipment, filling a backpack with two dozen stakes and a coil of orange survey tape.

As they prepared to leave, a white sedan pulled up and Carl Blenheim, the field supervisor, climbed out. He reached through the back window and pulled out a beer, popping it open and taking a long pull. Then he leaned against the car, tapping his fingers on the roof as he stared into the forest. The crew stood waiting. After a moment, he moved to the trunk, opening it and pulling out an armful of machetes. With his free hand, he waved Chancer and the others toward him.

He handed the machetes to Turley Weems along with several scabbards and a small sharpening stone before retrieving his beer. Turley looked at him askance, making no effort to hide his disgust. Recently back from Viet Nam, Turley had little toleration for authority. Angular and wiry, he still dressed in his standard issue fatigues. Wild hair jutted from beneath his canvas hat. Over the previous weeks, Chancer had come to know his unpredictable and restless nature, steering clear of him when necessary.

Days earlier he and Ben Ahote, the other crew member, were standing opposite Turley in a deep draw tying survey tape to the ends of stakes. The next thing Chancer knew a barrage of the four foot long stakes began raining down on them, the survey tape acting like feathers on an arrow. Ben managed to dodge several of the missiles before grabbing one and tossing it back just as Turley slipped on the steep slope. The point of the stake caught him just below the right eye.

Turley grabbed his face, the blood streaming through his fingers. Chancer watched as he slid down the slope, sure he had lost the eye. The doctor said a quarter of an inch was the difference between a bad cut and blindness.

As they strapped on the scabbards, Carl stared into the thicket again, his face grim. Chancer guessed he knew something about the place, something he would rather not tell. He followed Carl's gaze across the black water, wondering what it might be. They turned to leave and Carl raised a hand to stop them.

You boys best keep those blades sharp or you'll wear your arms out swinging. It's thick in there. They might come in handy for snakes too. Alright then, you can get on with it.

-Chancer decided to press for more.

Is there anything else we need to know, Carl?

This job will be slow going. You'll need to use the chainsaw a good bit, even take out some sizable trees.

-Turley squinted at him.

We know all that. What are you not telling us, Carl?

-He drained the can and tossed it aside, running a hand across his face.

Alright, then, you're probably wondering why you got pulled off a job to come out here. Well, truth is this is a priority tract with a bundle of developer's money waiting on our survey.

What else, Carl?

And the previous crew is in the hospital.

-Turley snorted.

I knew something kinky was up. Tell us what happened to the poor bastards.

They got into a nest of water moccasins.

All three of them got bit?

Yep, so you boys keep your eyes peeled and watch your step. And be careful when you're taking out the bigger trees. With a wind this big it could get dicey.

They waded across the swamp, careful to avoid piles of debris, before picking up a narrow trail that disappeared into the thicket. The pale winter light seemed to dim even further. As they moved away from the road an eerie silence surrounded them, broken only by their footsteps and the rush of an intermittent wind coursing overhead. Chancer thought it strange he heard no birds, no animals of any sort, only the murmur of Turley cursing under his breath.

The edge of a second swamp appeared beside the trail. Without a word, Turley turned, grinning at Chancer as he veered off the path. Chancer watched as he hopped onto to a half-submerged log, knelt and then jumped off holding a huge water moccasin by its tail. Mouth open wide, the snake bent one way then the other trying to reach him with its fangs as he whipped it in a tight circle above his head. With a whoop, he let the snake fly off into bushes not far from where Ben stood. Chancer stared at Turley in disbelief. Ben sighed and put his hand to Chancer's shoulder, pushing him down the trail.

Half an hour later, they came upon the broken remains of a stone house, its intact chimney still reaching toward the treetops. A short wall ran across the front. Beside the house, a circular water well stood beneath a rusted cast-iron pulley. Turley sat and pulled out a plastic bag filled with blue capsules. He popped one into his mouth then tossed the bag to Ben. After fishing out a pill, Ben turned to Chancer and held up the bag.

Want some Quaaludes?

-Chancer shook his head. He wanted to keep his wits about him. Ben broke a pill in half, swallowing it.

I got to have them. This place gives me the willies. It's not that different from 'Nam.

You were in the war too?

Damn right I was, and proud of it.

-He sat on the wall, spreading the survey map before him. Chancer peered over his shoulder.

Where do we start?

-Ben pointed to a small rectangle.

Here's the house. We shoot a line starting just beyond those trees. It looks like we're going to have a lot of cutting to do, like Carl said.

-Turley snorted again and spit into the powder-like dirt.

How would he know anything about it? He hasn't set foot in the field in twenty years, just like the damn higher-ups in 'Nam.

He knows enough to figure if we're working or not, so we better get to it.

-Ben stuffed the map in his shirt pocket, stood and then sat again.

Whoa, man, that's some powerful stuff.

-Turley lifted the bag, waving it at Chancer.

Sure you don't want one, man?

I'm sure I don't want to step on a snake.

You got to stay loose in a place like this. I'm feeling way mellow. Nothing's going to bother me. Besides, our Navaho friend here can smell a snake way before he sees it. Tell him, Ahote.

-Ben glared at him.

My great grandmother was Hopi, Turley, not Navaho. I'm about as Indian as Chancer here.

-Turley pulled out his machete.

I'm going to waste the vegetation nation. Where's the goddamn Agent Orange when you need it, huh? Tell me that, Cochise.

-Turley circled them, hacking through the surrounding brush with his machete, the sharp blade singing with every swing. He whooped and pointed the machete at Ben.

Hey, Injun Joe, where's the goddamn defoliant?

Take it easy, Turley.

-Turley vanished behind the house. A moment later, he reappeared with one arm behind his back, a grin on his face. Stopping before them, he swung out his hand. A squirming possum dangled by its hairless tail. He raised the animal for a better look and it managed to land a sharp claw on his arm. He yelped, dropping it to the ground and kicking at it. The possum turned, baring its teeth and hissing.

-Ben took a deep breath and again stood.

You better hope he doesn't have rabies. Now, let's get moving, Turley.

-Turley ignored him, raising his machete and bringing it down in a flash of metal, splitting the possum in two. Chancer turned away, a wave of nausea grabbing him. Lifting the chainsaw to his shoulder, Turley started down the trail, muttering to himself as he passed them.

An hour later they had chopped through a half mile of forest. Chancer stopped to catch his breath, the possum's gruesome face still dogging his thoughts, its lifeless eyes pleading with him to stay vigilant. He glanced at Turley, wondering what sort of torment leads a man to cruelty. Was it the war or something else, perhaps something from his childhood? Ben seemed to have none of his fierce anger.

Chancer stepped from the path and pulled the sharpening stone from his pocket, sliding the gray rectangle back and forth along the broad blade in smooth strokes. His shoulder ached from all the swinging. A chill wind coursed past him and on through the underbrush as a flash of movement caught his eye. He turned to find a huge owl perched not twenty feet away. The bird squinted at him, its thick talons shining even in the dim forest light. Then, in a blur of brown and beige, it vanished into the trees. He watched after it, grateful for a brief glimpse of beauty.

Replacing the stone, he ambled to where Ben knelt beside the trail studying the map. After a moment, he stood and lifted the transit level, flipping out the legs and adjusting it to check their line. Several yards ahead a thick pine stretched a hundred feet or more into the air. He looked up, sighed and nodded toward the tree.

You'd best fire up the chainsaw, Turley. That one has to come down.

It's about damn time I got to do some man's work. Chancer, get over here and lend a hand.

-Chancer cleared the underbrush from around the tree and stood back as Turley brought the popping chainsaw to life, pressing the whining blade into the trunk. A cloud of smoke and sawdust filled the air. A breeze whipped past him and Chancer stepped away from Turley, checking the treetops for movement. A wave of fear passed through his chest. He motioned to Ben and pointed into the sky. Ben leaned toward Turley, cupping his hands around his mouth.

Watch the wind, Turley.

-Turley yelled back over his shoulder.

Let me be, Ben! I know how the hell to waste a damn tree.

-Ben stepped away.

You're one stubborn son of a bitch, Turley.

-An instant later the trunk shifted, trapping the chainsaw like a vice. The engine sputtered to a stop. Turley cursed, again firing up the engine but with little effect. The tree still held the saw. He called over his shoulder.

Chancer, get over here and push on this tree.

-Chancer hesitated then stepped to the trunk, leaning into it with all his weight. Ben moved next to him and the saw blade again sang to life, covering Chancer with sawdust and oil, the fumes choking his throat. All at once, the crack of splintering wood sounded above them. Ben grabbed Chancer by the shirt, throwing him to one side. At the same instant the saw blade released, jumping from the trunk into Turley's knee. He cried out, collapsing beside the tree, his pant leg stained with blood.

-Flat against the ground, Chancer watched as the tree began splitting above him, the wind angling it directly at Turley. He jumped to his feet, running to Turley and grabbing his arm, dragging him into the brush. A falling limb cracked against his forehead and he hit the ground as the thicket beside him exploded beneath the huge tree, blinding him with dust. The next thing he knew, Ben was shaking him.

Are you hurt?

-Chancer stared up at him.

I... I think I'm alright.

-Ben lay stretched out next to him. He pointed to Chancer's head.

You're going to need stitches for that.

-Chancer reached up and wiped the blood from his forehead, feeling the already growing lump over his eye. Ben handed him a bandana, wincing as he leaned back against a small tree.

Tie that around your head.

Are you hurt, Ben?

You've got to get Turley to a doctor.

What about you?

My leg is broken so I'm stuck here. As soon as you get to the truck, call Carl and tell him to come find me.

-Chancer stopped tying the bandana

But I can't just leave you here, Ben.

I'll be alright. Turley's a regular pharmacy, remember? I'm sorry, Chancer, but you'll have to go it alone. I've done what I can to stop the bleeding but he needs help soon. You've got to get moving.

Wrapping Turley's arm across his shoulders, Chancer took a step then paused as the world spun about him. His eye throbbed beneath the bandana. Taking a last look at Ben, he turned and staggered down the path, Turley's blood-soaked pants slapping against his leg with every step. The endless trail passed beneath their feet, silent, dreamlike.

Byes' pale face appeared before him, her hair floating about her face like an auburn cloud. He stared into her azure-hued eyes, wondering how she could have found him. She reached out to him, her lips moving but her voice silent. An instant later she vanished beneath the fading light.

After what seemed hours, the trees fell away and the clearing came into view. Carl's sedan sat parked to one side. As soon as he saw Turley, he tossed aside his beer and rushed toward them, taking Turley and carrying him to the car. Chancer staggered behind.

Minutes later the wail of approaching sirens drifted through the trees. He sat, leaning his back against the car, pressing a cold can of beer to his head. An owl called from deep inside the forest. Chancer turned and stared into the black mass of trees, vowing he would find another way to pay for college.

Chapter Eight

Diego waited on the trailer steps as I angled the car next to a stunted scrub oak and climbed from behind the wheel. A warm February sun filled the cloudless sky. I preferred the nearby wooden bench to the trailer, so I rounded the car and sat, motioning him to join me. He ambled over, looking as carefree and unconcerned as the first time I saw him. During the past weeks, we had gotten to know each other but he had kept to small talk for the most part. I wondered when he would get to the truth behind his anger.

Relieved to see no sign of Omar's sports car, I again puzzled at what he might be doing with his time and money, and how flying lessons figured into it. Although he had avoided me after our first encounter, my intuition kept telling me he was up to no good. He had not laid a hand on Celia in weeks. I hoped my presence had something to do with the change. I tried to put all that out of mind as Diego sat opposite me in a rusted metal chair, leaning back against a small tree.

What up, miss?

I want to talk to the real Diego, not some tough guy act.

-He patted his chest.

It's me, for real, Miss.

I don't think so.

Why not, Miss?

Have you forgotten my name, Diego?

-He took a breath, letting it out slowly.

I know your name, Tegan.

Then talk to me.

What do you want to talk about?

I'm here to listen, remember?

I can't think of anything to talk about today.

Just say what's on your mind. You know how this works.

I'm trying but I don't have anything in there.

-I leaned back against the bench, familiar with this game.

I can wait.

We'll just be wasting time.

It's your time, Diego. You can waste it if you want to. I get paid either way.

Alright then, I'll just make something up so you'll be happy.

You'll still be wasting your time.

-Anger flashed across his face and he slammed the chair to the ground, leaning forward as if about to leave. Then he stopped himself.

You want me to get mad?

Is that what scares you, Diego, getting angry, letting go?

You don't want to see what happens when I lose it.

I know about the broken doors, the holes in walls. I'm still here.

-He slumped in the chair.

When do I go back to school, Tegan?

Weren't you about to tell me?

-His eyes grew dark.

I didn't mean to punch those holes. I just had to hit something and the wall was closest.

Punching a wall is better than a person. Who do you want to hit?

I don't want to hurt anyone. But sometimes I could punch Omar and it would be alright. I will too if he messes with my mom again.

Who else do you feel like punching?

The damn teacher when he gets in my face, the principal too.

Anyone else make you that angry, Diego?

No one else, I guess.

Are you sure?

-He squinted at me for a moment.

You mean my mom, don't you?

I don't know, do I?

-He leaned forward, his elbows on his knees.

I guess not because I'm not mad at her. She gets on my nerves sometimes but I can handle it.

Can you?

-His eyes again flashed with anger.

Hell yes, I can handle it.

How do you do that?

I just do.

What would happen if you didn't?

-He stood and began pacing.

How the hell should I know? Why do you keep asking me? You're not my mom.

I'm trying to understand what it's like for you.

Nobody can understand what it's like. She keeps bringing home these losers and they act like they can be my dad or something. Forget them. Forget him too. I still remember him, you know, even though I was young. The loser left when I was just a little kid, no more than five. Nobody can understand that.

I'll try if you'll help me.

Why did he leave then? Can you tell me, Tegan? Was it because I wasn't good...

-The bushes across the drive rustled to life and the old man appeared wearing the same rainbow-hued serape. The anguish in Diego's eyes vanished, the unconcern I had seen earlier again shaping his face.

Hey, Tegan, how do you figure Senor Fuego? Is he a nut case or what?

I thought we were talking about you, Diego.

I'm telling you he's crazy. You know all about that insanity stuff. What makes him so whacked out? Did he do too many hippie drugs or something when he was young?

-I could see he had gone as far as he was willing to for the time being, so I watched Senor Fuego move along the road with his crablike walk. A moment later, he stood before us. He lifted the heavy cane, pointing it at Diego.

Listen to me, mijo. You must tell your mother to release me. The devil is near. You must convince her so I may once again be free.

-Diego sat and leaned back in his chair.

Senor Fuego, you're a trip, man.

Yes, I am a man and you are a boy with the soul of an artist. You must protect your soul and free yourself of the devil.

-He pointed at me with his free hand.

Have you shown this lady your paintings?

That's just messing around, Senor Fuego. My mom should've never shown them to you.

No, mijo, you are wrong. I saw your future in them. You must protect the gift. Go get them for me.

But Senor Fuego…

Get them now, mijo.

-Diego pushed himself out of the chair and trudged toward the trailer. Seno Fuego turned to me.

You must see the paintings, senora. They have magic in them.

I'm Tegan.

-He took my hand and bowed.

Ah, la linda, the fair one. Your name, it suits you.

-I tried to hide my surprise.

You know what my name means?

Yes, I know names. Names, they have power in them. You must call me Eloy.

And your name, Eloy, what does it mean?

It is one who is chosen.

Chosen for what?

I still search for this. You must help the boy, Tegan.

I hope to, Eloy. I didn't know he was an artist. I've talked with him for weeks and he never mentioned anything of it.

He has the gift. The angels, they have blessed him. He paints a wolf standing on the thumb of a giant, a fish swimming through a sky of stars, a beautiful woman, her hair flowing like fire. She is not unlike you, I think.

-I could feel myself blush at the thought.

But he doesn't believe in his talent?

The boy, he lacks what you can never give him.

You mean a father.

You must find him.

How can I find his father? He left years ago.

You must find a man to show him how to be a man.

-I knew he was right. The idea had been eating at me for some time but I had found no answer. He held up his hand, turning a circle while sniffing the air.

Now I must go. The devil, he comes.

But, Eloy…

-He turned and hurried down the road, once again vanishing into the bushes. A moment later, Diego appeared with a stack of ink and watercolor images painted on thick paper. I thumbed through them, each image striking, filled with wonder. I'd never before seen anything like them. I looked up from the final painting and stared at him for a moment.

You asked me what I think of Senor Fuego so here's what I have to say. He may be a little eccentric but he knows talent when he sees it. You have a gift, Diego.

-He snorted and leaned back.

You're just messing with me, Tegan.

I'm serious, Diego. These are extraordinary.

-All at once he seemed like any other fourteen year old boy wanting to be proud of something, anything.

You think so, for real?

Yes I do, and I'd like to do whatever I can to encourage that talent. I think we should…

-I stopped speaking as the rumble of Omar's sports car drifted over the trees. Diego looked up and tensed, his face growing hard, his eyes dark, distant. Giving me a quick glance, he grabbed the paintings and stood without a word, moving toward the tree line before vanishing from sight.

-A moment later Omar's car turned into the drive, followed by a black van. Three men in loose shirts and dungarees climbed out, glaring at me as they talked among themselves. Walking to where they stood, Omar spoke to them in low tones, now and then gesturing toward me or the trailer. Then they climbed back into the van and sped off in a cloud of dust.

-My intuition told me they were up to no good but I had little idea what it might be. Then I had a chance to find out. Celia appeared in the doorway and Omar turned to face her, pointing his finger at me and yelling.

You do not tell me she is coming here today! I do not want to come here and be surprised by her! You know what happens when you do not obey me!

-I walked toward him, again reaching for my mace. He turned, surprised by my boldness. I glanced at Celia and she raised a hand of caution. Deciding I had held my tongue long enough, I stopped feet from him.

If your problem is with me, then talk to me not her.

-A look of disbelief crossed his face. I could see he expected something else from a woman. He sneered at me.

You do not belong here. You must leave this place.

I'll leave if Celia asks but not before.

-He again faced her, shaking his finger.

You tell her to leave.

-Celia turned her eyes to the ground. Seeing the helpless look on her face, the resignation to her fate, only added to my resolve. There she stood feet from her dilapidated sedan while his car sat gleaming in the bright sunlight. She had missed work twice in the last two weeks due to breakdowns. Suddenly, I saw a chance to catch him off guard.

What sort of business are you in that you can afford such an expensive car, Omar?

-He glared at me.

My affairs are none of your concern.

You're wrong. Diego's welfare is my concern. His mother's struggle to make ends meet is my concern. You make no effort to help when you clearly have the means. Why is that?

-He scoffed at the question.

You know nothing. I do help.

Sure you do. I can see what sort of car she has to drive. I'll ask again. What line of work are you in?

As I have said, it is not your concern.

Do those other men work for you? Are you an importer, maybe dealing through Mexico?

-An anxious look appeared in his dark eyes and I knew then I had hit a nerve. I realized I had a chance to make sure Diego and Celia would be safe. He pointed his chin at Celia.

How do you know this? Did she tell you? She will pay, if so.

No, she told me nothing about you. Your eyes were my answer.

-I followed as he started for his car. He turned, waving a finger at me as he climbed behind the wheel.

You ask no more. It is not your business.

-I leaned toward the window, measuring my words.

Listen to me, Omar. If you lay a hand on either Celia or Diego, I will report you to the authorities without hesitation. I have a feeling you don't want someone like that poking around in your business.

-A wave of fear crossed his face and he looked away, cranking the engine to life. Watching the car disappear, I wondered what I'd learned, if anything. I thought it likely he and the others were involved in something illicit. More important, I hoped he would leave Celia and Diego alone, at least for awhile.

Chapter Nine

A knock sounded on the front door as I rummaged through my purse searching for my keys. Beetie had invited me over for dinner and I was running late. Between work and settling into my new home, I had scarcely spoken to her or Pen in weeks. Even over the phone I could hear the hurt in her voice. I tried not to feel guilty as I slipped the key ring around my fingers.

The knock sounded again and I started toward the door, making my way across the small living room to the foyer. I guessed Vincent had decided to stop by on his way home from school but when I swung open the door I found Claude standing before me instead. He looked so good I had to remind myself of our first encounter.

I had only seen him in passing since then but felt his gaze linger on me more than once. I sensed an unspoken apology in his polite reticence. Part of me had wanted to know more but instead I put him out of mind. I still had little trust in men. He held out a bottle of wine.

It's a housewarming gift. I shouldn't have waited so long but I wasn't exactly friendly when we first met so I thought I'd give it some time. It wasn't personal, you know, the way I acted.

-I kept my guard up.

It felt personal.

I hadn't slept in days.

Why not?

-He took a deep breath, a defeated look settling on his face.

They're going to kick me out of school if I don't get my grades up.

That's not a good place to be.

Ever since I got back, I can't seem to focus no matter what I do. They warned me my concentration might be

66

shot, but the damn veterans' office hasn't been much help otherwise.

You were in the Iraqi war?

I was in Afghanistan and two weeks away from discharge when a blast wave threw me ninety feet. I fell into a ditch so the main force passed over me. If not for that piece of luck, I wouldn't be here.

-He spoke in a slow monotone, as if ordering off a menu. Suddenly I saw him as a real person, just someone trying to find his way.

That sounds like a nightmare, Claude.

I barely had a scratch when I woke up five days later. The other two guys didn't make it.

I'm so sorry.

Be sorry for them. I keep thinking there's something I should have done, something that might have prevented what happened, but I don't know what it is.

-My heart went out to him. Although tempted to talk with him as a professional, I knew better. We would be acquaintances, maybe more, or nothing. I checked the clock.

Claude, I'm sorry but I was just on my way out.

I'm not surprised someone as pretty as you has a date.

-I felt myself blush, not only for the compliment but also because I enjoyed hearing him say it.

The date is dinner with my grandparents, not exactly what you'd call an exciting evening. Can I have a rain check on the housewarming?

-His face seemed to relax a bit.

What time works best for you?

I'm not sure. I have a meeting about work late tomorrow so I'll need to get back to you.

I'll let you be on your way then.

-Without a word he turned and disappeared around the corner.

On the way to my grandparents' house Claude's sad face kept intruding on my thoughts, needling at me like a scene from an old movie. I wondered if my first impression of him had been mistaken. Part of me hoped so. But the optimist in me kept losing to the skeptic so that I scarcely heard what was said over dinner.

Trewin pulled a bottle from the cupboard and motioned Pen to the table as Beetie and I dried the last of the dishes. She hurried to return them to the bureau, nearly breaking a plate in the process. The way she looked at me, I knew she had something on her mind. Try as I might, I had been unable to stop her and Pen from feeling sorry for me. The last thing I wanted was a dose of her pity. She untied her apron and grabbed my arm, pushing me through the door.

Tegan, sweetheart, are you in some sort of trouble? Is it that new job of yours? Are you worried about paying bills?

-I was far from sure I wanted to let her in on my thoughts. On the other hand, I felt like I needed to talk to someone.

No, I love my work. I have enough cases to make ends meet if I watch my budget.

You seem preoccupied, is all. You hardly said two words at dinner. Is there a man in the picture?

-I looked at her, unable to speak, unnerved by her guess. I just nodded an answer. Her eyes grew wide.

You're not in the family way, are you, Tegan?

-I gasped at the thought.

Goodness, Beetie, it's bad luck to even mention such a thing.

But there is a man in the picture?

-I continued, deciding the conversation could get no worse.

Tonight, when I was on my way out, he brought by a housewarming gift. He lives next door.

My, that's convenient.

Or awkward, depending on what happens.

I know you've had your share of disappointment but try to think positive, sweetheart. He's bound to be an improvement over that Italian architect. What was his name?

-I felt a twinge in my side at the mere mention of Paolo.

That's in the past, Beetie. Let's leave it there.

What's your friend's name? What sort of work does he do?

His name is Claude and he's a student.

-Trewin's voice called from the kitchen.

Did you say he's a stewardess? Come in here so we can hear you.

-Beetie frowned and grabbed my wrist, pulling me back into the kitchen. She glared at Pen.

Old men are the worst eavesdroppers there are.

-He held up his hands.

I am not my brother's keeper.

-Trewin pulled out a chair and patted the seat.

Sit yourself down, Tegan and let your uncle Trewin ply you with a bit of his special truth serum.

-He held up the bottle, half-filling a tumbler. I sat while Beetie waved a finger at him.

Just because you don't do a lick of honest labor doesn't mean the rest of the world can be so lazy. She has to get up and go to work tomorrow, you know.

-He waved her toward a chair and poured another glass.

Beatrice, you'll live longer if you drink a bit more and worry a bit less. Now, Tegan, tell us about this new man of yours. Have you decided to rob the cradle and date a fresh-faced college student? Not that there's anything wrong with it, mind you. I'd date a good-looking forty year old, if she'd have me.

-Beetie snorted.

69

You'll be lucky to catch the eye of a plain-as-day eighty year old.

-I ignored her, hoping they would stop their sparring.

He's my age or older, I'd guess, but I've only just met him. He was injured in the war and now he's in school. I don't know much else.

-Beetie peered at me, worry in her eyes.

Was he hurt badly, Tegan?

It was a bomb. He's lucky to be alive by the sound of it.

Is he missing any...

-I shook my head, anticipating her question.

He said the blast knocked him out for a time but he got away without any serious physical injury. His buddies weren't so lucky. Both of them were killed.

Oh mercy, Tegan, why must men war?

-Pen reached over and patted my hand.

The loss of a young life is always a tragedy, Tegan, whatever one thinks of war. You bring him here anytime you like. We'll welcome him into our home.

-Trewin ran a hand through his silver hair and rapped the table with his finger.

Those goddamn bombers are cowards, blowing up innocents along with their own worthless carcasses. But there's too much anger and hate in the world as it is. I say we need more love. So, where's a good-looking forty year old when you need one? Ah well, if you can't have love at least there's Scotch whisky to make life worth living.

-Pen raised his glass and we did the same.

To love and new beginnings.

-I downed my glass in one swallow, wondering why I would have the slightest interest in Claude or any other man after what I'd been through. Did I even want a romantic relationship? I had no idea. Not the sort of answer that builds confidence. As I half-listened to Trewin holding forth on the merits of a good Scotch, I decided I'd let Claude make amends and leave it at that.

The following morning, instead of the sorry state of my social life my mind filled with thoughts of Diego and Celia. In the weeks since I had spoken with him, Omar had steered clear of them both, spending more time away from the trailer than at home. I hoped the relative calm would last. Diego needed to return to school. I mulled over what else I might do to prepare him as I made my way toward the door of their trailer.

Mounting the stairs, I peered through the screen door before knocking on the flimsy metal siding. I paused to listen. No sound came from inside. I knocked again and called out but got no response so I checked behind the trailer, finding no sign of Celia's car. Thinking Diego might be inside using his earphones, I walked back around the trailer, opening the screen door and stepping inside. I called out again as I wandered down the narrow hallway.

To my left, the door to what appeared to be Celia's bedroom stood open. Another room sat directly across the hall, also open. I peeked into the cluttered space, the walls littered with music posters and artwork clearly belonging to Diego. I turned back into the hallway. A third door, this one closed, marked the end of the hall.

I stood before it and twisted the knob, letting the door swing open on its own. On a large table before me blueprints, schematics and photos, all of the state capitol building, lay scattered about. Notes in some unrecognizable foreign script covered a yellow legal pad. In one corner, a laptop surrounded by several cell phones occupied a small desk.

I surveyed the contents of the room, puzzling over their purpose. Some of the photos were taken from the air. Could they explain the flying lessons? Was Omar doing some sort of work for the government, something involving the capitol? I pulled the door closed and walked back down the hall.

I had just stepped out the door when Omar's black car roared around the corner, passing the tree line and sliding to a stop feet from me. A cloud of white dust floated past the trailer. I slipped my fingers around my canister of mace as he jumped from the car, hurrying to where I waited on the stairs. He peered through the open door and then turned his black eyes on me.

What do you do here?
-I somehow managed to lie and tell the truth simultaneously.

I came to see Diego but I've knocked several times and no one answers. They must be out.
-The same worried look I had seen before altered his face.

You do not go in there?
I have no reason to go in if no one is at home, do I?
-He glanced over his shoulder and gestured toward my car.

If no one is here you must go. You must go now.
You seem in a hurry. Are you trying to meet some sort of deadline? What business did you say you're in?
-He glanced over his shoulder again.

Do not ask me more. You must go.
-I decided not to press my luck so I stepped past him and climbed into my car. As I drove back down the rutted road, I noticed Eloy in my rearview mirror. He stepped away from the roadside bushes, pointing his cane to the sky and raising his other hand in some sort of blessing, his mouth open as if singing to the heavens. I suddenly realized what I must do to help Diego return to school.

-Then a flash of light caught my eye. Turning toward it, I spotted the black van pulling from a side street and heading toward the trailer. Omar's men had obviously been waiting for his signal. I let my mind linger on what lay behind his shady business but only for a moment. Esther Schultz had another teenager for me to see, her home life even worse than Diego's by the sound of it. I hoped I was up to the task.

Chapter Ten

Chancer climbed into the small round space of the campus observatory, pulling Byes in behind him and shutting the metal hatch with a clang. The echo reverberated off the curved ceiling in waves of diminishing sound, as if they stood in the center of a huge bell. A single red bulb cast the space in a warm glow.

Byes watched as he darted about the cramped space. Lifting the wooden handle of a metal crank, he wound it clockwise and a slice of the curved ceiling began moving to one side, the cloudless night sky appearing beyond. A wave of cold air spilled through the opening. She stepped next to him, wrapping her arm around his elbow and leaning into him as he maneuvered the telescope into position.

Giving her a quick smile, he reached past her to flip a switch. The ancient electric tracking mechanism hummed to life. An instant later the metal roof lurched forward, creeping along the line of geared teeth edging the dome, the movement so slow as to be almost beyond notice. Chancer peered through the narrow opening at the black night. Turning to him, Byes studied the side of his angular face, his thick hair falling past his eyes. She brushed the strands from his forehead.

I won't have that unruly hair hiding those beautiful eyes.
-He felt himself blush and bent toward the eyepiece, trying to act nonchalant.
I've almost got it in place.
Chancer, I never imagined astronomy could be so romantic.
-He let go of the viewfinder, facing her.
You like it here?
I like cuddling up to you on a cold night.
Wait until you see this, Byes.

-He again bent over the telescope, adjusting the brass knobs before looking up and pointing into the night.

That group of stars is the constellation Orion, and those three stars in a row are his belt. In Greek mythology, Orion was a hunter who was made into a constellation after he died. You're going to be looking at something below the belt.

You make it sound so sexy.

-Chancer looked up, again feeling the blood rush to his face.

What?

Never mind. What will I see?

-He checked the eyepiece again and motioned her toward it.

Take a look at the Orion nebula.

-Byes peered through the lens at an oval cloud of violet and blue, gas-like and ethereal, with hazy points of light scattered throughout. She looked up at the sky again and then back through the eyepiece before facing him.

Chancer, it's amazing, not to mention beautiful. It's like some strange cloud.

That's just what it is, a cloud of gas and dust where stars sometime form. The Orion nebula was discovered by Christian Huygens, a Dutch astronomer in the seventeenth century.

-She leaned closed to him.

I like the way your lips say nebula. Say it for me.

-He whispered the word and she kissed him lightly. Then she drew back, smiling at him.

I'm sure glad this stargazer is not a fish.

-He squinted at her.

You're not going to let me forget that mistake, are you?

Where's the fun in that?

It was an honest mistake. There really is a fish called a stargazer.

You want to forget? I'll make you forget.

-Byes leaned into him again, kissing him hard. An instant later, the lights flashed on and the hatch flew open, followed by the top of a bald head. The man turned to them, his white eyebrows dancing about his coffee-colored face. Voices mixed with shuffling footsteps below him.

Oh mercy, I didn't know anyone was up here. Professor Greene is always forgetting to mark the sign-up sheet when he schedules a star party. I'm Professor Franklin and I'm covering for him tonight. Say, aren't you in my quantum physics class? Your name is Wylls, if I remember right.

-Chancer jumped from the stool.

I'm surprised you noticed me, Professor Franklin. It's a big class

I noticed your interest in the probability mathematics of Pascal and Fermat. I happen to share that interest.

-Chancer waved a hand at Byes.

This is Byes Byerson.

-The professor managed a slight bow in spite of his cramped position.

I am please to meet you, Miss Byerson.

Please call me Byes.

Then you must call me Franklin. Everyone does. You see, my full name is Franklin Jefferson Franklin so it works both ways. My father was a physicist with a great love for Ben Franklin, arguably the first American physicist.

-She gestured toward the telescope.

You need to use the observatory tonight, don't you, Franklin?

Right you are, Byes. I have no doubt you are signed up for the time.

Actually, it was Chancer that signed up.

-He sighed, nodding his round head.

Then, Chancer, I'm going to impose on your good nature and ask if we may use the telescope tonight. I have fifteen people who'll be much disappointed if you refuse us.

Of course, we'll get out of your way Professor...

-Franklin waved a finger at him.

It's just Franklin.

We have the Orion nebula in view, Franklin.

You've done me another favor, then. Follow me out here. I have something else to say.

-They climbed out of the small space, making their way through the crowded room to where Franklin stood waiting. He tugged on his white beard as he peered at Byes.

Byes, will you mind much if I ask Chancer to do something that may cut into your time together?

It's kind of you to ask, Franklin, but you don't need my permission. Chancer makes his own decisions.

-He faced Chancer.

Alright then, Chancer, I'd like you to help me with a project. It has to do with probability theory. Will you agree to it?

Chancer stood staring at him, speechless at the thought of a professor asking for his help. Byes gave him a quick nudge.

How long do you need to think it over, Chancer?

-He looked at her and then back at Franklin.

I wasn't thinking it over. I was trying to be sure I heard you right. You want me to assist you?

Yes, yes, that's precisely what I'm asking. I'm sorry to say I can't pay for your time. But, it promises to be an adventure. I should get back to my star party. What do you say?

I'm not sure if I'm up to the work but I'd like to try.

-He grabbed Chancer's hand while his brushy eyebrows danced above his eyes.

Excellent news, most excellent, I have to say. Come to my office before class and we'll discuss it.

-He took Byes' hand, giving her another quick bow before disappearing through the doorway.

A crescent moon balanced above the rooftops as Byes led Chancer along a bustling street, the lights from cafes and shops spilling onto the sidewalk in fantastic shapes. The calm quiet of the observatory seemed a distant memory. Students brushed past them in small groups, their voices mixed with music drifting from doors open in spite of the chill air.

At a street corner they passed a girl of no more than fourteen wearing a short dress and no coat, shivering in the chill air. She held up a tin can half-filled with coins, shaking it at Chancer. Reaching into his pants pocket, he pulled out what change he could find and dropped it into the can, trying to imagine her life on the street as he hurried to catch up with Byes.

She paused at the entrance to a bar, turned to him and smiled, then pulled him inside. Chancer peered into the dark interior. Dancers glowed under black lights, their faces pale and masklike, their silhouettes moving to the throbbing rhythm of a band. A hand appeared out of nowhere holding a lighted joint. He shook his head and instead followed Byes past the surreal scene. After a moment, they pushed through the back exit, stepping into a narrow alleyway.

Without a word she pointed to a half-open door across from them, starting toward it. Chancer followed her through the entrance and down a short hallway. A room opened before him. A line of windows facing a busy street corner covered the far wall. She waved to a table near the door then grabbed his hand, pulling him along. A moment later they stood before a young man, his long hair held in place by a bandana. A thin beard traced the outline of his jaw. Byes gestured toward Chancer.

Henry Rimes, this is my friend Chancer Wylls.
-He held up two fingers.
Peace, man, peace in our lifetime.
-Byes turned to Chancer.

Henry was leading the protest when the cops gassed us.

-He lifted the edge of his bandana to show a red mark above his right eye.

The war-mongers gave me this for loving peace. Violence begets violence, man. You know what I mean?

-Chancer glanced at Byes and nodded gravely.

I believe I do.

-He pointed at Chancer's chest.

Belief, man, that's where it's at. We've got to believe. Never forget that. You won't forget, will you?

-Chancer had no idea what he was talking about but felt Byes' gaze on him so he went along.

No, Henry, I won't forget.

Then have a seat and let's talk.

-Chancer pulled out a chair and sat. Byes moved to a seat across from him, next to Henry. He leaned across the table, peering into Chancer's face.

What's your draft number, Chancer?

I don't know yet.

You mean you don't have one?

I'll find out in the next lottery.

Whoa, that's heavy, just waiting for the axe to fall. My number is two hundred forty-seven. No chance they'll get that far down the list. What will you do if you get called up?

I guess I'll have to go.

-Henry peered at him.

Don't even kid about that, man. You don't want to support the military-industrial power brokers that are getting rich off the war, do you?

I'm not sure I have much choice.

That's no way to think, Chancer. You have to get your head straight about this. I'm serious, man. Your life depends on it. Don't you see that?

-Chancer glanced at Byes, wishing he could leave with her right then. She stared at him, waiting for an answer.

I guess I do.

You don't sound so sure, man. Look, I'm going to do you a favor.

What sort of favor?

-Henry grabbed a napkin and scribbled on it before handing it to him.

This is the name of a friend of mine at Middle Earth. Give this to him. He's going to tell it to you like it is. Promise me you'll hear him out, Chancer.

-Byes waited for his answer, an expectant look in her eyes. Chancer studied the napkin, nodding.

Sure, Henry, I'll go see him.

-Henry stood and pulled on his denim jacket.

Far out, man. Come to our next peace march. We meet three weeks from today on the south mall.

-Byes stood and faced him.

Henry, are you leaving?

I have a rally meeting. Since we're going on that dig, I won't have much planning time before the next march.

-Henry cupped her face in his hands, kissing her full on the lips. Chancer looked away, trying to hide his disappointment. He wondered what sort of friend Henry must be. Henry turned to face him.

She's a fox, isn't she? Thanks for sharing, man.

-Chancer had no idea what to say.

Uh… okay.

I guess you heard we're leaving tomorrow for a two week dig with our archaeology class down in Mexico. The site is a choice spot above an artesian spring that's prime for skinny-dipping. I'll tell you how it went after we get back. Now I have to get going. Later, man.

-He turned and vanished out the door before Chancer could find his voice. Byes peered into his face.

Did that bother you? It did, didn't it? Oh, Chancer, Henry and I are old friends, is all. We go back a long way.

Were you going to tell me you'd be gone for two weeks?

Didn't I tell you? Oh, I meant to, Chancer. I've just been busy trying to get ahead so I wouldn't fall behind in my classes. Let me make it up to you.

-She grabbed his hand, pulling him back down the hallway and into the alley. Moments later they were again pushing through the black-lighted dancers. Byes stopped and turned to face him. Raising her arms in the air, she stepped toward him, her hips matching the band's pulsating rhythms as she pressed herself against him then moved away. Closing her eyes, she danced a small circle. He watched her, mesmerized by her fluid beauty.

-She motioned for him to join in before closing her eyes again, lost to the music. Terrified, Chancer glanced around him. He had never danced before. After a moment of hopping from one foot to the other, he managed an awkward imitation of the crowd. A woman in a tie-died blouse sauntered between him and Byes. He stared at the glowing imprints of two hands covering her breasts.

-Smiling, she held up a joint and blew a thick cloud of smoke into his face. Chancer shook his head but instead of moving away, she thrust the end between his lips. A sudden image of Henry kissing Byes flashed through his mind, the disappointment again filling his chest. He nodded to the woman, taking a long pull and then another, his worries drifting away with the smoke. The woman smiled again and stepped toward him, rubbing her glow in the dark handprints against his chest before moving off.

-An instant later Byes appeared out of the glowing mass of figures, reaching for him as she moved to the beat. Her hand felt impossibly large in his. He leaned forward, peering into her face. For a moment it seemed she could read his mind. Her red hair floated about her head in an undulating cloud, the ends dripping with lime green and fuchsia. The crowd seemed to close in, their faces pale and menacing, as if they too could read his thoughts.

-A sudden wave of panic pulsed through him, taking his breath. He turned toward the exit, pulling Byes behind him. Moments later they stumbled into the alleyway. Laughing, Byes reached up and brushed the hair from his eyes. All at once, he could breathe again. As his mind cleared, he peered into her face, wondering if he would ever know the truth about her and Henry, unsure whether he wanted to. He felt the odds turning against him.

Chancer paid little notice to the cloud-scrubbed sky as he walked away from Byes' dorm, a dull ache lodged in his throat. Did Byes care for him or was he just another of her 'friends'? Where did Henry fit into her life? What would he do if he was drafted? He wondered if he had a say in any of it.

A familiar urge to retreat into his studies intruded on his thoughts. His brief foray into the real world, the world of protests and 'friends', a world he failed to understand, now seemed a mistake. At least Franklin's invitation was something he could look forward to. He needed something solid, something he could feel sure of. The mathematics of Fermat and Pascal drifted before him like a raft on an empty sea.

Chapter Eleven

Esther Schultz stood on her front porch waiting for me as I pulled to the curb and climbed out of my car. She wore a simple orange shift and sandals, the sun-drenched afternoon feeling unusually warm for late February. Earlier she had told me she had a sensitive case and asked that I come to her home rather than the office to discuss it. Perched on a limestone bluff, the modest solidity of the rock house somehow seemed a physical version of her.

She led me around the corner to a limestone patio overlooking a narrow valley and the haze-shrouded hills beyond. The rush of flowing water drifted up the bluff. In the distance, a silver line marking the creek wound between the hills, winking like light off a cellophane ribbon. Esther poured a glass of ice tea and handed it to me, nodding toward a nearby chair. She sat and filled a glass for herself. In the resulting silence, I suddenly wondered if the sensitive case she mentioned was me.

I know I may have sounded a bit dramatic on the phone, asking you here instead of meeting at the office, but I have my reasons.

Have I done something wrong, Esther?

-She cackled and waved off the question.

No, I'd say the opposite is true. I need your help with a situation.

Oh, that's a relief. You had me worried.

School districts can be small worlds and the politics that go along with them tricky to navigate. But before we get into that, tell me about yourself, Tegan. I've been so busy I haven't had a chance to visit with you the way I'd like to.

-I peered at her, surprised by the question.

Where should I start?

Jump in anyplace you like. Where are you from? Do you have family here?

-I leaned back in the chair, thinking of Chancer.

I was born in Houston but I've lived here most of my life. My grandparents helped my father raise me.

-Her blue eyes danced about as she considered what she'd heard.

That's an unusual arrangement.

He was a single parent and sort of an absent-minded professor so he needed the help.

I imagine that could be useful in working with these kids.

I suppose it is. Fortunately, I was lucky enough to have grandparents willing and able to do their part. My life would've turned out very different without them.

-Esther smoothed back her reddish-brown hair, giving her head a shake.

My father used to say that the older I got the smarter he'd get. He was right about that.

I called my father by his first name, if that tells you anything. He was sweet-natured but too smart for his own good. He got along better in the world of ideas than the world of people.

I understand he died recently.

He was killed in a one-car accident.

-I looked away, unused to the strangeness of hearing myself say it. She leaned toward me.

He must have been far too young.

-I nodded, again thinking about our recent time together.

In the last couple of years he had been trying hard to be a father. We even went on a couple of trips together, something he never liked much.

And what happened to your mother?

I wish I could tell you but she left soon after I was born. I know almost nothing about her.

-She peered at me.

You become more interesting by the moment, Tegan Wylls. But I don't want to take too much of your time, at least not right now. We'd better move on to the problem at hand.

Sounds serious, whatever it is. I hope I'm up to the task.

Rather than serious, I'd call it sensitive, and you're better suited than you realize. You're going to be working with a girl, a fourteen year old. Her name is Cheering Sanders. She's had a rough time of it, taken from her home by family services after her mother got involved with drugs.

There's not a father in the picture?

Unsurprisingly, he and the girl's mother couldn't get along so he left for parts unknown.

Where is the girl now?

They've placed her with her grandparents.

Now there's a coincidence.

I'd call it fate to have you with us right now, Tegan.

Fate or luck, I'm looking forward to meeting her. When do I start?

There's more to her story than I've told you so far.

What haven't you told me?

Her grandfather is my boss.

-I tried to hide my surprise.

She's the granddaughter of the district superintendent?

His daughter got involved with cocaine when she was quite young. Unfortunately, she got pregnant early on as well. She managed to get clean for some years but took a downward turn when her husband, the girl's father, left. That went on for months, with the girl running away to her grandparents on a regular basis. Finally, family services stepped in.

Did something in particular happen?

She was molested by one of the mother's many boyfriends.

How long did it go on?

She won't talk about it, at least not yet.

So that's where I come in?

You can see the sensitive nature of your work. Don't misunderstand me. I have no worries about you keeping it confidential. But the superintendent is sensitive to the girl's position as his granddaughter and wants to avoid making things worse for her.

Then where I see her will be important.

That's right. We've arranged a comfortable space for you next door to our office. She'll be starting school here next week and you can see her then.

The small but strange coincidences in my life filled my thoughts as I climbed into my car. How many young girls end up being raised by their grandparents? What are the chances I would end up counseling one? I had decided to go see Vincent and talk to him about Diego. As I stepped onto his porch, rapping twice on the screen door, I realized by asking for his help I was playing the odds in a different sense.

Vincent's thin face appeared behind the screen like a pale image of himself, ephemeral, ghost-like. I tried to hide my concern as I stepped past him into the spare living room. He was the key to my plan. I hoped he would be willing to help but more important, able to. I avoided facing him for a moment, wondering if he had developed some new illness.

Looking about the room, I stopped in mid-step. A luminous painting of a woman, her profile to the viewer, stood on an easel before me. Blown by an unseen wind, her auburn hair swirled about her head, partially obscuring her face. I realized at once I was looking at myself. I turned to him with the question on my lips but he spoke before I had a chance to.

I hope you don't mind, Tegan. I just had this vision of you standing in an open field with the wind in your hair. I became so obsessed with the idea I went for two nights without sleep trying to finish. If it's any consolation, I only paint people I'm fond of. Please don't be offended.

I'm surprised, Vincent, not offended. But I can't imagine why you'd want to paint me.

Ideas just come to me and I have to see them through. It's sort of a compulsion. Besides, you're a good subject with your red hair and fair skin.

I suppose we should thank my mother for that.

Does it look alright? I'm beginning to mistrust my sight, especially when it comes to color combinations and detail work.

It looks good to me.

That's a relief. I may have to ask your advice on some others.

I'm glad I could be of help, Vincent. In return I'm going to ask you for a favor.

Anything for you, fair Tegan.

One of my students is a talented artist and he's in need of a man's influence. I'm hoping he can assist you.

You want me to take on an assistant?

I think it might be helpful on both your parts.

He's not a serial killer or anything like that, is he? I don't want a young Charles Manson roaming around the house.

He has a temper but I think you'll get along, especially when you see his paintings. Besides, he can see just fine.

That would help. Some days I waste half an hour searching for something that's right in front of me.

His name is Diego Rivera.

You're joking.

No, that's his real name.

As in the well-known Mexican painter?

If you say so.

In that case, I agree to your plan. Now I have to leave. I have a date.

-I cocked my head, squinting at him.

87

You have a date as in a romantic evening?

-He frowned.

Don't look so surprised, Tegan. I do take a break from painting now and then.

-He grabbed his phone and brushed past me.

Don't forget to lock the door when you leave.

-I decided to take another look at the painting before I left. A moment later footsteps sounded behind me. Thinking Vincent had forgotten something, I turned but found Claude standing in the doorway instead. He nodded toward the painting.

That's one of Vincent's best, but mostly because of the subject.

-I felt myself blush.

I was just leaving.

-He raised a hand to stop me.

I still have that housewarming gift.

-I blushed again, knowing how I had avoided him.

I didn't forget, Claude. It's just that I've been busy with work.

Can you stay for a glass of wine? I won't take much of your time. Just a toast to your new home and that'll be it. Otherwise, I'll hand over the bottle. It is for you, after all.

-He was so polite about it, I felt like I had to do more than just take the wine and leave. I nodded, managing a smile in spite of my reluctance. He motioned for me to sit before vanishing into the kitchen. Moments later he reappeared with two half-filled tumblers. Ruby-tinged light glinted through the wine. He held up his glass.

Here's to new beginnings. In addition to your new home, I hear you have a new job as well.

-That he made the same toast as Pen flashed through my mind, and I again wondered if I had misjudged him.

I suppose so, although neither feels new anymore.

Vincent said you work with troubled kids. That can be difficult work. I admire people willing to take it on.

-His flattery, along with the wine, was beginning to work. I sat back in the chair, feeling myself relax a bit.

Ah, so you've been talking about me behind my back.

I needed to do my research so I could make amends properly.

Is that what this is, making amends?

Like I said, I was less than friendly when we first met. I hope that wine is alright.

-I took a sip.

I could get used to this.

I got Vincent's help picking out the wine. Most of the guys in my program drink beer.

What are you studying?

I'm in criminal justice. I plan to go into the Border Patrol.

-Omar and his black van intruded on my thoughts and I again wondered what he was up to. Without intending to, I suddenly found myself telling Claude.

One of my students is caught up in a puzzling situation. Can I talk to you about it? You may have some thoughts from the criminal justice perspective.

-He leaned toward me, a surprised but intrigued look in his eyes.

I doubt I'll be much help but I'm willing to try.

The student's name is Diego. His mother's boyfriend is from somewhere outside the country. I think he may have come here through Mexico, legally or not. He seems to be up to no good.

What makes you think so, Tegan?

-I liked hearing him say my name but I tried to focus on my questions.

I won't say how but I found blueprints and photos of the capitol at the house. The boyfriend acts nervous and suspicious anytime I ask about his work. He has a group of men, also of the same nationality more or less, that seem to work for him. They get upset when I show up unannounced and generally act as suspicious as him.

-I sat back, trying to catch my breath after rushing through all I knew in seconds. He ran a hand through his thick hair and squinted at me.

If I was an agent along the border and came across that, I'd definitely call it in.

You would?

Mexico is an easy entryway for criminal types. Then again, I'm a student. What do I know?

My guess is they are involved in some sort of smuggling.

Considering how close we are to the border, that makes the most sense. We have stolen artwork, black market goods and high-tech secrets crossing the border all the time. That's in addition to the human trafficking and drug smuggling you hear about in the news.

I can't imagine what the blueprints are about.

It would make more sense if they had the layout of a bank or new type of computer.

What should I do?

You should be careful, and smart. Smugglers in this part of the world don't think twice about eliminating a threat. Unless they're believed to have something illegal in their possession there's little the authorities can do. You didn't see anything like that, did you?

No, I guess not.

Could you get some evidence of what you saw?

Maybe, but it would be tricky.

I don't want you to put yourself in a risky situation. I tell you what, Tegan. I'll ask one of my professors about it. That is, if I don't get kicked out beforehand.

-I suddenly recalled him confiding his injury and school troubles to me when we last met. My heart again went out to him and I fished a business card from my purse, scribbling a name on the back and handing it to him.

This is a friend at the university who may have some useful ideas. Will you talk to him?

-He held the card up to the light.

Sure, Tegan, I'll give him a call.

In the meantime, I'll look forward to hearing what your professors say about our mystery.

Getting them to stop long enough to take a question is a challenge. Most of them are ex-lawmen and used to being on the go.

You don't strike me as a man of action, Claude.

Don't I? Well, if you'll let me take you to my favorite pub maybe I can change your mind.

-I looked into his handsome face, realizing that my initial hesitation had been replaced with interest. I finished my glass and stood. Then I stepped out the door without another word, afraid I might look too eager if I said so much as good-bye.

Chapter Twelve

Although crisp sunlight filtered through a green canopy of live oaks, dappling the broken sidewalk before him, Chancer's thoughts were instead focused on the cosmos. At that very moment the planet Jupiter was poised to move past Aldebaran, a massive star in the constellation Taurus. Also known as the eye of the bull, follower of the Seven Sisters, the giant star roamed his thoughts like a wayward comet, or perhaps an avenging angel. After weeks of avoiding it, he had decided to visit Turley.

He pushed through the entrance of Ben Taub Hospital, the county trauma center, coming face to face with a sea of jostling people. Taking a breath, he scurried across the lobby then threaded his way down a hallway crammed with empty gurneys and shelves stacked with medical supplies. Out of nowhere an image of Turley, his pants soaked with blood, filled his mind. In some inexplicable way, he felt responsible for the accident.

Turning to his left, he hurried down a secondary hall trying to dismiss his guilt with a litany of excuses. He turned again and a wall of odors, antiseptic mixed with sweat and garbage, swirled around and past him, leaving him light-headed and nauseous. He forced himself to press on.

A moment later, he came to a broad set of doors and pushed through into a room filled with beds. He scanned the rows for Turley. Seeing no sign of him, he turned to leave and instead found himself face to face with Ben Ahote. Chancer blinked, wondering if he could trust his eyes. Ben smiled and waved a finger at him.

It's about time you made it down here, Chancer. I was beginning to think that bump on the head was worse than it looked.

-Chancer took a step back.

Ben, what are you doing here?

I work here.

-He glanced at Ben's leg.

But you broke your leg.

Turns out it was just a fractured tibia, painful as hell but quick to mend. I still have a brace on under these scrubs.

But how did you end up here of all places?

I was a medic in 'Nam so I know the ropes, more or less. I worked the survey crew because the money was good, but after the accident my advisor told me working in a hospital gives me a better shot at getting into medical school. She sent me here.

You're in college? How come you never talked about it?

The same reason you didn't. That's the last thing guys like Turley want to hear.

Where is he?

The doctor is with him. I'll take you over in a minute. First, tell me where you ended up.

-Chancer grimaced at the thought.

I ended up nowhere, Ben. I'll go broke if something doesn't come along soon.

Why not work here? The place can get a little intense but it's steady work.

-Chancer shrugged, feeling inept.

I don't have any hospital experience, Ben.

That's not a problem. Just come with me.

-He vanished around the corner. Chancer hurried behind, catching up with him at a low counter where a nurse sat scribbling on a paper-filled clipboard, mumbling to herself. Her mahogany-hued skin shone smooth beneath the fluorescent lights. After a moment she looked up, giving Ben a pained look.

Ben Ahote, a smart college student such as yourself must have better things to do than stand around watching me write. And who is that young man you have with you? This ward is not your personal fraternity house, you know.

-He nodded at Chancer.

This is Chancer Wylls, Nurse Berry. He's in need of a job.

-She stood and raised her eyebrows, studying him.

Is he now? Well, Mister Wylls, can you assure me that you are in no trouble with the law?

Am I in trouble with the law?

And that you have no communicable diseases?

Diseases?

And you are sound in mind and body?

I…

-She moved her broad face close to his.

And you are able to speak the English language in an understandable manner?

What?

Perhaps it is your understanding of the language that is in question, Mr. Wylls.

No… I, uh… I understand. I know how to talk.

-She stepped back smiling.

I'm relieved to hear it. We can schedule around your classes. We don't want to interfere with the education of young people. Are you able to start on Wednesday?

-Chancer grunted in the affirmative, so unsettled by her rapid pace he could barely speak.

Then be here at seven sharp. Ben can show you the locker room and whatever else you have time for today. I will expect you bright and early.

-She grabbed several clipboards from the counter, disappearing down the hall. Chancer turned to Ben, trying to believe what he had just heard.

I have a job?

Welcome to Ward Six, Chancer. Now I'll take you to Turley.

-He pivoted and started back down the hallway, Chancer on his heels.

How's his leg, Ben? He's been here quite awhile.

A chainsaw is a powerful machine. The doctors had to reconstruct his knee. But they found something else, something having to do with his blood, and they're still trying to figure out what it is.

That sounds serious.

He thinks it's Agent Orange.

What is that?

Agent Orange is a defoliant. The geniuses at the Pentagon decided to spray 'Nam with millions of gallons of the stuff to clear out the jungle. Sounds like a good idea, right? The problem is they sprayed a lot of us on the ground too. There's no telling what slogging around in plant poison does to you.

-They found Turley sitting up in bed, his eyes closed, his back against the wall. Ben slapped the rail with his palm. Turley turned toward the sound, his features gaunt and glassy-eyed. Chancer looked away, trying to hide his surprise. A bitter smile crossed Turley's lips.

You really missed it not getting hurt any worse than you did, Wylls. The pain meds here are choice.

-Ben snorted.

You ought to know, Turley, you've tried them all.

You're damn right I have, Injun Joe.

-He shoved a finger in Chancer's face.

You took your damn sweet time getting your ass up here.

-Chancer managed to face him.

How are you feeling, Turley?

How in the hell do you think? Take a closer look.

-Chancer leaned toward him.

You don't look so bad.

-He grabbed the rail and pulled himself forward.

Don't lie to me, Chancer. I look like hell and I know it. The goddamn Yellow Rain has got its claws in me. The freaking army brass couldn't kill me off in 'Nam but they might still do it. I'd like to drop a load of napalm on the bastards.

-Ben lifted a pitcher from the bedside table and filled a paper cup, handing it to him.

Take it easy, Turley. Have the doctors found out anything yet?

-He drained the glass and lowered it, out of breath at the effort.

They still have some tests to run but they think it's leukemia.

-Ben reached across the rail, taking him by the shoulder, leaning in close.

'To know your enemy, you must become your enemy'.

That's Sun Tzu?

-Ben nodded and Turley's faced changed in an instant, the bravado gone.

You'll fight with me, won't you Ben? I need you to, man. Tell me you will.

-He clasped Turley's forearm.

Did once and will again, brother.

-Turley fell back against the wall, clearly exhausted. Ben glanced at Chancer before patting the mattress.

I'll be checking back on you but first I need to show Chancer around. He just got hired.

-Turley's eyes fluttered as he spoke, his voice a near whisper.

Welcome to the war, Wylls.

They passed though a long hallway, stopping at an open set of doors. Beyond the entrance, two rows of beds lined the opposing walls of a narrow, rectangular room. A sign beside the doors read "Pre/Post Recovery". Ben motioned Chancer to follow as he strolled along the beds.

Halfway down the row they came upon a nun in a gray and white habit standing over an old man, his face as gray as her cloak. Chancer watched as she bent toward him and pressed her ear to his chest. An instant later she sighed and stood, raising her fist and bringing it down on him with

96

a solid thump. The man jumped at the blow and opened his eyes wide, staring up at her with a questioning look, his voice like a rusty hinge.

What the… what happened, Sister Beatrice?

Your heart stopped again, William. I'm sorry I had to wake you in such a way.

- She smiled and moved off down the row. The old man eased back onto the bed as Chancer turned to Ben.

What did she just do?

We have an order of nuns that work here as nurses. Sister Beatrice has been keeping the old man alive like that for years.

-Ben moved down the row, stopping in front of a white-haired woman with a hardback book propped on her chest. Age spots mottled her gnarled brown hands. Lowering the book, she looked up at him

Why, Mister Ben Ahote, I thought you had forgotten your promise to come see me before my surgery.

-Ben pulled Chancer next to him.

I ran into an unexpected surprise. Miss Beulah King, this is Chancer Wylls. We used to work together and just found out we're going to be working together again.

-A grave expression crossed her coffee-colored face.

You're coming to work here, Mister Wylls?

Yes 'mam.

This is important work. This is the Lord's work that you come to do. Never forget that.

Yes 'mam.

-She tapped the front of the book.

Do you enjoy a good read, Mister Wylls?

I'm just Chancer, Miss King.

You may call me Beulah, if you please.

I do like books, Beulah.

Have you read *A Tale of Two Cities*, Chancer? The novel is set during the time of the French Revolution. Mister Charles Dickens does a fine job telling the tale.

97

No, I haven't read it.

Then may I give you this book of mine?

But don't you want to finish it?

-She winked at him, a smile spreading across her red lips.

I read the last chapter this morning. I was just rereading bits of the story here and there but I believe I'll be going in soon. Mister Dickens had a special feeling for the poor people of his time, you know, perhaps because as a child he was poor himself.

-She held out the book, clutching it for a moment while she studied his face.

Chancer, will you sit and talk with me until they take me in?

-Ben placed a hand on his shoulder, directing him to a nearby chair.

I need to go check on my ward. Bad things happen if I'm away too long. Come find me when you've finished your talk.

-He vanished through the doorway. Beulah grabbed the rail and leaned toward Chancer, her voice just above a whisper.

Don't tell Ben but I get a bit nervous waiting. I have never spent a day in the hospital before now. I don't quite know what to make of it.

I guess it's new to me too.

-She studied him again, her eyes dancing about.

Am I right in guessing you do not hope to attend medical school like our friend, Ben Ahote?

I'm going to study astronomy.

Well, that *is* something different. I do love to gaze into the night sky on a warm summer night. I believe I can see the hand of God in all that beauty, all that grandeur, the stars as they move above us season after season, the cycle of time sweeping past in one constellation after the other.

That's very poetic, Beulah.

Why, it's kind of you to say so, Chancer. My mother read poetry, most especially the poetry of Langston Hughes. It is because of her that I love books.

Does she live here?

-Beulah leaned back, staring out the window as she spoke.

My mother died when I was still a girl.

What about your father? Is he around?

My father was killed in an automobile accident four years after my mother passed on. Losing a parent is a hard thing for a young person to understand, Chancer, but losing both is almost unbearable. No child should be left alone in this hard world.

Do you have any family close by?

No, I'm all that's left. All my relations, all my aunts and uncles, all my brothers and sisters, they're all gone.

I'm sorry, Beulah.

-She shook her head, patting the rail with her hand.

Now don't you be sorry for me, Chancer. I'm old now and all that was long ago. Besides, I'll be joining them someday.

-She let out a slow, hoarse laugh.

But let's hope it's just not today, huh, Chancer? Knock on wood.

-She tapped her knuckle on the bedside table. Footsteps sounded behind him and she looked past him.

I believe my good luck wish was just in time. Here they are to take me.

-Two orderlies in green scrubs went to each end of the bed. She reached out to Chancer, taking his hand.

Now, you come and see me when you have a spare moment.

-She squeezed his hand. As she disappeared down the hallway, Chancer stood watching, a knot rising in his throat. He puzzled over why. Did his ill father weigh on his mind? Could coming to see Turley be the cause? Then an image of Henry kissing Byes flashed before him. Taking a breath, he stepped through the door, struggling to put her from thought.

Ben led Chancer up a narrow staircase that opened onto a circular arena ringed with seats. In the center of the room an oval glass-covered window overlooked the room below. A metal rail edged the opening. Chancer peered through the window, wondering why Ben had brought him there. An empty metal table stood in the center of their view surrounded by moveable lights, monitors and a large, rectangular box lined with tubes.

Chancer moved to the rail as two orderlies wheeled a gurney into the room. He leaned his elbows against the cold metal, suddenly realizing the window looked down on an operating room. Though crossed with tubes and partially hidden by a blue sheet, the patient below him was a black woman. A red birthmark stretched across her left wrist. A sudden fear gripped his chest. Could he be looking down on Beulah King? He strained to remember if she had such a mark. Ben sat next to him and Chancer glanced at him without a word, afraid to ask.

Below them, a crowd of green-robed figures entered the room, obscuring Chancer's view as they moved about the table attaching tubes and checking machinery. Within minutes, blood began streaming through the rectangular box, following a line of tubes that snaked from one end to the other. Then the box began rocking back and forth in a slow, jerking motion. Ben nudged him, pointing to the contraption.

That's a heart-lung machine, Chancer. It keeps oxygen in the patient's blood while the surgeon repairs the heart.

She's having heart surgery?

-Ben leaned against the rail.

She? Oh, right, the patient is a woman. According to the schedule, they have an aorta repair and a double bypass set up for this afternoon. I'm guessing this is the aorta.

That sounds serious.

Damn right it's serious, Wylls.

Do you think she'll make it?

-Ben turned, studying him for a moment.

Listen up, Chancer. You can't be thinking of the patients as people while you work here. It'll eat you up if you do.

Not think of them as people? I'm not sure if I can do that, Ben.

I don't mean you can't be friendly and all when you're on the ward but you have to stay objective. Keep your distance. Remember that it's just part of your job to put them at ease.

I'll try to remember.

Trust me, Chancer. You won't last if you don't.

So, you were just putting Beulah King at ease?

-Ben leaned back, pointing into the space between them.

In 'Nam, everyone in my unit had a different date they got sent over and a different date they got sent home. We were all flying solo, all on our own. Most of the guys just tried to do their time and get out. We had each other's backs but I learned real quick not to get too friendly. Odds were the poor bastard next to you would get killed sooner than later and if you weren't careful it would tear you up. It's not that different here.

-He turned back to the window as the surgeon opened a section of sheet, running a scalpel down the middle of the woman's chest. Blood gushed from the incision. Chancer peered into the room, at once both fascinated and horrified as the doctors wiped away the flow, tossing blood-soaked wads of gauze into metal pans one after the other. He gripped the railing, speaking under his breath.

I never imagined surgery was so primitive.

-Ben pointed at him again.

Are you a philosophical man, Wylls?

I don't know, maybe. I study the stars, trying to understand the origin of the universe and where we all came from. Does that count?

Have you ever noticed how the world can change around you? How your perspective, what you actually see, can change completely from one time to the next?

You mean like when you go back to your hometown and it looks nothing like you remember it?

-He nodded and gestured toward the overlook.

There was a time when I thought like you do, that what they're doing down there is primitive. But what I saw in 'Nam changed me. The things I saw over there makes what they're doing right now seem skillful beyond belief, almost miraculous. What Beulah said is true, Chancer. This *is* important work. But you have to do it right to do it for long.

-Chancer turned his eyes back to the operating room, admiring the courage it takes to heal another human being and wondering if he was up to the task.

Chapter Thirteen

In 1654, two mathematicians, Pierre de Fermat and Blaise Pascal, decided to work together on the problem of figuring a winner's take in an unfinished game of dice. In the process they created probability theory. Chancer had come across the theory in his search to understand the unpredictability central to quantum mechanics, but probability itself soon became his obsession.

He sat staring at a page of equations, trying to keep his mind off Byes and her archaeology trip with Henry. The chances they were more than mere 'friends' seemed to increase by the day. But if probability theory could determine winning stakes, why not a winning hand of cards, or a winning horse? Could he use probability for that purpose? Perhaps Byes would be impressed if he did. In any event, he would need the knowledge for his work with Professor Franklin.

A faint knock pulled him from his thoughts. Opening the door, he found Gammie on the stairway landing, her back to him. On the lawn below, Trewin stood with his arms outstretched, his eyes closed. His lips appeared to move in silent prayer. Gammie sighed and turned to Chancer, a pained look on her face.

I do believe some evil person switched your uncle with my real child at birth. I have no other way to explain the strangeness of that man.

What's he doing, Gammie?

Probably some nonsense he picked up on all those travels of his. I've never known such a restless wanderer as my first-born son. I thought the eldest was supposed to be mature and responsible. He has about as much responsibility as a blue jay.

-Trewin dropped his arms and looked up at her.

Mother, I can hear you. All your talk is keeping me from paying proper homage to the four directions. That's bad luck, if you want to know.

Well, I don't. You can find more ways to waste time than anyone on earth.

-Chancer stepped next to her, curious about his uncle's ritual. He leaned over the rail.

How do you honor the four directions, Uncle Trewin?

-Gammie nudged him, speaking under her breath.

Don't encourage him, sugar. Ever since his poor wife died, he just hasn't been right. Right in the head, I mean.

-Trewin ignored her whisperings.

Some people believe the practice comes from the ancient Druids. Whatever the case, I learned it from a Welsh witch.

You met a witch?

She's not only a witch but a beauty too.

What did she teach you?

Well, I can't go into that in mixed company.

I mean, what did she teach you about the four directions?

-He turned a slow circle.

North provides us logic and reason, east gives us hope, and the south brings comfort. Most important of all, west is the home of those no longer with us.

-Gammie shook a finger at him.

Trewin, if you went to church more often you wouldn't need all this mumbo-jumbo to make you happy. And you might even meet a nice girl rather than some so-called witch. Instead you're filling Chancer's head with all your strange ideas.

Chancer has a curious mind, mother. There's nothing wrong with that.

He has stars enough in his eyes without your help.

-Trewin turned and walked away without another word. Chancer faced his grandmother.

Gammie, I'm studying science not sorcery.

104

I just don't want you to take after him, sugar.

Is that what you came to tell me?

What? No, of course it isn't. I'm here to see why you haven't come down for breakfast. Sister has made some of her special biscuits. You need to eat a good breakfast, sugar. You're burning the candle at both ends these days, working *and* going to school.

-He glanced at his watch.

I don't have time, Gammie.

-He pulled the door to and hurried down the stairs. Gammie followed then disappeared inside the house. Moments later, footsteps approached from behind as he climbed onto his bicycle. The two sisters appeared before him.

Now, Chancer, we've been through this too many times. You know Sister and I won't let you leave without having some breakfast. Take some biscuits with you. They're buttered and still warm.

-Weesie held out a grease-stained paper bag.

Sweetheart, someday when I'm dead and gone you'll find yourself wishing for some of Weesie's special biscuits and you'll look back with regret on those times you were just too busy to eat.

-He frowned and grabbed the bag from her, dropping in the wire basket.

Thanks for the biscuits, Weesie.

-Gammie leaned over the handlebars.

You promise to eat them, sugar?

-He nodded slowly for effect.

I'm in college now, Gammie. You can stop treating me like I'm six years old.

-Weesie leaned in next to her.

Men must eat, sweetheart. Not eating was the downfall of my Gerald, may he rest in peace. He was thin as a rail, a mere ghost of a man, when he passed on.

Listen to Sister, sugar. She knows firsthand the heartache of a man who won't eat right.

-Chancer sighed and pushed the bicycle past them.
I have to go.

An ambulance sounded in the distance, echoing
between buildings scattered along a curving loop just off
Main Street. A nearby grove of live oaks rattled in hushed
counterpoint before the morning breeze. As he had for
weeks, Chancer parked his bicycle next to the loading dock
and made his way toward the rear entrance where steam
poured from the hospital laundry in shifting clouds.
Pushing through the door, he headed for the stairwell.

Moments later he stepped into the second floor
hallway and began winding along the maze of connecting
throughways. Sirens came to life in the street below, their
high-pitched wails echoing up the stairwells. The eerie
sound still rattled him.

Continuing along the endless hallway, he sensed a
tension in the nurses and doctors moving past. A moment
later Ben appeared briefly then vanished through a double
doorway. Chancer hurried after him. Rounding a corner, he
found him waiting at the ward entrance. He motioned
Chancer to follow as he walked among the rows of newly
arrived patients.

Midway down the aisle, two stout nurses stood before
a shrouded figure. Chancer hesitated, suddenly realizing
the figure beneath the sheet was dead. Ben stopped and
hastened back to him, grabbing his arm and pulling him
toward a nearby gurney.

You have to concentrate, Chancer. We've got a
multiple shooting on the way and we don't have enough
beds. Steady the gurney while we move this one onto it.

-Ben and the nurses shoved the gurney next to the bed
before grabbing the sheet corners and sliding the body into
place. A coffee-colored arm, clearly a woman's, fell from
beneath the sheet, a red birthmark crossing the wrist.
Chancer felt the blood rush from his face as he took a step

back, the image of Beulah King filling his mind. An instant later, Ben's face appeared between him and the gurney.

Don't you faint on me, Wylls. This place is about to get crazy and I need your help.

-Chancer pointed to the sheet.

But this is...

-Ben shoved a finger in his face.

You do not go there! You do not think about anything but what needs to be done right now. This ward will be a war zone in minutes. Do you understand me?

-Chancer stared at him without speaking, his mind a whirl of confusion. Ben took him by both shoulders and leaned in, his clay-hued skin only inches from Chancer's face.

Listen to me, Chancer. You have got to breathe. Take a breath. Are you hearing me?

-Ben's face suddenly came into focus and Chancer pulled away.

I hear you.

You're back with me, aren't you? I can see it.

-Chancer looked about the ward, dazed but determined not to embarrass himself.

What do we do now?

The body needs to go to the morgue. Take the elevator to the basement, drop it off and get back here as fast as you can. You can do that, right?

-He nodded his agreement and Ben vanished between the rows.

Trying to avoid the thought of what lay stretched before him, Chancer pushed the gurney through the basement door. A wave of cold air smelling of decay and formaldehyde surrounded him. The dimly lighted passageway suddenly seemed to tilt like the deck of a sinking ship. He thought he might get sick. Clutching the gurney, he closed his eyes, trying with effort to steady himself.

Moments later the door opposite him flew open and a young man in blue scrubs stepped through, a tangled mass of hair jutting from beneath his white surgeon's cap. Noticing Chancer, he stopped and pointed toward the doorway behind him, his voice rising and falling beneath his accent like a song.

Put the vessel just beside the door, if you please. Then you must join me for tea.
-He held up an empty mug and smiled, his teeth shining white against his dark skin. Chancer stared at him, unsure what to think.
What vessel do you mean?
You may call it a body, if you wish.
-Chancer wheeled the gurney next to the doorway and turned, relieved to be rid of it. The young man nodded toward a doorway before continuing.
Some consider the body a vessel for the soul until it moves into the next life. It is a poetic image, of course. Do you like it?
-Chancer followed him into a narrow room crowded with a table and chairs. Dirty coffee mugs and half-used packets of sugar littered the counters. The man tossed three teabags into the mug before filling it with water. Chancer glanced in the direction of the gurney.
I've never heard anyone call a body a vessel before.
Being an unbeliever myself, I prefer to think of death as a return to the pure physical elements of neutrons, protons and electrons, not to mention smaller particles yet to be properly understood. There is also poetry in such thinking, don't you think?
-Chancer sat across from him.
I suppose so. Are you a doctor?
-He laughed, his smile again flashing.
I am just a lowly student. And medicine is far too messy for my taste. I prefer the solid nature of the physical. That is why I am majoring in physics at the university.

108

-Chancer peered at him, shocked by the coincidence.

You're a physics major? I'm majoring in physics too. What are the odds we'd both be working at the same hospital?

My uncle would say there is no coincidence, but fate only, a meeting meant to be. Oh, please forgive me. My name is Rajesh but often people here call me Russell. I don't know why.

-They shook hands.

I'm Chancer Wylls.

Ah yes, as in chance meeting of two physics students. What would you like me to call you?

You mean to call me other than Russell?

How about if you go by something else, like a nickname?

What is a nickname?

It's a shortened version of a name.

You wish to call me Rash? Is that not a disease of the skin?

You have a point. Rash wouldn't do, especially working in a hospital. What if I call you Raz?

-He nodded emphatically.

Ah, yes, I would very much like such a name.

-Chancer watched in disbelief as he emptied three packs of sugar into the mug.

You like your tea sweet.

Yes, strong and sweet is the only way. Wouldn't you like a taste?

-Chancer grimaced at the thought.

No thanks.

-Raz discarded the teabags, frowning into the mug.

In India, they say it is impossible to find good tea in America. They say that American tea is only the sweepings from the tearoom floor. I came to understand this after I ran out of tea from my home and now must drink these tea sweepings.

-Chancer watched him stir the black liquid.

I don't guess I know the difference.

Ah, but a difference there is, Chancer Wylls. Perhaps in time my mother will send more and I will show you. But enough talk of tea. We are in common with the physics. Have you chanced to take a class from Professor Franklin?

I'm taking his class now. He's asked me to help him with a project.

-Raz stared at him in surprise.

What sort of project must this be, Chancer Wylls?

It has something to do with probability theory.

-Raz leaned across the table.

Ah, perhaps fate does move us about like pawns on a board. Probability is a part of mathematics I wish to understand more completely. My uncle is obsessed with the racing of horses and he has enlisted me to find mathematics that will help him make the good wagers.

Does he win much?

Yes, but he believes he can win much more. I don't like it but I am obligated to him because he arranged for me to come here. Will you help me also with these predictions?

It'll involve some work but I suppose it might be interesting to try.

Speaking of work, where are you assigned, Chancer?

-Chancer jumped from his seat.

Work! What the hell am I doing still here?

-Calling out his regrets, he rushed out the door.

The cackling tenor of competing voices greeted him as he stepped off the elevator. Nurses crisscrossing the crowded hallway called out directions to orderlies and aides before hurrying on. He pressed his way through them, the noise and chaos growing as he neared the ward. Several tattoo-marked teenagers huddled near the doorway, two of the girls in tears.

Halfway down the aisle, Ben held a large x-ray in front of a nearby window, the gray outline of someone's ribcage light against the dark background. Several green-robed doctors huddled around him, studying the image. A moment later they turned their attention to a nearby bed, their barked calls echoing off the hospital walls.

Chancer hurried toward them. Blood pooled at their feet, spreading in all directions beneath the bed. He turned his eyes away with effort. Ben nodded him closer, handing him the x-ray. He pointed toward the lowest rib, speaking under his breath.

This kid is one of our shootings.
-Chancer glanced at the boy's face but had to look away.
He's so young, Ben.
Wylls, look at what I'm showing you, not the patient.
-Chancer watched Ben trace his finger across the image.
The goddamn .32 caliber bullet entered here and this is where it ended up. The surgeons hate these small caliber guns because the slug ricochets off bone, causing damage all along its path.
How do they know where to operate?
They don't. That's why they've had to open him up again in the freaking recovery ward. They missed an artery somewhere.
How bad is it?
He probably won't make it.
-Ben grabbed the x-ray as one of the surgeons pivoted for another look. He squinted at the image, tossing aside a blood-soaked bandage before turning back to the bed. Chancer glanced about the ward, feeling useless.
Give me something to do, Ben. I can't just stand here while some kid dies.
-Ben nodded down the aisle.
Check on the other gunshot cases.

-Chancer started down the aisle but Nurse Berry waved him over. She stood in the doorway with the teenagers grouped before her.

Now you children have to move downstairs, you hear me? This is a recovery room not a waiting room.

-A girl with tear-stained cheeks peered at her, speaking with difficulty.

Will he be alright?

The doctors are doing everything they can for your friend. Now do what I ask.

-Sobbing, she started toward the elevator without a word. Nurse Berry watched her then faced the others.

You go on with her, now. Mr. Wylls here will keep you informed.

-The boy with the tattoos glared at Chancer.

What are you, some kind of junior doctor?

-Nurse Berry leaned close to the boy's face.

This man has important work to do. He is not hammering nails or bagging groceries. We rely on him. These patients rely on him. Do you understand me?

-He looked away and nodded.

Yes, 'mam.

-She pointed down the hall.

Now go on and take care of your friend. Anyone can see how upset she is.

-She glanced into the ward then faced Chancer, giving her head a slight shake.

Those poor children are too young to see such grief, Mr. Wylls. You'd better start thinking how you'll go about giving them the sad news. You can do that, now can't you?

-He nodded, trying to convince himself he was up to the request. She pursed her lips, placing a hand on his shoulder and nodding into the room.

We have two gunshots, a stabbing and a young person nearly killed on a motorcycle. I meant what I said about how we rely on you and Mr. Ahote.

Spring

\\'spriŋ\: the season after winter and before summer,
in the northern hemisphere from March to May; the season
in which vegetation begins to appear

Middle English, from Old English *springan*; of
Germanic origin; related to Dutch and German *springen* or
to Greek *sperchesthai*, to hasten

the period from the vernal equinox to the summer
solstice

I measure every grief I meet
With analytic eyes;
I wonder if it weighs like mine,
Or has an easier size

-Emily Dickinson

Chapter Fourteen

I stepped from the steamy heat of early March into the air conditioned office set aside for my meetings with Cheering Sanders, the district superintendent's granddaughter. The room stood quiet except for the hum of an oscillating fan. Half an hour earlier I had stopped by the high school to check on Diego. Although he had managed to avoid any real trouble since resuming his classes, he seemed edgy and distant, avoiding eye contact and skirting around my questions with vague answers. I tried to console myself with what progress he had made.

Cheering was another story. Living up to her unusual name, she remained ever so polite, confining her conversation to the trivial and mundane. I'd seen her for weeks yet barely knew her. I much preferred the oversized passion of Diego. Yet I liked her and felt empathy for her to a degree that worried me. In spite of doing my best to stay objective, I had begun to fear I could not help her.

I turned at the sound of footsteps to find her standing in the doorway, Esther Schultz beside her. A police officer waited just outside. Slouching against the wall, her eyes to the floor, Cheering's face held no expression. Esther, on the other hand, seemed barely able to contain her exasperation. I looked at each of them, saying nothing as I tried to work out an explanation. Just as I was about to ask, Esther managed to find her voice.

Cheering is here for her appointment but I need a word first.

-She directed Cheering to a chair before stepping back outside. The officer stood by as we walked to the porch of the adjacent building, beyond the girl's hearing. I waited as Esther thumbed through Cheering's thick file. Pushing her glasses up over her reddish hair, she took a breath and faced me.

How do you think she's doing?

So far, she's keeping her distance and giving me next to nothing to work with. She never gets in trouble but she's failing all her classes.

Well, she's doing more than nothing now. Your young charge ran away from home last night. The campus police managed to track her down early this morning.

-I glanced at the doorway, sensing there was more to the story.

A teenager running away isn't unusual. Why is the officer still here?

She met up with a man, a twenty-eight year old. So far, she's staying quiet but her grandparents are beside themselves. It's one thing for a girl her age to sneak away to see some classmate but a man twice her age is another matter.

I'm guessing he's in jail.

-Esther nodded.

I hope she'll talk with you about it but I'm not holding my breath. If she keeps this up the authorities will find her another home. That would be disastrous for her and her grandparents. I don't have to tell you how important it is for her make some visible progress, and soon.

-I wondered again if I could manage the task but kept the thought to myself.

I think this is her way of dealing with the abuse. The trick will be in helping her find a better way to get past what happened to her.

-Esther chewed on her thumbnail, lost in thought, then looked up at me.

You're her best hope, Tegan. I know you'll find a way. The officer will make sure she gets home when the time comes.

-She turned without another word, disappearing around the corner. I took my time getting back to the room, stalling as I considered how I might approach Cheering. My gut told me I had gone too easy with her. But if I pushed too hard I would lose her, perhaps for good.

116

-I stopped in the doorway and studied her pale features. Framed by clipped, satin-like hair, her oval face carried a deep but beautiful sadness. She wore all black, purple nail polish and heavy black eyeliner. I pulled a chair within inches of hers and sat facing her but saying nothing. She kept her eyes to the floor. After what seemed an eternity, she looked up, glaring at me, a sneer on her over-red lips.

This is so lame. Don't you think I've had the silent treatment before?

-I shrugged.

I never thought about it.

Well, I have and I hate it. I've seen so many counselors in my life it makes me sick. You're just like all the rest.

How is that, Cheering?

-Tossing back her dark hair, she leaned forward mocking me.

'How is that, Cheering?' Is that all you can say?

You were brought here by the police. I'm here to try to understand what happened, if you'll let me.

-She sat back, anger lighting her eyes.

You don't care what happens to me.

Don't I?

All you want to do is collect a paycheck so you can go out and party all night.

How should I be, then?

-She squinted at me, practically yelling her words.

How the hell do I know? You're the counselor, not me!

-I'd never heard her raise her voice, much less swear. She seemed almost a different person from the depressed and passive girl I'd come to know.

But if you could choose, how would you like me to be?

If I could choose, you wouldn't be here.

But I am here, Cheering. So, how should I be?

You could try not being so stupid.

Alright, I can try. But I need to know what that means.

It means listening.

I can listen.

No, I mean really listening and not just faking it like most people.

Is that what people do?

-She stood and began pacing around her chair.

People can't be trusted.

The people in your life have been less than honest?

You make it sound so nice. People lie.

What do they lie about?

They make promises they don't keep.

What sort of promises?

I don't know.

Are they important promises, the kind that matter?

All promises matter.

Which promises get broken, then?

Which don't? They say they'll stay but then they leave you. They say they'll take care of you but they only care about themselves.

Are all people are like that?

-She sat, considering the question.

No, not all of them.

Who, then?

I don't know.

I'm confused. You're saying people have let you down, people close to you, but you can't figure out who they are?

Who hasn't? I mean, look at my screwed up mother. Look at how she went out partying every night. She said she'd stop but she didn't, of course, so I was left at home not knowing if she'd ever come back, so worried I couldn't sleep.

So now it's your time to party?

Why not? She doesn't care. I mean, look at the losers she hooks up with. They act all nice and bring you things.

They seem like they want to be your friend. But then they start putting their hands…

-She stopped, catching herself as tears welled in her dark eyes. Searching my mind for what to say, I reached for her hand, knowing that doing nothing might be the best course. She flinched and pulled away. In spite of my misgivings, I decided to push on.

People have let you down, Cheering, people you trusted, people you counted on. It's unfair. It's wrong. But we can't go back and change what's already happened. We have to go on from here. We have to decide what happens next.

-She wiped her eyes with the back of her hand and peered into my face, her expression a mixture of sadness and defiance.

You make it sound so easy. Well, it's not easy.

I understand. Going on from here may seem difficult. Change is never easy but...

-She leaned forward.

How can you understand what happened to me? No one can understand.

I can try if you'll let me.

You weren't there. It didn't happen to you. You'll never understand.

But that doesn't mean you can't find a way beyond what's happened, beyond the abuse.

-She flinched at the word. Glaring at me, she sat back and turned to face the exit.

I don't want to talk about this anymore.

But Cheering, you can do this.

-She stood.

I want to go home.

-I could see she had gone as far as she was willing. As I followed her into the dappled sunlight, I wondered if I was trying to convince her or myself.

Although I tried to avoid them, Cheering's words flew through my thoughts like frightened birds. I feared I had pushed her too far. Stepping into the cool light of a low-slung cafe tucked around the corner from my office, I surveyed the sprawling room, half-expecting to see Esther Schultz. I had told her I was meeting a friend. An instant later, I spotted Claude waving at me from the bar.

We moved to a corner table. As he ordered two of his favorite beers, I studied his profile, letting myself wonder where the evening might lead. I wanted a distraction from the discouraging day. The waitress left and he turned to me, his face carrying the expectant look of a child at his first day of school. He waved his hand over the glasses.

This ale is brewed not far from here. I know beer is sort of a guy thing but I hope you'll like these.

So, you think drinking beer is manly?

-He squinted at me, unsure what I was getting at.

Some people say so.

But if I like men, shouldn't I like beer too?

-A hint of a smile crossed his lips.

I guess so. Then you do like men?

Well, that depends, doesn't it?

Does it?

Of course it does. Not all men are alike.

What sort of men do you prefer?

I haven't decided.

Ah, so your opinion is a work in progress?

You could say that.

Like one of Vincent's paintings?

-I chuckled.

They all seem to be in progress.

He's a perfectionist so he never stops tinkering with them. Except for the painting he did of you. I'd say that one is just about perfect.

-I felt myself blush but managed a skeptical frown.

You think so, do you?

How could it be otherwise?

You don't have to keep trying to make up for our first meeting, Claude.

That's just how I see it, Tegan.

Oh, I'm as far from perfect as anyone. To tell the truth, after the day I've had I'm feeling pretty imperfect.

Has something happened to the kid you were telling me about?

Let's not talk about my work. I want to hear about you, Claude.

-He looked about the room as if searching for a place to start.

What do you want to know?

Anything. Are you from around here? What about your family?

I grew up here. My father was shot down over Viet Nam before I was born.

-An image of Chancer flashed through my mind.

Those were difficult times. So your mother raised you by herself?

-His eyes grew dark.

She tried to. She never really got over my father's death. She died the year I graduated high school.

That's a hard age to be without both of your parents. Is that when you joined the service?

No, I knocked around for a few years, going in and out of college but never taking anything very seriously. It's a strange feeling to be without a family. I suppose I joined because I needed direction, something to give me a purpose instead of just living day to day. Losing my father to the war had something to do with it too. Those soldiers were treated badly. My mother said he was spit on when he came home on leave. I wanted to honor what he did.

I'll bet your father would be proud of you.

-His turned his gaze, looking into the distance.

I don't know. I'm not sure anyone should be proud of just surviving.

-I again studied his handsome face, wondering what it must have been like for him.

But you did survive, Claude.

After I was blown into that ditch, I had a few moments before I passed out. The brush all around me was on fire. Everything seemed incredibly clear, as if I was seeing the world as it is for the first time. Then I saw God there in the middle of it all. Or, I thought I did. It seemed so real. My unit… my friends, were scattered along the road dead or dying. I thought of all the times for God to show himself, this would be it.

What did you see?

That's just it. I saw nothing except fire and smoke.

Like Moses and the burning bush?

-His eyes narrowed as he recalled the moment.

I believed because God is unknowable, by not seeing God I saw God.

You were badly injured, Claude.

I know it sounds crazy but at the time it was very real. I now know what I saw, Tegan. Fire and smoke surrounded me, nothing more. If there is a God, he was nowhere to be found that day.

I'm sorry, Claude.

I made it through and my friends didn't. That's what I can't understand. Why am I still here and they're not?

I wish I had an answer for you but I don't. I'm just glad you survived, Claude.

-He peered into my face.

I've never told anyone what I just told you, Tegan.

-I leaned across the table, gazing into his blue eyes.

I'd like to hear whatever you want to tell me, Claude. Maybe we could…

-Esther Schultz appeared out of nowhere, her face flushed even in the bar's dim light. Unable to hide my disappointment, I turned from Claude with difficulty. She tossed her hair back, looking from me to Claude and back.

I'm sorry to interrupt but I just got off the phone with Diego's mother. I could barely understand her but she was close to hysterical. You'd better get out there right away.

What's happened, Esther?

I'm not sure. There's something about a girlfriend. I couldn't follow her. She said you're the only one the boy will listen to.

-I faced Claude to apologize but he interrupted me.

That boy needs you, Tegan. We'll have time to talk later. You should get moving.

-Mumbling a farewell, I hurried toward the exit.

Chapter Fifteen

Shadows stretched across the rutted road as I pulled past the familiar line of trees and onto the circular driveway leading to Celia's trailer. I was relieved that the sun had yet to set. Celia stood on the other side of the dusty yard, hugging herself and glancing toward a nearby wall of brush. She pulled back her thick mane of hair, motioning me over with a nervous wave. As I walked toward her I surveyed the open area for Diego but found no sign of him.

Shuffling footsteps sounded behind me just as I reached her, and I turned to find Eloy hobbling toward us with his sideways gait, his gnarled cane cutting the air between steps. He stopped feet away. Raising his arms, his palms up, his face contorted, he leaned toward Celia.

Daughter, you must cut these chains and release me. You must turn the devil from this place.
-She waved a finger at him.
Senor Feugo, I have no time for you. Diego, he is in trouble.
Yes, mija, your son, he is in danger. The devil, he does his work.
-With that he again began singing his strange tune, dancing about us in a slow circle.

> The trees they hide a hairless bird
> he flies above a treeless world
> he makes his song in wordless call
> to turn a heart away from all
> a boy takes fire in his hands
> the fire burns, the fire brands

-Stopping, he again held out his arms.
Daughter, release me, your slave. Turn the devil away.
-She pleaded with him.
Please, Senor Fuego, I must go find Diego.

Yes, mija, you must release him also. The time, it grows short.

-He pivoted, hurrying back down the road and disappearing into the thicket. I turned to face her.

Celia, what's happened? Why did you call?

-She raised a hand to her cheek as I followed her into the trailer.

Omar started yelling and said he would hit me. Diego, he went crazy with his anger.

When was this?

Five days, maybe a week ago. Diego and Omar, they had a fight. After Omar left, Diego found his grandfather's rifle.

Diego has a gun?

-She pointed to a nearby shelf. In the center, a single bullet sat perched upright, the brass case shining dully in the half-light.

He keeps the gun there. Sometimes he points it at me when he gets so angry. He scares me, Tegan. I do not know what to do with him.

Where is he now, Celia?

This is what scares me so much. He gets angry with his girlfriend as with me. He has taken her into the woods.

He has the gun with him?

-She nodded and I grabbed her arm, heading for the door. Moments later we entered the thicket. A web of shadows crisscrossed the leaf-littered floor as we picked our way forward, pressing past the low-hanging branches. The sound of voices rose and fell in the undergrowth ahead. All at once the shadows thinned and Celia nodded toward a small clearing just beyond the trees.

-In the center of the circular space a blonde-haired girl lay stretched on her back. My heart sank. Diego paced before her mumbling to himself, one hand clasping the rifle, the other pressed to his forehead. He stopped and looked down at her, waving the rifle through the air as he spoke.

125

I saw you with him! How can I trust you now?

-She raised her head.

But Diego…

-He pointed the barrel at her.

Don't you move!

-I watched her ease back into place. She followed him with her eyes as she spoke.

Jason likes my friend, Chrissie. He wants me to set him up with her. That's all it was, Diego.

Why should I believe you? You females are all alike. You say one thing but mean something else.

I'm telling you the truth, Diego. Why won't you believe me?

-I pushed through the brush and he swung around, still holding the rifle at his hip. His eyes grew wide at the sight of me.

Tegan, what are you doing here?

Your mother told me where to find you. She's worried about you, Diego.

-He glared at me, his face full of anger, his voice rising with every word.

She should mind her own damn business!

-I struggled to stay calm as I stared into the muzzle.

Diego, what's happened to make you act like this?

She should have never brought that bastard into the house!

Your mother is not responsible for what Omar does.

-He spoke slowly, his voice shaking with anger.

I'll kill him the next time he touches her.

-I stepped toward him, my voice just above a whisper as I spoke.

Diego, listen to me. This is not you. This is not the Diego I know, the young man with an artist's heart, the one that wants to protect his mother.

-Sadness replaced the anger in his eyes.

You shouldn't be here, Tegan.

I'm not leaving until you set down that gun. Talk to me, Diego.

I'm tired of people using me, lying to me.

I'm on your side, Diego. You know that. I want to understand what you're saying but I can't with a gun pointing at me.

-He stared at me as if in a trance. In spite of the rifle, I took another step toward him.

Let the girl leave.

-He turned his eyes to the ground and gave his head a slight nod. The girl watched him a moment then jumped up, disappearing into the trees. I moved to where he stood and gently pushed the barrel to one side.

You don't need that, Diego. No one here wants to hurt you.

-He tossed it to the ground. I could see he was on the verge of tears but would not let me see him cry so I nudged him toward the trailer and we made our way back through the woods in silence. Celia followed at a distance. As soon as we reached the drive, Diego walked to the bench and sat. I took the chair opposite him.

I want you to let me take the rifle and keep it for you. I have an uncle who knows all about guns and he'll put it in a safe place.

The rifle belonged to my grandfather.

I know it did. Your mother told me.

My grandfather was a cabinetmaker and he carved saints and painted alters for churches and rich people. He was good to my mom and me. He would never hit me or even yell at me. He let me use that rifle when we went hunting together. But then he got sick and couldn't go hunting anymore. Just before he died, he gave it to me. I never go hunting but I keep the rifle because it reminds me of him.

That's why I'm going to be sure to put it in a safe place until you're ready to have it back. Is that alright?

-He nodded and peered into my face.

Do you remember your grandfather, Tegan?

-I sat back, thinking of Pen.

Sure, it's easy. He and my grandmother are still alive. They raised me, mostly.

Did your father leave you too?

Not exactly. He just wasn't cut out for being a father. Does your father have something to do with what happened today?

I hardly remember him. But if he'd been a real dad to me, I wouldn't have to be around that baldheaded bastard.

And you're angry about that, angry at him?

Why shouldn't I be?

And you're angry at Omar?

I hate Omar.

It makes sense you'd be angry at him and your father. But what happens now?

What do you mean?

Are you going to let Omar rule you for the rest of your life?

He doesn't rule me.

But he's the reason you got so angry today?

I guess so.

It sounds like he's in charge.

No, he's not.

You were in control out there? Be honest with yourself, Diego.

-He picked up a twig, breaking into tiny pieces.

I don't know what happened to me, Tegan. I got so mad I couldn't think.

Sometimes you get so angry you do what you don't mean to. Is that how you want to be?

It just happens.

You haven't learned to see it coming?

I've done better lately.

Yes you have, but not this time. What could you have done differently?

I could've told you about what Omar did instead of letting him get to me.

Is he the only one you were angry with?

Most of it was because of him.

You didn't sound too happy with your mom.

I'm mad about the way she lets him treat her.

So, you were angry at her too?

Wouldn't you be?

I might be. But she's not the same as Omar, is she?

-He stared at his hands, considering the question.

She doesn't hit me.

Have you told her what you just told me?

-His face wore a mixture of sadness and anger.

She ought to know without me telling her.

Do you know what it's like for her? Have you ever asked?

-He stared at me, his eyes glistening. Looking away, he wiped them with the back of his hand before facing me again.

How can I? She starts crying whenever I say anything about my father or Omar or any of the others. If only she hadn't hooked up with him in the first place…

-His voice trailed off and he seemed to sink into the bench.

You can blame her, Diego, or you can get on with your life. That is, if you want to be in charge of it. Maybe you don't. Maybe you want someone else calling the shots and making your decisions for you.

No, that's not what I want.

Then talk to me when something like this happens.

-He stared at the ground, speaking under his breath.

I could've done something bad to her, Tegan.

-I leaned toward him.

Listen to me, Diego. You are a strong person to have made it through all you have. You do not have to be like your father. You do not have to be like Omar. You can be who you want to be. But only you can decide.

-He looked up at me.

But how do I, Tegan?

We'll find a way, Diego. Your grandfather would be a good place to start.

Chapter Sixteen

Images of Blaise Pascal and Pierre de Fermat floated through Chancer's thoughts as he stepped out of the warm spring night and into the three story brick building housing both math and physics departments. Imagining himself linked to the great mathematicians by a common history, he wondered if his work with Professor Franklin would lead to some undiscovered theorem and the notoriety that would surround such a find. And, if so, would Byes care?

With Spring Break only a week away, time seemed to be racing past. He had hoped to spend the holiday with her but his obligations to Franklin and the project kept pressing in. When they talked it over, she had been vague about making plans, seeming distant in a way he was still at a loss to explain. The slippery details of probability seemed infinitely easier to understand.

Two weeks earlier she had returned from her archaeology class trip tanned and energized by the experience. At least he guessed that was the reason. With a pile of class work to make up, she'd had little time for him, and a bothersome distance had crept between them, leaving him dejected and lonely. Mounting the stairs, he realized he had little idea what to do about it.

The second floor hallway stretched before him dark and empty. At the far end, the half-glass door of the professor's office cast a feeble glow across the polished floor, reminding him of the hospital and Turley's ashen face the last time he had seen him. He and the other patients constantly flickered through Chancer's exhausted mind like a silent movie, morphing sleep into an endless nightmare of suffering and pain. He took a breath, trying to concentrate on why he was there.

A moment later, he stopped before Franklin's door. Staring at the frosted glass, he again thought of Byes and where he stood with her, if anywhere. He felt a sudden urge to rush off and find her. Half-turning toward the hallway, he stopped as Franklin's voice sounded through the glass.

Are you waiting out there for a reason, Chancer?
-He turned the knob and pushed open the door, keeping his eyes to the floor as his dark thoughts lodged in his throat. Franklin looked up from a desk scattered with papers and studied him, tugging at his wiry beard for a moment before speaking.

You're not looking so good, son. Are you unwell?
-Chancer shook his head.

I'm a little tired is all.

You look more than a little tired.

I have a lot on my mind right now.

Ah, well, allow me to guess. If I was a betting man, I'd say you're having women trouble.
-Chancer looked up at him, alarmed that he could know.

Well... I... how did you...?
-Franklin held up a hand to silence him.

As old as I am, I've had plenty of such troubles myself. Besides, if you'll remember, I did meet Byes. Perhaps we should postpone our work to another time.
-Chancer leapt into the chair, suddenly realizing what he most needed was to stay busy.

But we can't postpone, Franklin. We have too much to do.

You're sure, son?
-He leaned toward the desk.

What's our next step?
-Franklin lifted a stack of papers from the desktop.

We're shifting gears and moving on to a more important project. What I have here is a proposal to test the use of Bayesian probability and the Markov chain Monte Carlo method in predicting the movements of stars and galaxies. Are you familiar with the work of Andrei Markov or Thomas Bayes?

132

I've heard of them but that's about it.

How about Stanislaw Ulam?

Wasn't he at Los Alamos during World War II?

That's right. The Monte Carlo name comes from the fact that Ulam's uncle often gambled there. The method has to do with using algorithms to run repeated simulations in order to calculate the probability of a particular outcome.

The outcome we're trying to predict is the movement of star and planetary systems?

Exactly so. I want you to familiarize yourself with these processes so once I get a green light for the proposal we'll be ready to move. Does that sound agreeable, Chancer?

This sounds like a big project.

I know you have job responsibilities in addition to your schoolwork. I'd understand if you felt unable to manage this project on top of all that.

-Chancer leaned toward him.

Franklin, this is the one thing I look forward to more than anything else. I'll do whatever it takes to continue. I'll find a way.

-Franklin stood and came around the desk, putting a broad hand on Chancer's shoulder.

Listen to me, son. I want you here working with me as much as you want to be here. But a human body has its limits. I don't want to ask too much of you. And I can see you've been working hard.

I'll be alright, Franklin. So, I can be part of the project?

-Franklin pulled at his beard.

I have an idea but I'm not ready to say what it is just yet. In any event, you must promise to tell me if this gets to be too much. Otherwise, read the paper and we'll get started tomorrow evening.

Chancer stepped into the warm night as a brisk wind whipped past the building, carrying with it a trace of rotting leaves and newly turned earth. Streetlights rattled before the coursing breeze. Before him, the grass-covered mall where weeks earlier he had pulled Byes from the panicked crowd stood empty. Dim pools of light dotted the narrow sidewalk bisecting the lawn.

As he started along the walkway, a faint clang of metal against metal caught his attention and he turned toward the sound, surveying the area but finding nothing. He waited a moment then started for home again, following the passageway under the darkened arches of the portico.

Halfway along the passage the clanging sounded again. He paused to listen, careful to keep to the shadows, and then backtracked along the portico, stepping behind the end archway and leaning around the brick wall. The sound appeared to come from the administration building. Muffled voices echoed through the passageway.

Chancer stood still, peering into the darkness as three men emerged from the shadow cast by the nearby buildings. Raising a metal ladder, they set it in place above the main entrance and began scurrying up and down with cans of paint. Their brushes scraped along the rough brick in rasping strokes.

All at once they pulled down the ladder, grabbing the spare cans and rushing across the mall within yards of him. They had just passed when a brush clattered to the ground. Chancer froze. One of the men turned and moved directly toward him. As he bent to retrieve the brush, his face appeared beneath the streetlight. Chancer gasped in surprise, recognizing him as Byes' friend, Henry. He stood and looked up and down the portico, squinting into the shadows as if he sensed Chancer's presence. An instant later, he vanished into the night.

An image of Henry's illuminated face dogged Chancer the following afternoon as he stepped into the stillness of the hospital's second floor hallway. A rare calm had descended upon the ward. His shift over, he glanced through the door before turning toward the stairwell. He had an errand left before heading home. Turley had been moved to the third floor and he felt obligated to go check on him. He dreaded what he might find when he got there.

A moment later, a voice called his name and he turned to find Beulah King waving to him from a wheelchair. Chancer hurried toward her, the memory of his trip to the morgue still fresh. She motioned for the aide to push her to one side and leave her.

Why, Chancer Wylls, I was hoping I might see you before they took me in for my procedure. They sent me home so quickly the last time, I missed saying goodbye.

-She offered him her bony hand and he took it, surprised at the cool of her fingers. He peered into her face, relieved to see her alive.

I thought that you might have…

-He stopped, unable to finish. She studied his face.

Why, you poor man. When you missed seeing me leave this place, you thought I had come to an unfortunate end.

I'm glad I was wrong, Beulah.

I can see that in your face and I am touched. When you get to be of a certain age, you begin to wonder if anyone at all notices you or cares in the least what fate might visit you. I sometimes feel as if not only my hair and skin has lost substance, but even my very self has faded like some old photograph left in the sun too long.

Why did they send you home so quickly?

Chancer, I believe I experienced one of God's little miracles. The doctors thought I had something serious but that was not so. After they did my procedure, they decided I should try some medicine rather than what they had planned for me. Now it's time for them to take a second look.

That sounds encouraging.

-She pointed toward him.

135

What's that you have in your hand?

I've brought a book for a friend. I borrowed the idea from you.

Your friend is very ill, Chancer?

He's been here for quite awhile and will be for a good while longer.

-The aide reappeared and nodded toward the elevator. Beulah again took his hand, squeezing it lightly.

I fear I must leave you.

-The elevator bell sounded and the aide turned her toward it. Chancer moved around to face her.

If I miss you again, how will I get your book back to you?

-She waved off his concern.

You needn't return Mister Charles Dickens but I would love to discuss your impression of him sometime. I always put my address on the back page of a book in the hope a kind person will return the tome if I should lose it. In this case, you may return your opinion to me if you wish.

-Chancer watched her disappear into the elevator, wondering when he would see her again.

He emerged from the third floor stairwell into a dimly lighted waiting area surrounded by rooms, each fronted with a single plate glass window. The doorways all stood open. Moving from room to room, he searched for Turley's name. The featureless walls and shining floors seemed unnaturally sterile beneath the fluorescent lights. A growing sense of unease settled in his chest.

As he came to the last doorway a blast of frigid air swept past him. Across the doorway a chain barring entry read 'Keep Out'. Taking care to avoid crossing the threshold, Chancer craned his neck to get a better view of the room. In a bed crammed into the far corner, he spotted a figure curled into a tight ball beneath a pile of blankets. Chancer could see no movement.

He took a step back and surveyed the area, quickly spotting Turley's name taped between the doorframe and window. Below the window, a pair of rubber gloves reached through two holes into the room. Chancer again peered at the unmoving figure, puzzling at the reason behind the strange rooms. He turned as footsteps echoed in the hallway behind him.

Don't you even think of going in there, Mr. Wylls. That chain is there for a reason.

-Relieved to see a familiar face, Chancer gestured around the waiting area.

Nurse Berry, what brings you to this strange ward?

Take care with your choice of words, Mr. Wylls. This strange ward, as you call it, is my new baby.

What sort of ward is it? It seems so sterile.

You have the right idea. We're treating leukemia patients here. These high pressure rooms are designed to use moving air to keep the germs away from our patients.

-Chancer turned his face into the steady stream of air.

Yes, I can feel it.

-She pointed toward the far wall.

You see all those little holes? Filtered air is forced through them at all times. A cold virus would have to swim upstream to get into that room. That's the way we want it. You see, the chemotherapy will kill the cancer but will also take away the patient's immune system for a time. We must protect them during that dangerous period.

They can't leave the rooms?

Exposure to even a minor infection could kill these patients. They are prisoners to their treatment and can have no direct contact with anyone but specially trained staff members.

That sounds lonely.

I see you have found your friend, Mr. Weems. You even beat Mr. Ahote. We do have concern for the patient's isolation. Human contact is very important in recovery.

That's why we installed those arm holes. Not only can you shake hands, but you can also play chess.

-Chancer leaned toward the window, spotting a chess set on a table just below.

Can I talk to Turley? I brought him a book.

-She nodded and moved toward the door.

After you show him what you've brought, leave the book at the nurses' station. They will need to send it through the autoclave for sterilization before giving it to him.

You have to sterilize a book?

Everything must be sterilized, even his meals. His life will depend on it. Now, let me see if he feels like having a visitor.

-She pressed a button on a metal panel next to the door and leaned toward it.

Mr. Weems, you have a visitor if you feel up to it. He has something for you.

-The form beneath the covers stirred and a raspy voice crackled through the intercom.

It better be whisky or I'm going back to sleep.

-Turley crawled out of bed and shuffled toward the window, dragging the blanket with him. Chancer watched him move from bed to chair, shocked at his gray pallor. He sat hard and squinted through the window.

It's only you, Wylls. I was hoping for Johnnie Walker or Jack Daniels.

-Nurse Berry pulled a chair next to the window and motioned for Chancer to sit. Easing onto the seat, he watched her leave before turning to the window, trying to hide his concern.

I heard you got yourself a room all to yourself so I came up to see the place. How do you like it?

How in the hell do you think, Wylls? They've half killed me already. The bad food should finish the job. I'm telling you the damn Viet Cong treated our P.O.W.'s better than this.

They're trying to help you get better, Turley.

-He pulled the blanket around his shoulders.

They've taken me prisoner. They're shooting me up with all kinds of poison to kill the cancer. The stuff leaves me sick as a dog and freezing my ass off most of the time.

-Chancer held up the book.

I thought you might like something to read.

-Giving it little more than a glance, Turley sat back frowning at him.

I don't have any use for books. Why don't you tell me what it's about so I won't have to read it?

You don't like to read at all?

Hell no I don't like to read at all. I'm not a college boy like you and Ahote.

You don't have to go to college to like books. Why not give them a try?

Listen, Wylls, my reasons are not your business.

But you don't even know what I brought.

I can see it's a book. That's enough for me.

-Chancer pressed the cover to the window. Turley glanced at it with a dismissive sneer before turning his gaze back to the window. A look of surprise passed across his face.

That's Sun Tzu. You brought me *The Art of War*.

I heard you and Ben talk about it, so I decided to find a copy.

-Turley pressed his hand to the window.

You brought Sun Tzu for me? I can have it?

You can if you want it.

Buy why would you do that?

-Chancer shrugged, unsure what to say.

I thought having it close by might help, even if you don't actually read it.

-Turley starred through the window, his eyes focused on some distant time and place.

My father was a mean son of a bitch. He used to beat me for bringing home bad reports from school.

139

Your father beat you just for that?

-He peered into the palms of his hands.

Sometimes he would tell me to hold out my hands like some parents do when they have a gift for you. Then he would lay into me. The bastard used a half-inch bamboo cane, something he learned as a prisoner during the war. He thought the beatings would get me to do better but they only made me hate anything to do with school, reading, math, homework or whatever. School became my battleground in the war with my parents.

With both of them?

My mother was too cowed to do anything but go along with the program. As soon as I was old enough I enlisted and got the hell out.

It makes sense you would hate books. Do your parents know you're in here?

-He sank back into the chair, a look of resignation moving across his face.

I haven't talked to them in years.

Not at all?

Not once, not ever.

There's no one else?

-He stared at Chancer for a moment before reaching into the pocket of his robe, pulling out a tattered snapshot and pressing it to the window. Chancer peered at the photo. A blonde-haired girl stood before a frame house, her image yellowed with age.

Who is it, Turley?

-He wrapped the blanket around his head, his teeth chattering as he spoke.

She's my sister. I lost touch with her a long time ago but we were close as kids in spite of the problems on the home front. Last I heard she had gotten accepted into the university. Find her for me, Wylls. Tell her where I am.

-Without a word Turley stood, stuffing the photo into his robe before shuffling back across the room. Chancer watched him climb beneath the covers, the weight of his request just beginning to sink in.

Chapter Seventeen

Turley's ghost-like image haunted Chancer's thoughts as he crossed the mall on his way to the physics building. He stopped to peer into the night sky. Ropes of cloud raced overhead, obscuring the stars beyond. He tried to focus his mind on Franklin's paper. Admitting that he understood the paper's main concepts but only in part, he puzzled over the ways simulation probabilities might predict the movements of planets and galaxies... or horse races. Answers remained as elusive as the stars.

He pushed through the building doors and hurried up the stairs, anxious to hear Franklin's views. As he approached the office, a trio of voices rumbled beyond the door. He guessed Franklin had a late meeting. He tapped on the frosted glass and a moment later Franklin opened the door, locking eyes with him and giving his head a slight shake. Two men in police uniforms stood behind him, one young, angular, with ears like trumpets, the other thick-necked and bald. The older officer's belly stretched the buttons on his blue shirt to near breaking. Franklin nodded for Chancer to come in.

Chancer, these officers are looking into an incident that happened near here. They're asking those of us with offices in the area if we saw anything unusual. I told them you and I had a meeting last night.

-Franklin moved aside as the bald officer stepped forward, his lower lip bulging with snuff. He gestured at Chancer with his notepad.

Show me your hands, son.

-Chancer cast a glance at Franklin then peered at the officer, confused by the question.

Why do you want to see my hands?

-He lifted a paper cup from Franklin's desk and spit into it.

I'm the one to ask the questions, boy. Now do as I say or Sergeant Weston here will do it for you.

-Chancer held out his hands.

My, my, you keep your hands good and clean. You must spend plenty of time washing and scrubbing to have hands that nice, fingernails included, just like some sorority girl. Take a look sergeant.

-The younger office thrust his pale face toward Chancer, leering at him with a tobacco-stained grin.

Why, I do believe they look just like a girl's hands, Captain Schmidt. Right you are, as always, sir, just like I was telling...

-He waved the sergeant back into place.

Alright, alright, let's move on here. Where were you last night between the hours of six and seven, Mr. Wylls?

But don't you know that already?

What did I say about not asking the questions, boy? Now, tell me your whereabouts last evening.

I was here with Professor Franklin, just like he just told you.

Don't you get smart with me, son.

- Franklin leaned toward the officer, speaking under his breath.

Captain, as a man of obvious intelligence and ability, not to mention vast law enforcement experience, you can surely see he is doing his best to be cooperative. Perhaps an analytical mind like yours can achieve your goal by allowing some latitude in his answering.

-Captain Schmidt took a breath. Chancer thought he heard a button snap.

And after you reprimanded yourself from the premises of this vicinity, whereabouts did you travel to?

I walked straight home.

-He squinted at Chancer.

You didn't make any stops for any extracurricular activities like your average college boy?

I have a job and take a full course load so I can keep my scholarship. I don't have time for much else.

Why work when the college gives you money for school? A curious mind might wonder what you need all those funds for. Could it maybe be for paint and brushes, that kind of thing, Mr. Wylls? Is that right?

-Chancer realized with a start the officers thought he, not Henry, had vandalized the administration building. Not knowing what else to do, he decided to stall.

Are you going to tell me why you're asking all these questions?

You don't listen too good, do you? You answer, not ask.

It might help if you'd tell me why I'm here.

First, you need to answer my question. What do you do with all that money you make, Mr. Working Man?

The scholarship pays only part of my tuition. My salary is barely enough to cover books, meals and all the rest.

You're telling me you didn't buy brushes and paint with that salary? I have ways of finding out these things, you know.

Then you don't need me.

-The officer's wide face turned crimson.

Answer the dang question, boy!

I don't have any use for paint. I live in a garage apartment behind my grandmother's house. If she wanted her house painted, she'd pay somebody to do it.

-The younger officer sneered at him.

This paint wasn't used for granny's house, boy.

-Officer Schmidt glared at the younger man.

You can let me handle this, Wally. Now you best listen up, Mr. Wylls. We know you're part of a group that's got nothing better to do than protest the war.

I'm not part of any group.

You've been seen fraternizing with the peaceniks. We keep a close eye on them. This country has to guard against hippie, longhair subversives taking over.

-Franklin leaned in again.

Captain, a physics student hardly meets the definition of a subversive.

-The officer shook his head.

We know what we know, professor. He's one of them activists.

-Chancer searched his mind for a diversion.

What does long hair and war protests have to do with brushes and paint?

-An unfriendly smile spread across the captain's face.

You know much about locoweed, Mr. Wylls?

Not really. I know it's a plant that's bad for cows.

-He lifted the paper cup again and spit. Still grinning, he leaned toward Chancer, black specs of snuff peppering his teeth.

That's right. Cows that get into the stuff act a little crazy, sometimes a lot crazy. And why is that?

I have no idea.

It's because locoweed is just another word for marijuana. You been getting into the locoweed. Mr. Wylls?

-Chancer glanced at Franklin again.

What? No, I haven't gotten into locoweed or any other kind of weed. This is ridiculous. Your questions make no sense.

-Wally thrust a finger in Chancer's face.

Don't you mouth off to Captain Schmidt, you little twerp!

-Franklin stepped between the officer and Chancer, his voice low but firm.

The only disrespect I hear is coming out of your mouth, Sergeant Weston.

-Captain Schmidt moved Wally aside before turning back to Chancer.

Now, a college student such as yourself should be able to understand this, Mr. Wylls. We're here because we had us a crime sometime last evening, a crime right here close by.

-Franklin moved next to Chancer.

I believe he has a right to know something more specific than that, captain. Is there a reason you can't tell him what happened? After all, he only has to step outside to see it.

-Captain Schmidt stared at Franklin a moment before continuing.

Several persons vandalized the administration building, painting a wall and leaving a foul message to the university regents on the main door.

-He nodded at Franklin.

I'll let you explain the particulars, professor.

-Franklin leaned against his desk.

Chancer, the group in question painted the side of the building with the words 'war criminals' and nailed a petition listing their demands to the door. The message said the group is opposed to the university having investments in munitions manufacturing, specifically the making of cluster bombs used in the war.

The university makes money off bombs? Is that legal?

Apparently it is. Whether it's right, as in ethical, is another question.

-Chancer faced the officers, looking from one to the other.

What does all of this have to do with me? I don't know anything about cluster bombs or university investments.

I believe you are at least involved if not the outright leader of the gang.

-Chancer felt the blood rush from his face and for a moment thought he might pass out. He took a breath, trying to gather his thoughts.

146

But I was here. Tell them, Professor Franklin. I didn't have any paint with me, did I?

-The captain spit into the cup.

You're bound to be involved, son. We've got you in the area within minutes of the crime. We know you associate with the antiwar types. And, you have the funds to buy the materials.

But just because I was here doesn't mean I did it.

Maybe you didn't get any paint on your hands but a brainy kid like you would have no problem thinking up and leading a crime all full of big words and demands.

I'm not the leader of anything.

Oh, you might not be the only egghead with big ideas in the group. Maybe you were just one of them following along. We'll find out who the rest are sooner or later and they're bound to talk. Why don't you do us all a favor and come clean now?

I won't admit to something I didn't do.

It won't be as bad as you think. A judge is likely to go easy on a first-timer. You'll probably just get a fine and some community service time. You'll get kicked out of the university, of course, but there's lots of other schools out there. What do you say, son? The president will be real happy if we can get this thing wrapped up quick. In the meantime, at least we have you in the bag. He'll like that too.

-An image of Henry kissing Byes flashed through Chancer's mind and he suddenly realized he could separate her from him merely by telling the truth. He glanced at Franklin and a wave of shame passed over him. Should he tell the officers what he saw and free himself of blame knowing Henry would, at the least, be expelled from school? Or should he say nothing and wait for the university to locate the culprits? No one but him could be certain of what he had seen last night.

-Byes' face again flashed through his mind, the possibility of having her to himself pulling at him, sending his thoughts into chaos. Yet, in spite of his confusion, he knew the vandalism was not a crime in the usual sense but another means of protesting the war. Rather than greed, making a statement had been the purpose.

-He glanced around the room and wiped the sweat from his lip, knowing he could stall no longer. Franklin locked eyes with him. Then the captain grabbed his cup and spit again before thrusting his face within inches of Chancer.

We've wasted enough time dillydallying around here, Mr. Wylls. I'm taking you to headquarters so we can proceed with booking you. That's unless you want to own up and give us a statement right here and now.

-Chancer stared at him, locked in indecision. Captain Schmidt turned to Wally.

Alright sergeant, take him in.

-All at once he snapped out of his stupor.

No, wait, I'll tell you what I know.

-The captain nodded.

You best not be wasting my time, boy.

I was there but not in the way you think. After I left here, I was walking along the east portico on my way home when I heard noises coming from behind me. I backtracked and saw three men using a ladder to paint something on the side of the building.

Who were these men you claim you saw?

It was dark and they were moving fast.

-Captain Schmidt snorted and motioned toward Wally.

That's not going to do you any good, son. You've only told us what we already knew. Let's get on with it, sergeant.

-Chancer took a step back.

I did get a glimpse of one of them when he dropped a paintbrush. His name is Henry Rimes.

What does he look like, this Henry?

He has a beard and long hair that he ties back with a bandana.

What did you say to this feller?

I didn't know who they were or what they were doing so I kept out of sight. When he stopped to pick up the brush, he leaned into the light. That's when I recognized him.

Why didn't you report it?

I had no idea what they were up to. I just figured it was some harmless college prank.

What did you do after that?

Like I said before, I went straight home. That's the truth.

Well, sonny, you took your time in getting around to it. Of course, stool pigeons usually do. But you're not out of the woods. We'll hold off on the booking for now. I know where to find you if I need you.

-The captain nodded to him before stepping through the door, the sergeant close behind. Chancer watched Franklin move to his chair, lost in thought, his fingers absently tapping the front of a small desk calendar. Chancer stared at it, recognizing the day as the Ides of March. His betrayal of Henry was now complete. After a moment, Franklin looked up.

There's something more, isn't there?

-Chancer avoided his gaze.

What do you mean?

It's not my business but I hope you know what you're doing.

I didn't see I had much choice.

Perhaps you didn't. The captain is a buffoon but he's determined.

I need to stay in school, Franklin, not to mention avoid blame for something I didn't do.

Yes, yes, of course. No one would expect that. But was naming the student who did do it really necessary?

You heard the captain. He had just about decided I was guilty. What else could I do?

There was nothing more, I suppose. You'll have to forgive me. My mind is always putting unrelated things together, trying to find connections.

What connections?

Well, you have been having women problems, have you not?

What does that have to do with this?

I see you do something I don't expect, so I try to connect your romantic trouble to this police business. Understanding the effect of one galaxy on another, the way they connect, is what I do for a living. Sometimes I see connections that aren't there.

I didn't want to go to jail, Franklin.

Of course you didn't, Chancer.

I can still be a part of the project?

Nothing has changed. But in view of the events let's take time to clear our minds. We'll begin again tomorrow.

-Chancer took a breath and nodded, his thoughts a jumble of relief and fear as he turned toward the door.

Summer

/ˈsəmər/: the warmest season of the year, in the
northern hemisphere from June to August

Old English *sumor*, of Germanic origin; related to
Dutch *zomer*, German *sommer*, also to Sanskrit *sama*

the period from the summer solstice to the autumnal
equinox

To learn the transport by the pain,
As blind men learn the sun;
To die of thirst, suspecting
That brooks in meadows run

-Emily Dickinson

Chapter Eighteen

Chancer woke with a start, the creak of floorboards breaking onto his consciousness like splintered wood. He lay still, fear gripping his chest. An image of Henry and the others rose before him, retribution in their eyes. Then out of the darkness Byes' voice whispered his name as her silhouetted form slipped across the room. She quickly climbed out of her clothes and into the narrow bed, pressing herself to him.

He breathed in her familiar scent, feeling he had fallen into a dream unlike any he had ever known. Nothing seemed real, the brush of her hair, the heat of her skin. All at once he began to shiver uncontrollably, as if caught in a sudden fever. Byes pressed her cheek to his face, her breath mingling with his, her hands touching him, snapping him back into the moment. With a voice full of emotion, she whispered into his ear.

Love me, Chancer.

Yellow light, thin and without warmth, filtered through the blinds of Chancer's small apartment. He sat up in bed and looked around, trying to recall the previous night. A chill moved over him and he pulled the blanket up around his shoulders, listening as Byes' voice drifted in from the living room, her words beyond understanding.

He stood and shuffled across the room, the blanket still draped across his shoulders, stopping in the doorway and peering around the corner. Byes set down the phone and slumped against the couch, her eyes red and swollen. Shivering, he stepped into the room.

Byes, what is it?
-She turned at the sound of his voice but seemed not to see him.

They sent Henry away, Chancer.

-He tried to act surprised.

They did what?

The police said he vandalized a building on campus. They put his things on the sidewalk outside the dorm and, just like that, told him he had to go.

-For an instant, Chancer dared to be hopeful.

Did he leave?

Of course he did. They've banned him from school, Chancer. They said if he agreed to leave they wouldn't refer the matter to the local authorities. He didn't want to be arrested so he left.

-He felt an uneasy sense of victory.

Where is Henry now?

He's gone to stay with his parents in New Orleans until he can figure out what to do next. I'm so sad and angry. Why did this happen to Henry, of all people?

He was just unlucky, I guess.

-She squinted at him, her voice holding a trace of disdain, barely there yet unmistakable.

Luck had nothing to do with it, Chancer. Henry was targeted because of his antiwar work.

Where did you get that idea?

He told me.

Why would he think that?

The police said someone turned him in. Do you believe that?

I suppose so, if that's what they said.

-She stared at him, the look in her eyes less than friendly.

Who would do that to him, Chancer?

-A sudden fear that Byes somehow knew what he had done gripped him.

I don't know.

-She stood.

I have a class in ten minutes.

Can I see you later?

154

-She stepped through the doorway without looking back.

A lot has happened, Chancer. I need time to think.

I sat in my car trying to understand what my father had written about himself. Though I was often exasperated with him and the way he managed to waste time, I never imagined he could be so devious. He seemed too gentle and unassuming for such dishonesty. Recently, that sweet image of him had started to overtake me at inconvenient moments, and without warning I would find myself tearing up. Now I had another picture of him to contend with, one at odds with those memories.

One memory in particular seemed to descend on me at will. I lay in the semidarkness of my grandparents' bedroom, a washcloth draped across my forehead as Chancer read aloud from my favorite book, *The Secret Garden*. I'd been ill for days, so weak I could barely get out of bed. In my feverish state, his calm voice made the garden, the door in the wall, the robin all seem very close and very real.

That first night he set an old army cot next to me and never left my side. That was the Chancer I remembered, not the conniving young man from his almanac. Yet why would he paint a dark and unflattering portrait of himself if not true? To see him in such a light was a shock.

I tried to squeeze the two images of him into one as I stepped through the open door of Vincent's house. The sweet and sour odors of linseed oil and turpentine surrounded me. Since starting his apprenticeship, Diego had changed in ways I never could have imagined, and the incident with his girlfriend now seemed a distant memory.

I followed their voices to Vincent's studio. They stood before a brightly painted canvass, both of them completely absorbed in the image. I mouthed a silent thank you to Eloy Fuego for his insight, tainted with madness though it might be. Vincent pointed at the canvas.

You have it now. See how her face seems to rise out of the background? The reflection from her arm casts a soft glow onto her cheek, taking it out of complete shadow.

-Diego nodded and stepped back for a better view.

That's wild, Vincent. She looks like a real person.

-He clasped Diego on the shoulder.

She looks like your mother.

-Diego stepped aside to reveal an incomplete yet beautiful image of Celia, capturing her cascade of hair, dark and silken. I knocked lightly on the doorframe.

Your mother will love that, Diego.

-Frowning, he turned to face me.

Is it time to go already?

I'm sorry to interrupt your party but, yes, we need to get you home.

-Vincent squinted in my direction.

Is there someone here, Diego? I can barely make out a figure.

-I stifled a smile.

Knock it off, Vincent. You're not blind yet.

Is that any way to treat a starving artist?

You know Diego would help out even if you had perfect sight, don't you?

-He reached into the air with both hands, wandering in my direction.

I do need his help. Diego, are you there? A painter must have his wine.

That wine better be for one painter only, and I don't mean the young one.

-Vincent dropped his arms.

Tegan, you're destroying the atmosphere we artists need to stoke our creative fires.

Stoke all you want after Diego and I leave. Is there anything you want him to do before we go?

-Vincent surveyed the room, shaking his head.

He can go if you'll stay behind a moment. I have something I want to ask you.

-A worried Diego looked at us.

Did I do something wrong, Vincent?

No, no, you're a pleasure to have around, not to mention a big help.

Are you sure, Vincent? If I need to do something before we go, I can take the time. My mom will understand.

There's no reason to worry, Diego. I just need Tegan's advice about a project I'm working on.

-I watched Diego amble out the door, the worried look never leaving his face. I looked about the room.

What's your project, Vincent?

He's even better than I imagined, Tegan. I'm sure I can sell his work.

That's the project? How sure are you?

I've already showed the paintings to my contacts and they're in.

Are we talking good money or just charity change?

He's really good. He could do well.

-A little voice sounded a warning in the back of my mind. Fortunately, for once I paid attention.

Have you told him?

I thought I should talk to you first. Do you see a problem?

I'm not sure he's mature enough to handle that kind of money.

Tegan, most artists would die for a chance to sell to these people.

Go ahead and talk to your contacts. But I want to hold off on anything official until I can think this through.

-Seeing the disappointed look in his eyes, I took his hand in mine.

I know you care about Diego and want to see him succeed, Vincent. All I'm asking is for a little time.

Okay but I'm not through working on you, Tegan Wylls.

-He squeezed my hand before pushing me out the door.

As Diego and I bumped along the rutted road leading to his house, Claude's idea of getting evidence on Omar kept running through my mind. Maybe I could find a way after all. Considering the pile of drawings and photos I'd seen in that backroom, I figured one or two fewer would hardly be noticeable.

I decided to see what Diego knew but before I had a chance to ask, Eloy Fuego appeared in the middle of the road. I slammed my foot against the brake, narrowly missing him. A wall of yellow dust drifted over the car. A moment later he emerged from the cloud, standing before my window in his rainbow-hued serape, white hair framing his head like a halo. He raised his hands as if cradling an invisible ball.

I see the devil. He rides the wind. He poisons the air. You must stop him, daughter.

-Diego leaned toward the window.

Senor Fuego, the devil doesn't exist for real, man. He's just a symbol, a way for people to explain evil and the bad things that happen to them.

-Eloy bent towards the car, his eyes wild, his voice rising with each word.

He is evil, young one. That is the truth you speak. But he does exist. He is near and he is poison.

-Diego waved off the admonition.

Take it easy, old dude. You're going to give yourself a heart attack.

-Eloy held a gnarled hand before my face.

Protect the young one, daughter. The poison grows. You have seen it. You must stop it.

158

-He turned and slipped into the thicket. I gripped the steering wheel, trying to stop my hands from shaking.

Jesus, that was close. How does he just appear like that? I could've run him over.

Maybe he's a Mexican witch. My mother believes in stuff like that. She calls them brujos.

Whatever he is, I like him in spite of his strange behavior. Sometimes he sounds like anyone else and then other times like what we just saw. I wish I knew why.

I like him too but he's crazy, Tegan. Haven't you figured that out yet?

I don't know, Diego. There's something more to him, something I can't quite put my finger on.

You're starting to sound like my mother. When we get to the house, I'll make some tea to help you snap out of it.

-As the trailer came into view, I surveyed the area, finding no sign of Omar or Celia. I decided to take my chances. After following Diego through the trailer door, I stopped in the small living room and pointed to the end of the hall.

What's the room at the end used for?

-He frowned at the question.

Omar stores his junk in there. He kept the door locked until I disabled it. Now, he just threatens us, telling us to stay out like it's all secret and stuff. I've been in there and there's nothing but a bunch of boring pictures and drawings. I thought maybe he had some pot or money stashed but it's only something to do with his work, whatever that is. I'm going to make iced tea. Do you want some?

-I nodded and pointed down the hallway again.

Do you think I could take a look? I want to know what he's up to.

Sure, but like I said, it's nothing much.

-He disappeared into the kitchen. I glanced through the front window to check the driveway before hurrying down the hall and through the door. The room looked

159

much as I remembered, with piles of photos and blueprints scattered about. Scribbled notes and drawings sat beneath coffee cups and overfull ashtrays.

-As I hoped, the mess provided a cover. I thumbed through the piles, pulling photos and drawings from the middle, careful to disturb them as little as possible. The instant I slipped the last snapshot into my purse, voices sounded from the front steps. Diego was arguing with Omar, clearly trying to stall him.

-I stepped behind the door and closed it as a wave of panic gripped my chest. Turning toward the cluttered room, I tried to clear my mind. In the back corner opposite me a window stood half-open, the screen missing. I knew my car had given me away but not necessarily inside the house, so I slipped around the table, slid open the window and pushed one leg through. As I swung my foot around, my shoe grazed a coffee cup just enough to tip it, spilling the dregs onto a notepad. I cringed at the sight but seeing there was nothing I could do, I slipped to the ground behind the trailer.

-Omar's voice echoed from inside. Staying beneath the windows, I crept around to the front of the trailer and knocked loudly on the metal siding. A moment later, the door flew open. Omar stood glaring at me though the torn screen. I tried to manage an innocent smile.

I've been looking for Diego. I think he's avoiding me.

-He looked at me askance.

You do not come into the house?

When I drove up, I spotted Diego walking toward the back so I went looking for him. Have you seen him?

-He nodded toward the tree line.

He is there. He lies to me. I can see when he does this.

Maybe you give him reason to lie.

-He ignored my comment, instead pointing his chin at my car.

You did not bring him here from his lesson?

I was tied up with another student so a friend brought him.

Why did you come, then?

-The ease of lying to him shocked me, and I again puzzled over my father's deceits.

I came by to ask him how it went.

-He eyed me suspiciously, the tone of his voice filled with contempt.

But you did not come into here, counselor or whatever you truly are?

-I felt my patience drain away.

I've already told you I was looking for Diego, not that it's any of your business. Why are you so worried about me coming into the trailer? I've been inside many times before, you know. Does it have something to do with your work, whatever you truly do?

-A wave of anger crossed his face.

He is not here so you must go.

This is Celia's home, not yours. If she was here I wouldn't leave.

You must go now.

If you do anything to hurt Diego, you'll answer to the authorities.

He has no respect. If he hits me, I will hit him.

If you hit him, you will go to jail. I'll make sure of it.

-With that, I turned toward my car, deciding not to press my luck. As I drove back down the rugged lane, I promised myself I'd find a way to remove him from Diego's life.

Chapter Nineteen

A light breeze stirred the damp heat of late-summer, leaving a sauna-like stillness in its wake. I stood waiting on the porch as my grandparents climbed out of their blue sedan and ambled toward the sidewalk like two ancient turtles. Beetie had called to ask if they could come see me and, by her tone, I feared I was in store for bad news.

She approached the house with a purposeful frown, a sign she was on a mission, carrying a brown paper bag no doubt filled with home cooking. They lived in fear that as a young, single woman living alone, I would somehow die of malnutrition. That I would turn thirty in a few months made no difference.

I held the door open as they stepped past me into the cool of air conditioning. Once in the kitchen, they looked about the room as if they had never seen it before. I began to suspect they had a different sort of news for me. Beetie emptied the bag onto the table and eyed me for a moment.

Tegan, you look positively emaciated. I brought you some coffee cake and nut bread for your breakfasts, and a pecan pie for whenever you like. We must put some weight on you.

-I stared at the baked goods and sighed.

I can cook for myself, you know.

-Pen gave me a quick wink.

Now Tegan, there's nothing like your grandmother's cooking, is there?

-Knowing I was beaten, I decided to change the subject.

So, what brings you two out this way?

-Beetie turned to me, looking hurt.

Your old grandparents can't come for a visit? Have you washed your hands of us, then?

-I peered at her, wondering what she was up to.

Beetie, what on earth are you talking about? I just saw you and Pen last week. Or, was it the week before?

See, it's been so long you can't even remember.

Okay, so you're here now.

Aren't you going to ask us to sit?

-I glared at them both.

Since when do I have to do that? What's gotten into you?

-Pen helped her into a chair and then sat across from me, leaning his elbows on the table.

We're just worried about you, Tegan.

But why, Pen? I love my job. I have a nice house and I'm making enough to pay the bills and save a little. What's worrisome about that?

-Beetie put her hands together and faced me with such concern I thought she might start praying. She had recently started watching one of those twenty-four hour religious programs on cable.

Tegan, sweetheart, are you going to waste away your life as a lonely spinster?

-I struggled to stay calm.

Is that word even in the dictionary anymore?

Don't you like men, honey? If you don't, we understand... well, sort of. Anyway, your grandfather and I would learn to manage.

You don't have to manage anything, Beetie. I like men fine.

But here you are nearly thirty and still unmarried. How will you ever have children at such an advanced age?

-I tried to remind myself these were my grandparents, after all, and two generations removed from me.

Beetie, women my age and older have children all the time. Besides, I don't know if I even want kids.

Oh, but you do want to, Tegan, even if you don't know it just yet.

Well, we'll see about that.

Still, you first need to find a husband, Tegan. Don't you know any men?

Of course I do.

Then where are they? You never bring them to our house.

I've been seeing someone for quite awhile, if you must know.

Do you mean that young soldier you told us about? Is he your boyfriend?

He's long past being a boy, Beetie.

Whatever happened to him? Is it a serious romance between the two of you?

-I felt myself blush at the thought. Claude and I had been sleeping together for months.

We like each other, if that's what you mean.

Then why have you never brought him to meet us, sweetheart?

I don't know, Beetie.

Are we an embarrassment to you, then?

-I turned to Pen.

Has she started some new medication or something?

-Beetie glared at me as Pen reached across the table, taking my hand.

We just want to know you'll have someone to see after you when we're gone.

-There was no sweeter man than my grandfather but I was tiring of their game.

I can see after myself just fine. Is there something you're not telling me? Are you feeling alright?

-Pen's expression grew grim.

The truth is, there's another reason we're here. We've come to ask your help with Trewin. He's taken to bed and we can't roust him out of there no matter what we try. For the first time in my life I'm worried about my older brother.

That *is* worrisome, Pen. Trewin is never sick. But what can I do? I'm no doctor.

164

The problem is with his head.

-Beetie nodded in agreement.

Or you might rather say the problem is with his heart. He seems to have given up on life.

What brought this on?

We can only guess, sweetheart. We do know a lady friend of his decided to move closer to her kids. But he's had so many come and go, I can't imagine why this one would have such an effect on him.

-I glanced at the clock. I was due to meet Claude at French Street Dancehall, a newly opened bar.

Alright, I'll try to stop by and check on him sometime. Right now, I have to go meet someone.

-Beetie perked up.

Does that mean you have a date?

-I searched for a way to avoid her question.

In a manner of speaking, I suppose you might say that.

Then is your date with that handsome soldier?

-Ignoring the question, I started for the door, calling back over my shoulder.

If I don't leave now I'll be late. Lock up on your way out.

I puzzled over my reluctance to talk about Claude as I pulled into a gravel parking lot fronting what looked to be an old, high-roofed warehouse, the outside covered with corrugated tin. A tree-shaded beer garden sat off to one side. Climbing the wooden stairs to a small landing, I pushed through the door and into the dim interior. Off-color light cast by the trees filtered through the windows, clashing with the reds and blues of neon beer signs hanging above the bar.

As I moved along the elevated entry I squinted into the broad interior, surveying the room for Claude. Below me a hardwood dance floor stretched from the bar to a low stage scattered with drums, guitars and microphones. Musicians milled about the space checking their equipment. Opposite the stage, couples sat in the near-darkness, leaning close and speaking in low tones. I decided Claude must be running late.

Thinking I'd find a table, I wandered into the room. A group of men standing along the bar all turned at once, ogling me as I passed by. I started to say something, annoyed by their brazenness, then thought better of it. Instead, Claude's lateness and choice of meeting place began to wear on me. Before I knew it, my annoyance became a simmering anger. The room suddenly seemed stifling. I decided to leave.

I had turned toward the door when Claude's voice called my name from across the room. I hesitated in spite of an anger that continued to sweep me along. Part of me wanted to keep walking but instead I turned back toward the dance floor, spotting Claude's face amid the dim confines of the far corner. The mere sight of him gave me a chill.

As I approached him my emotions began to settle. Then I noticed a young woman sitting at his table. Her jet black hair, lost to the surrounding shadows, gave her pale face an intimidating beauty. Her gray eyes held a flint-like hardness.

I nodded a greeting and sat on the bench opposite her, expecting Claude to join me. Instead, he sat next to her. I tried to hide my disappointment as he grinned and gestured toward her, barely able to contain his excitement.

Tegan, this is Kat Gunter, my internship partner.
-She nodded without smiling, her accent unidentifiable.

It is my luck to partner with Claude. We think the same on everything.
-He glanced at her and leaned toward me.

Speaking of luck, we just found out we've been assigned to a border patrol unit working south of town. Isn't that great?

166

-I tried to sound excited but something about her made me uneasy. She seemed so confident, as if she had some sort of hold on him. I studied her face.

That's good news. So, you'll be working together, then?

-She peered back at me, her eyes reflecting all light, revealing nothing.

You should be proud of Claude. He has earned the respect of his professors through much hard work.

-I felt my anger returning.

What makes you think I'm not glad for him?

Glad is not the same as proud.

I know as well as anyone how hard he works.

-Claude waved his hand between us.

Okay, okay, we've established that I've worked hard, but the point is this internship is a big deal. The word from on top is something is about to happen, something big involving foreign nationals. We've been told it's hush-hush, very secret. We'll be joining a stakeout team to watch a suspected group, I forget from what country, and every extra pair of eyes is important. This is a plum assignment, Tegan.

-I thought again of Omar and my promise to myself.

Maybe your supervisors can make something of the photos and papers I gave you.

-He sat back, clearly disappointed that I had changed the subject.

I already gave them to one of my professors but I don't know when he'll take a look, if ever. He didn't seem too impressed.

I have to find a way to get rid of that guy, Claude. He's bad news for Diego.

I'll try to ask someone at the stakeout.

When's that going to happen?

That's the best part, Tegan. The timing is great. We don't have to wait forever like the other interns. We start tonight.

-I looked across the table at them, my mind racing. Was the stakeout real or some excuse to get rid of me? Was she really an intern? I chided myself for having such thoughts but my insecurities only grew. An image of Chancer deceiving my mother flashed before my eyes as I leaned toward Claude.

I thought we came here to dance.

We will sometime, just not tonight. This is a big break, Tegan. Interns have a good chance of getting hired if they're willing to do what it takes.

-Kat nudged him.

He won't say so but with such ability, his chances are excellent.

-I had the sudden urge to pull him out of there and away from her. I stared into his eyes, lying without hesitation.

Claude, I have something I need to talk with you about, something private.

-He glanced at his watch.

We'll have time to talk after the stakeout is over, Tegan, just not tonight. In fact, Kat and I need to get moving.

-They stood but I stayed put, as if not standing might stop him. She moved to the end of the table and waited while Claude looked down at me.

Tegan, we really need to get going. Are you staying here?

-I made no effort to hide my disappointment.

Maybe someone will ask me to dance.

-He fidgeted with his keys.

I'm sorry for the change of plans but I hope you can understand how important to me this is.

Go roust some aliens, Claude. I'm not stopping you.

-He hesitated and then started for the door, Kat next to him. I refused to let myself watch them leave. Staring into the tabletop, I thought again of Chancer, wondering how and when his deceit finally caught up with him.

Chapter Twenty

The damp heat of August followed Chancer as he pushed through the back door of his grandmother's house and into the kitchen. Thunder rolled in the distance, vibrating the windowpanes and china. The cramped room felt like an oven.

Gammie took no notice as she peered at a small television balanced on the countertop. Sitting across the table from her sister, she motioned him to a chair without a word. Instead, he wandered about the room looking for something to distract himself. Gammie turned her eyes from the screen, craning her neck to see him.

Chancer, you sit yourself down and pay attention. This draft lottery is the most important thing ever to happen in your young life. Don't you know that?

I know the odds, Gammie. A lottery is determined by the mathematics of probability.

-Weesie pulled her eyes from the television.

Mathematics won't mean much if someone is shooting at you, sweetheart.

-Gammie glared at her.

Sister, you mustn't talk like that. It's bad luck.

Oh, you worry too much. He'll probably end up number three hundred and sixty-five. But if not, we always have our communist brother for backup. He's offered more than once to take in Chancer. And I can think of worse places to live than Vancouver, Canada.

Sister, I don't recall him offering any such thing.

Of course you do. But you don't like to admit to things you don't agree with. Besides, you know how opposed to the war Brother is. He's always on the lookout for ways to fight against it.

Well, I don't want him influencing Chancer with his communist views.

He's not a real communist. He just thinks Americans are greedy, is all.

-Gammie pulled a handkerchief from her apron, dabbing sweat from her cheeks as she spoke.

I just don't understand why we must have a war lottery. In the last war, men joined up willingly, including our brother. They felt it was their duty and most were proud to serve. We all did. We saw the war as an unpleasant but necessary responsibility, a just cause. But no one seems to understand what this present war is all about. All I hear is a lot of doubletalk.

At least we didn't have to watch the last war on television. The sight of those body bags lined up on the runway is something I fear I'll never forget.

Sister, please stop. I'm already beside myself with worry.

-Weesie pointed to the screen.

Look, they're about to pick number thirteen. Someone will have to be unlucky twice over to get that one.

Sister! You're going to give me heart failure.

-Raindrops splattered the window screen as Gammie fanned herself. Unable to resist, Chancer turned his eyes to the screen as a man in a dark suit and glasses reached into a glass bin, pulling out a small ball. He handed it to a colleague who snapped it open. An instant later, the third of October, Chancer's birthday, flashed across the screen.

-Gammie gasped and leaned toward the screen, reaching for Weesie's hand. Chancer stared at the date, the reality of the numbers escaping him. Then a dull numbness settled over him and he turned from the television, starting for the back door. Gammie jumped from her chair as if to stop him.

Sugar! Where are you going?

-Chancer stepped into the rain, calling over his shoulder.

I've seen all I need to.

The rain had stopped by the time Chancer had reached the hospital. Wisps of steam drifted from the sidewalk. He crossed the loading dock, pushing through the back exit and into the empty hallway. An outdated wall calendar hung from the storeroom door.

He thought again of the lottery. He knew he would be drafted yet he felt no different. The hospital still smelled of alcohol and disinfectant. His grandmother, no doubt, was still sitting across the kitchen table from her sister anxiously discussing his fate. He could find nothing out of the ordinary to explain what had just happened to him. Yet he sensed that the brief, mundane, all too civilized television moment had forever altered his life.

Voices drifted down the stairwell as he started up the steps, approaching the ward Turley had called home for the past few months. Chancer had last come by over a week earlier and he now felt the familiar unease of not knowing Turley's current condition. Would he be well enough for a game of chess or curled into a ball beneath the blankets?

He stepped through the doorway, surprised to find a room bustling with people. For an instant he thought he heard Turley's rough voice above the noise, but then shrugged it off as wishful thinking. He wandered among the crowd, puzzling over the reason until he emerged at a table filled with food. At the far end Turley stood talking with someone, stuffing chocolate cake into his mouth between words. Chancer blinked, trying to believe his eyes. An instant later Turley spotted him, letting out a cackle of laughter.

It's about damn time you showed up, Wylls. Where the hell have you been?

What's happened, Turley? You're not in your room.

Did you figure that out all on your own, Einstein? They let me out of the goddamn prison, Wylls. Can you believe it?

That's great but why, Turley?

171

My white cells are back to normal and I just ate a freaking cheeseburger. I never tasted anything so good.

So, they're sending you back to the ward?

Hell, no, I'm not going back to the ward. They're graduating me from this hellhole, Wylls. The goddamn army didn't kill me after all. I guess that means I won't be seeing your ugly face anymore.

Why do you say that?

Do-gooders like you and Ahote only hang around if you can take pity on a man.

That's not true.

Sure it is. Being sorry for someone makes you college boys all warm and fuzzy inside.

You're wrong, Turley.

I know the type. You like feeling superior.

That's not fair, Turley. Ben is trying to support you through a bad time. He's the opposite of superior.

That's just his Injun act.

It's no act but I'm beginning to wonder why he bothers. How are people going to support you when you talk about them like that?

I'm not asking for anything.

And we do what we do because we choose to. We're on your side, Turley. You know I'm right, don't you?

I don't know, maybe.

Besides, I heard Ben quote Sun Tzu to you. That sounded like friendship, not pity.

What about you, Wylls? Are you friend or foe?

Give me your address and I'll come see you.

I would if I had an address. I'm officially homeless.

You don't have a house or apartment?

I had a nice place but I've been in here too long so I lost it.

Where will you go?

I don't know. I thought I might shack up with Ahote but his younger brother is staying with him while he looks

172

for a job. Thanks to you college boys, finding an apartment around here is next to impossible.

It can't be that hard.

Last time, I searched for three weeks before I found a place. I hear there are a lot of vets on the street these days. I guess I'll be meeting some of them.

You've been sick, Turley. You can't start sleeping under some bridge. That's tempting the fates. You don't want Aisa turning her attentions on you.

Who in the hell is she, some damn social worker?

She's one of the Fates in Greek mythology whose job was to cut a person's thread of life when it was their time to die.

I've fooled her once already, Wylls. I can do it again.

I have a better idea, Turley. My place has a big couch. Why not stay there while you look for an apartment?

You mean it, Chancer?

-Chancer scribbled his address on a napkin and handed it to him. He peered at Turley, considering what he wanted to say.

Can I ask you something, Turley?

Don't' tell me you've already changed your mind.

I just got my draft number.

Damn, Wylls, we're standing around wasting time when you've got that hanging over your head? You should've said so.

I'm saying so now. My number is thirteen.

Hell, Wylls, no wonder you're not looking so good. What are you going to do?

I just wish I could continue being a physics student.

No, no, no. Wishing isn't any good when fate deals you a bad hand. You need to have a plan. Think, Chancer. This is no time for indecision.

With a number that low, I don't know what I can do. I guess I'll just wait and see what happens.

You'll wait and see what happens? That's the last thing you want to do. You've got to be on your game, Wylls. I say pack up and head north.

Head north to where?

For a college boy, you're sure out of touch. You get your ass to Canada.

But my family expects me to go to Vietnam.

Listen to me, Wylls. You do not want to go to that hellhole. You can evade the draft by going to Canada. They've let in plenty of draft dodgers already.

But I'd have to drop out of school. I'm in the middle of summer term.

You don't have to leave school until they call you up. That's after you've had your physical.

If I become a draft dodger, my parents will disown me.

Maybe the damn politicians will come to their senses and end the war before then. Anyway, your parents will get over it. In the meantime, make your plans. Now, I promised I'd go see Nurse Berry before I leave here. We can talk more later.

Chancer wandered back through the crowd, imagining the look on his mother's face if he announced he was moving out of the country. As bad as getting drafted sounded, facing the disapproval of his family seemed worse. He needed time to think. He had decided to return home when Raz appeared before him.

Chancer, thank the gods I found you. My uncle, he is going to the racetrack in the morning and is begging for my consultations. You must help me, please. I believe he has become indebted to men who do not accept his habit of making excuses.

Raz, I gave you the formulas I worked out. All you have to do is rank the horses in each race.

But I am too slow, Chancer. We must both work the formulas. Besides, this is not just any day at the races for

174

my uncle. He is betting my parents money, money they saved for my college. If he loses I will have to drop out of school and return home. That would be a fate worse than horrible, I can tell you.

Chapter Twenty-one

Weeks had passed and still I had yet to go see Trewin. I tried to lessen my guilt by convincing myself I had important work to do but the truth is I was not up to the task. Claude and I had barely spoken since he reneged on our date and I was feeling sorry for myself. Knowing he was involved in an important and secret operation made little difference. To pull myself together, I dove into work.

As I neared Celia's trailer, I tried not to think about my love life. I had seen little of her since Diego started working with Vincent. But earlier in the day when Diego told me Omar had gone missing, I decided I needed to make a visit. I wondered if pilfering the drawings and photos had anything to do with his disappearance.

Eloy Fuego stepped into the roadway, pointing his cane at my windshield. I pulled to the side and climbed out the car, glad to avoid another near-miss. He peered at me with his drooping eyes, looking more subdued that I had ever seen him, and a sudden dread filled my throat. He faced the sky, raising his cane into the air.

The sun, he shines but he brings no warmth to this old man.

-I felt the sweat trickling down the back of my neck.

Eloy, the temperature has to be at least ninety-five out here. How can you be anything but hot?

The devil does his work unseen, like the maggots of the flies.

-I winced at his grim language but wanted to understand what he had long tried to tell me.

Eloy, what do you mean when you speak of the devil?

Yes, it is of him that I speak. Beauty falls beneath his blade.

-I liked the sound of that even less.

Help me understand, Eloy.

-He swung his cane toward the trailer.

You must go to her, daughter.

-I peered down the drive.

You mean Celia? What is it, Eloy? Has something happened to her?

-He again raised the cane.

The Queen of Egypt gives her hair but it is not enough!

-I turned and hurried toward the trailer, pushing through the glass door without knocking. The shades were all drawn. In the dim shadows of one corner Celia sat with her knees to her chest, uneven patches of stubble checkering her bruised scalp. Her beautiful mane of hair was gone.

-I stood frozen in place, anger and frustration blotting out all thought. When finally I was able to move, I knelt next to her, taking her hand in mine, refusing to let myself cry.

Omar did this to you?

-She nodded without facing me.

Why, Celia?

-Her voice was hoarse, just above a whisper.

He said I stole from him. He said he should cut off my hand for doing this, but instead he would cut off my hair. I tried to fight him but he knocked me down and held me by my throat. Even now, I have no voice.

-I winced, knowing my willfulness had led to this. I tried to concentrate on how I could help her.

Diego told me Omar had gone missing. I was hoping it was for good.

He has been strange in the last weeks, going away without saying where or why, bringing men here I never saw before. I think they are preparing for something.

Where is he now?

-She glanced toward the door.

He left after he did this to me but he said nothing. I'm afraid he will change his mind and…

177

-She stopped as the rumble of his sports car rattled the windows. I stood and faced the doorway, trying to control my anger. An instant later, the door flew open and Omar strode through, his face grim but determined. I pointed a finger at him.

You don't touch her! She might not call the law on you but make no mistake, I will.

Your law, it means nothing.

In this country, the law keeps men like you from bullying women.

I do not bully. I give justice to thieves.

-Guilt again rose into my throat. I pointed to Celia, reminding myself that his wrong was many times worse than mine.

You had no right to do this to her.

-He glared at Celia, thrusting his finger at her.

I warn you not to allow her here again!

-He took a step toward Celia and I suddenly realized I had left my purse, and my can of mace, in the car. I glanced around the room, looking for something to use against him. To my left, a heavy wooden candlestick sat on the mantle. I reached for it just as he lunged past, knocking me aside as he reached out and slapped Celia across the face. The candlestick clattered to the floor.

-Without thinking, I leapt at him, grabbing his arm before he could strike her a second time. She scurried past us and out the door. Expecting him to follow, I grabbed at him again but he shook off my grip, pushing me to the floor and pressing his forearm to my throat. The candlestick lay just out of reach.

-I struggled to free myself but one arm was pinned beneath me, the other he held with a sure grip. I struggled for a breath as the ceiling above me began to lose focus, the colors draining of hue, fading to white. I tried to call out but no sound came from my throat. A sudden realization I would die gripped me.

-Jerking to one side, I managed to free my arm and feel about the floor for the candlestick. An image of my father flashed across my mind, his wrinkled collar and his splayed hair. I thought again of my promise to see Trewin, regretting my negligence.

-Then my fingers brushed the end of the candlestick and I grabbed it, swinging the heavy wood up and around in an arc, aiming for his face. The glancing blow stunned him and I raised the heavy wood again but he knocked it from my hand, pressing down harder onto my throat.

-A blurred figure moved across my vision, arms outstretched, wing-like, hovering. I thought of angels. An instant later, a sharp crack snapped me back to consciousness. Omar slumped across me and onto the floor. Suddenly I could breathe again.

-A man's face emerged from the formless world above me. Still dazed, I stared at his halo of white hair, imagining some unnamed saint had chosen me for saving. I blinked and took a breath. Instead of a saint, the face of Eloy Fuego peered down at me with his watery eyes. At that moment I could imagine no better candidate for sainthood.

-Omar groaned as I pushed him aside. After helping me into the chair, Eloy lifted his serape, pulling out a rope he used in place of a belt and deftly tying Omar's hands to his feet while I called the police. Once I hung up, Eloy tapped his cane on the floor.

You see, daughter, the devil, he must be stopped. He will poison the air, set fire to the sky.

-My mind still in a fog, I stared at him, again trying to understand his words.

You mean Omar is a devil, don't you?

He and the others bring evil upon the land, on all they touch.

He's evil alright.

You free us of him, Tegan. You free us of this devil.

179

I'll do my best to see he goes to jail but you mean something more, don't you, Eloy?

-He leaned forward pointing a gnarled finger into the air but before he could answer, a knock sounded from outside. I stumbled to the door and opened it. Two men stood before me, neither in uniform. Confused, I peered at them.

How did you get here so fast?

-The taller one took off his sunglasses.

Excuse me, 'mam?

You're with the police, aren't you?

We work for the Federal Bureau of Investigation.

-I took a step back, unsure if I'd heard right.

You're not the police?

That is correct, 'mam, we're FBI.

I don't want the FBI, I want the police.

We intercepted your call to the authorities. If you'll give me a moment to explain, I think Agent Fritch and I can help you understand...

-My patience gone, I interrupted him.

No, you're the one that doesn't understand. We need the police here right now. A man just tried to kill me. I want him in jail.

-The shorter agent stepped forward, a forced smile spreading across his lips.

I believe Agent Price and I can take Mr. Smith off your hands, 'mam.

-A part of me wanted to slap that fake smile right off his face.

I don't know any Mr. Smith, agent. A man just tried to strangle me. I want him arrested.

The man is also known as Omar Gil or Ottmar Garza or Olivier Gilbert. You do know a man who goes by Omar do you not, Ms. Wylls?

How do you know my name?

We've been running an investigation on this man for over two weeks.

180

-I nodded, hopeful that my thievery might help Celia after all.

I knew he was up to no good. What's he done? My guess is he's running drugs across the border. That should put him away for a long stretch.

We're not at liberty to say, Ms. Wylls. Now, if you'll just stand aside.

-I wanted to know for sure if I'd had a part in determining Omar's fate.

Hold on a minute. How did you find him?

-Agent Fritch shook his head, a look a smug indifference on his face.

That's classified information.

Someone from the university gave you the tip, didn't they?

-He glanced at his partner and again shook his head.

Like I said...

-Agent Price took a step forward and held up his hand, silencing his partner.

We do have a contact at the university. He gave us a description that fit a criminal known to have crossed the border illegally. That's all we can tell you, Ms. Wylls.

-That was enough. I stood aside and watched as they hauled him though the door like a pig on a spit. A moment later, the black sedan sped off in a cloud of dust. I walked to where Celia sat nursing a split lip. She looked up at me, beautiful despite her lost mane.

The men, they have taken him away?

He won't hurt you anymore, Celia.

What will they do to him, Tegan?

Whatever it is, it won't be enough to suit me.

Omar, he was not all bad.

-I stared at her in disbelief.

How can you say that, Celia? Look what he did to you.

Sometimes he would buy me things, nice things, and food to cook. But I must protect Diego. Now, I have nothing. I will lose the trailer.

There's assistance out there, Celia. I'll help you find it.

But I am alone, Tegan.

You have a son, Celia. You were right to protect him from that evil.

-Reminded of Eloy, I turned and looked for him.

Where is Senor Fuego?

He is gone.

He just left?

He is a strange man. He is always afraid to go into my house and then today for some reason he is not.

Did he say where he was going?

-She looked up at me with her dark eyes, clearly dazed by what she had been through.

He said to tell you he knows.

-I had no idea what she meant.

What, Celia, what does he know?

Oh... yes... he knows why he was chosen. I don't know what he means by this.

His name means the chosen one. What he meant, I can't say.

-She reached out, taking my hand.

You are the reason, Tegan. He tells me he was chosen for you.

As I drove back down the rutted drive, I wondered at the odds of showing up at Celia's moments before Omar walked in. What might have happened to her if I had not been there? And why did Eloy go into her house, a place he had always refused to enter? Where would I be if he had not shown up when he did? I shuddered at the thought.

My father would have had something to say about it, no doubt. His face flashed through my mind, and I again tried to guess at where he and my mother had gone wrong.

Was their romance what had so changed him that year? Or did fate have something more in store?

Autumn

/'ôtəm/: the third season of the year in the northern
hemisphere, from September to November; time when
fruits and crop are harvested and leaves fall

Late Middle English: from Old French *autompne*, or
later directly from Latin *autumnus*

the period from the autumnal equinox to the winter
solstice

I many times thought peace had come
When peace was far away
As wrecked men deem they sight the land
At center of the sea

-Emily Dickinson

Chapter Twenty-two

Yellowed strings of party lights drifted above Chancer as he and Byes spun a tight circle, shuffling to the two-step rhythm of an old country and western song. Cornmeal grit hissed beneath their feet. Though he tried to catch her eye, she would not face him, going through the motions but little more.

On the way to the dancehall that evening, the pink, misshapen sun had perched above the highway like the broken head of a porcelain doll. Tree-cast shade stretched to the north in narrowing lines, jailing the road behind its dark bars. Autumn, his favorite time of year, was less than a week away yet at that moment he dreaded the passage of time caught within the sun's southward tilt.

He glanced at Byes, trying to guess her mood. Though she loved to dance, he'd had to beg her to join him. Since then she had scarcely said a word. He could make no sense of it. Try as he might, he could not stop the feeling that his world was spinning out of control, and her with it. Each day that slipped past brought his draft call-up closer.

As the song ended, Byes pulled free and started for a row of tables near the back corner. He watched her walk away, searching his memory for something to explain her unpredictable moodiness. Maybe her semester had gotten off to a difficult start, or perhaps she was unhappy with her looks. She had recently put on weight. He sat across from her, hoping to change the tone of the evening.

I'm still not much of a dancer, am I? Are your feet sore?

-She shook her head, still unwilling to face him. He tried again.

You look nice tonight, Byes.

-She looked up.

I know I'm not good company, Chancer.

What's wrong, Byes?

186

I'm not feeling well. I'd like to go home.

-Half an hour later a wave of dread spread through his chest as he drove away from her dorm, the feeling vague but unmistakable, as if his body could sense what his mind could not. He resisted the urge to turn around and go find her. Instead, he retreated into the solid, unambiguous world of mathematics. The formulas he had given Raz hovered in his thoughts like hoarfrost on a windowpane. He had finally mastered the Monte Carlo method for predicting probability.

Late the following morning, Chancer angled his car past a parking attendant, stopping next to a sign reading 'County Fairgrounds'. Pickups and flatbed trucks littered the grass-covered parking area, dwarfing his car as he climbed from behind the steering wheel and started toward a broad gate marking the race track entrance. Past the gate an open lawn split by a wide sidewalk led to a county livestock barn and, beyond it, a race track fronted by bleachers stretching three stories into the sky. The air smelled of straw and horses.

At the ticket window an old man counted out Chancer's change with shaking hands, tapping the bills with his forefinger three times before pushing them through. His wizened face grinned through the bars. Chancer turned from the window, ambling toward the track and wondering if the taps meant good luck or bad.

Beneath the stands, men in straw hats huddled together clutching racing bulletins and speaking in low tones. Though the morning air held the latent heat of a summer day, they wore long-sleeve shirts and jeans. September sunlight played across their stitched boots. The men went silent as Chancer passed by in his shorts and sneakers.

He climbed the bleacher stairs and scanned the seats for Raz, instead spotting two men wearing sunglasses, looking out of place in slacks and silk shirts. They eyed him with interest. Recalling Raz's worry over his uncle's debts, Chancer moved away without looking back, the hair on his neck tingling beneath their stares.

He had decided to leave when a hand landed on his shoulder. Flinching, he turned to find Raz and his uncle standing before him in white shirts and pants, plastic sandals on their bare feet. Raz moved aside as his uncle stepped forward. Taking Chancer's hand in his damp palm, he peered into his face. After a moment he turned back to Raz, his heavy cheeks drooping in disapproval.

Nephew, you have brought me a mere student, and a disheveled one at that. You were to bring a mathematician.

But uncle, Chancer is a gifted mathematician. He is sure to assist in your racing venture.

-He mopped his wide forehead with a sweat-stained handkerchief.

You cannot do this yourself, Rajesh? You are not a gifted student mathematician also?

But, uncle…

Why am I spending all my money to keep you in this place, then?

Uncle Talin, it is my parents' money that allows me to be here.

Yes, well, possibly, but they named you after Rajeshwer, the king of gods. Such a god should be able to do simple mathematics.

Uncle, probability calculations are far from simple. Besides, with Chancer here we can work twice as fast. He will not do the calculations all by himself.

-Talin glanced at the men in silk shirts.

Yes, that is good. These men I do not know. I am quite nervous about them, actually. Let us place ourselves far away.

-They moved to the top of the stands and Talin maneuvered himself next to Chancer, hunching over a

188

racing bulletin while stealing glances at the two men. Chancer leaned toward Raz, speaking beneath his breath.

Who are they, Raz?

-Talin tapped Chancer's knee.

What is it that you name my nephew?

I call him Raz.

-He nodded gravely, his cheeks flapping.

Yes, that is better than Russell. And what shall I call you?

Chancer is fine.

You may call me Mister Jones... or Uncle, if you so wish.

Is your name really Jones?

-Talin frowned, looking around as if someone might be listening.

Of course it is not Jones. My surname is Jodhpur but I must take care to be unnoticed in my work.

Unnoticed?

-Raz chuckled.

Uncle wants to pay no taxes on his winnings. He is travelling incognito, as they say.

-Chancer nodded toward the silk-shirted men.

Do you think those men are from the government? Is that why they make you nervous?

-Talin waved his handkerchief before Chancer's face.

You must not say such things, young man. I have enough troubles as it is.

-Raz leaned toward his uncle.

Then one of them is not Ling?

-Talin grimmaced at the name, bending his jiggling face even lower.

Keep down your voice, nephew!

But I'm whispering already, uncle. What else shall I do?

-Chancer leaned in with them.

Who is this Ling?

-Talin blew out his cheeks, his face growing redder by the minute.

He is to be avoided at all costs. He is employed by men I have dealings with. If one happens to be late with a payment only the slightest bit, Ling will pay them a visit, a most unfortunate visit.

What does he look like? His name sounds Chinese.

I have seen him only once. They say his father comes from Hong Kong but his mother is Panamanian.

Do you think the two men that keep staring at us work for him?

-A voice sounded over the loudspeakers announcing the first race. Talin sat up.

We have had enough of this most unfortunate talk. Please, you must now use your mathematics to calculate the winning horses so I may never again see Mr. Ling.

-Chancer picked up a racing bulletin and began jotting notes in the margin, using a calculator to run the formula. A moment later, he handed the program to Talin.

Bet on numbers three, twelve and seven in the first three races, Mr. Jones.

You don't observe the horseflesh?

There's no point. I know nothing about horses.

-Cradling the form in both hands, Talin disappeared down the stairs. Chancer turned to Raz.

You saw how I used the formula? The system is based on five factors for each horse.

-Raz nodded.

It is just as I imagined. The algorithm uses progressive approximations to arrive at the most likely winner.

Let's split up the list and figure the races so we can get out of here. All this talk of Mr. Ling makes me nervous.

-They hunched over their calculations, oblivious to the restless crowd. Chancer had nearly completed his portion of the list when a pair of shoes appeared at his feet. Determined to finish, he kept working. Raz looked up,

190

gasping as the two men stood before them, their silk shirts flapping in the warm breeze. He bent toward his racing program, speaking under his breath.

Good god, Chancer, the men, they are standing before us in their sunglasses. I am believing they wish to do us harm.

-Chancer looked up from his program. One of the men removed his sunglasses, giving him a slight bow. A thick accent bent his words.

Please excuse but we do not bet before. You can tell us how?

-The other man bowed before leaning toward Chancer.

We are geologist from Bulgaria. We wish to wager on the horse.

-Chancer studied them.

Ling didn't send you?

Ling? Who is this?

Never mind.

-He scribbled across his program before tearing out the page and handing it to them.

Go to the windows below the stairs and say you want these two for the daily double. The minimum bet is two dollars but you can wager as much as you like. I've written it all down there.

-The men studied the paper then bowed again, hurrying away without another word. Raz sat back, wiping the sweat from his forehead.

I do not like this business, Chancer. If only my uncle was not my uncle. Then I would not put us in danger so he can pay back his losses. We must calculate well so we can finish with this unfortunate work. I do not like to think what will happen if we fail.

-Chancer tapped his pencil against Raz's program.

These are probabilities, Raz, not guarantees. But I think your uncle will beat the odds.

191

-Raz took a breath and turned back to his program as the crowd stood, erupting with cheers. Chancer ignored the commotion. Completing his calculations, he sat back and watched as farm tractors moved around the track smoothing the surface. Jockeys in bright colors perched atop their mounts, the nervous horses tracing small circles in the dirt, their nostrils twitching. Old women clutched their betting stubs in both hands as if praying.

-Minutes later, the Bulgarians scrambled up the stairs, their hands full of funnel cakes. Smiling, they thrust one at Chancer. A puff of powdered sugar rose off the fried dough, disappearing in the wind.

We take the chance and wager ten dollars, and then we are winning three hundred and thirty-four.

-Chancer held up the cake.

Would you like to join us?

We thank you for your instruction but we must return. Two ladies ask us to join with them.

-They bowed and disappeared down the stairs. Chancer handed the cake to Raz and stood.

I'll get us something cold to drink.

-Seeing the line at the concession booth stretched across the plaza, he decided to wait for the crowd to ease and instead wandered into a show barn adjacent to the stands. The metal building housed a vast room used for livestock shows, its shaded interior offering a cool respite from the fuming heat. A row of offices sat just inside the entrance.

-Ambling past an office window, Chancer heard the rising tone of angry voices. In spite of all the worry raised by Raz and his uncle, he stopped to listen.

I don't want any maybes from you types!

But Mr. Maceio...

You better hear what I'm saying to you, Sidney! I want to know for sure he's going to win that number, uh... which race is it, Leo?

We got the fourth race, Mr. M.

Tell me why he'll win the fourth, Sidney.

-A man's voice answered, high and nervous.

We held him back in nine races, Mr. Maceio. We got his handicap down as far as they allow for a horse his size. Plus we got our jockey listed ten pounds higher than what he is. And we got the vet in our pocket. That sorrel gelding is juiced to the max. He can't lose with all that going for him.

What odds we expect, Leo?

They're predicting thirty-four to one, Mr. M.

Thirty-four to one, that's good. We all set, then, Sid?

We got it, Mr. Maceio. Nobody but us should be betting on that horse. When he wins, we score big.

That's what I wanted to hear. Okay, you get moving.

-Three men exited the office, one of them pausing to eye him before disappearing into the crowd. Chancer rushed up the stairs, meeting Talin halfway as he hurried down to place a bet. Grabbing the program from his hands, Chancer scanned the fourth race, finding *Major Tom's Surprise*, the only sorrel gelding. He held the paper in Talin's face, pointing to the name.

Bet on this horse, the sorrel gelding, not the one I picked.

-Talin looked at him askance.

Now the mathematician has learned to judge horse flesh?

Bet as much as you can, Mr. Jones.

-Talin's eyes grew wide, his cheeks quivering as he spoke.

You think there is something special about this horse, do you not? That even I can see. How do you come to learn this?

All you need to know is the gelding is your pick. If you don't hurry you'll miss your chance.

-He glanced at the race clock and rushed down the stairs. Chancer walked to the pre-race arena trying to understand all he'd overheard. Moving to the fence, he stood watching the trainers as they led their horses into the paddock. A veterinarian moved among the stalls, checking horses and making notes. Chancer wondered how many other drugged horses he had let pass. A jockey stood next to him looking confident.

-He had decided to give the concession stand another try when a voice sounded behind him. He turned to find one of the men from the show barn office, a muscular, dark-haired man, his chiseled face the color of green tea. He faced the paddock as he spoke.

The fat man, your friend, he has again won a race, his third. He bets much.

-Chancer looked to either side.

Are you talking to me?

-The man ignored the question. His wide nose and full lips seemed out of place, as if two faces had been smashed together.

I must wonder how this can happen, the odds being much against it.

-Chancer shifted his eyes back to the paddock, his worry growing.

What does that have to do with me?

-The man turned to face him.

You can answer this question, I believe.

-Chancer looked at him.

I don't know what you're talking about.

That is a disappointment. My employer expects businessmen like your friend to honor their commitments. It is possible they will turn to drastic measures if he should fail to do so.

-The man peered into his face, his dark eyes absorbing all light, reflecting nothing. Chancer swallowed, trying to hide his fear.

What makes you think I'm helping this man?

You have been seen advising him.

I don't deny talking to him. What's wrong with that?

The man, he must cheat to win.

-Chancer stared at the man, his past disappointments and failures rising in his chest, growing into a careless anger.

I don't cheat.

-The man stared back, a cold smile crossing his lips.

The young, they have no fear. You deny your uncle cheats?

He's my friend's uncle, not mine.

-The smile disappeared.

I am Ling. Perhaps you have heard of me.

I don't think so.

Does lying always come so easy?

What do you want?

-He leaned his face close to Chancer's.

The man owes much but now he wins. He must cheat. How do you help him?

I use mathematics to predict races. There's no cheating to it. Anyway, why should you care?

This man, this uncle of a friend, he owes a large sum to my employer.

Then your employer should be glad he's winning.

-The cold smile returned to Ling's face as he shook his head.

The money he owes is not the only problem. My employer profits off the betting of fools like your friend's uncle. But the fool must lose, as fools always do.

And what if the fool wins?

You must convince him to leave.

What if he refuses?

-Ling turned back to the paddock.

A man used to wager here often and lose often. Then he sold his house to bribe his way to winning, and he won… for a time.

And then?

They say his body washed up on Quintana beach. They never found his head.

-Ling turned and vanished into the crowd. Chancer stared after him for a moment then pivoted, hurrying back up the stairs. Raz had nearly finished the funnel cake. He held out the remaining bits.

I am sorry but I could not resist the goodness.

-Chancer searched the surrounding bleachers.

Where is Talin? We must find him right away.

-Raz jumped from his seat, a finger to his lips. He leaned toward Chancer, speaking under his breath.

Mr. Jones has gone to make a wager. What is wrong?

Ling is here.

Good god, Chancer, he is here in this place?

He told me your uncle must stop betting.

But he is winning.

That's the problem. He's winning too much and the owners are losing money. Ling threatened him, Raz. Your uncle is in for serious trouble if he doesn't leave.

He will not, Chancer. I know him.

It's worse than that, Raz. I overheard a conversation about fixing the fourth race so I gave your uncle the name of the horse.

So, he will win again?

-Chancer glanced at the television monitor hanging above them.

He already has, Raz, He won big, too. That only makes the situation worse. He's got to leave here.

-Talin appeared below them, red-faced and puffing as he climbed the stairs. He held up a thick finger, speaking in low tones, his cheeks quivering.

Quickly, you mathematicians, give me my numbers. I must try for the trifecta. The possible winnings are quite large, huge even.

-Raz grabbed his arm, pulling him closer.

But you just won again, uncle, did you not?

-He waved his index finger in the air.

Your uncle has won more than he ever has before, a miracle of modern mathematics I must tell you. But I am not finished. If I can win just a bit more, well more than a bit but doable, I am out from beneath the horrible debt I owe.

No, uncle, please…

I must confess to you, nephew. I lost nearly all of your college money in a fit of betting insanity. But I am back on the right track now and I will keep on until I have returned the full of your parents' savings.

-Raz peered into Chancer's face, the disappointment clear in his dark eyes. Chancer gave his head a slight shake. Then Raz turned to his uncle.

No, uncle, you must wager no more. We are leaving this undesirable place with much haste.

-Talin jerked his arm free.

What are you talking about, boy? I am winning most spectacularly. And I will go on winning.

But uncle, Ling is here.

-His wide eyes darted about.

What? How do you know this?

Chancer saw him.

-He glared at Chancer, disdain in his voice.

What does a mathematical genius know about such men? He must be mistaken.

But uncle…

Do not argue with me, boy, or I will tell your parents you spend your time at the race track instead of on your studies.

Uncle, you are in danger.

Enough of your schoolboy nonsense! Now, you go from me. You and your genius leave this place.

-He grabbed the racing program from Raz's hands and hurried back down the stairs. Raz watched after him.

My god, where does one learn such greed, Chancer? What will become of him?

We'll go find him and try again. He'll listen.

No, he will not. I know my uncle. If we push him he will be even more stubborn and he will tell my parents of

197

my shameful deeds, real or imaginary. At least he is winning.

But Raz, what about Ling's warning? I'm sure Talin is headed for serious trouble.

-Raz shook his head, starting down the stairs.

Fate will decide my uncle's future. We have no choice but to leave him to it.

Chapter Twenty-three

Chancer climbed a narrow stairway, stepping into the cramped two-room office of *Middle Earth*, the volunteer draft counseling center located across the street from campus. The place appeared to be empty. In one corner, the Door's *Strange Days* blared on a dust-covered turntable, its scratched grooves popping like distant gunfire.

'Strange days have found us,
Strange days have tracked us down'

He looked about the room, wondering what sort of people volunteer in such an office. Antiwar posters crowded the walls. In the middle of the room a cement pillar held a dozen fliers announcing speakers, marches and rallies. Directly before him, a Vietnamese prisoner stared out from a black and white photograph, a pistol to his head, taken at the moment of his execution.

Chancer tried to banish the image from his thoughts as footsteps sounded on the stairs behind him. A moment later, a man in t-shirt and jeans appeared in the doorway, a faded peace symbol covering his chest. He ran his hand through a wild mass of hair and tucked a handful behind his ear, surveying the office from side to side until his gaze settled on Chancer.

You the only one here, man?
-Chancer glanced behind him.
I think so. Do you volunteer here?
-The man strode toward him, his head bobbing.
Damn right I do. So, what do you need? We got books, brochures and rally dates. Or are you here to talk?
My draft physical is tomorrow.
Whoa, that's heinous news, brother. Uncle Sam is coming for you. What's your plan?
I don't have a plan. That's why I'm here.

Oh, right on, man. You need information. Knowledge is power, man. And power belongs to the people.

-Chancer had no idea what he was talking about. The man busied himself around the office, grabbing booklets and handouts before pointing him to a chair. He sat on the edge of a desk.

Man, you must be freaking. I mean your draft physical is tomorrow and all. Once you're processed they can nab your ass with ease. That's heavy.

After the physical they can call you up?

And likely sooner than later, man. Haven't you seen the way those body bags from 'Nam are piling up?

I try to avoid the television.

-He held up his hands, his head bobbing.

Oh, right, sorry. Talk about freaking you out. That would do it. But you've got to see a draft physical as your chance to beat the system and keep yourself out of this illegal war.

-Chancer sat up, the words piquing his interest.

How can I do that?

Some guys are getting their doctor to write up a fake illness or injury, like a bad back or arthritis, something hard to diagnose one way or the other. Other guys make like they're crazy.

I wouldn't know how to do either.

I knew a guy who wore lipstick and mascara, with a bra and pantyhose hidden beneath his clothes. The military docs freaked when he stripped down.

What did they do to him?

They sent him home, what do you think? They don't want any weirdoes in their army, man.

Are you telling me I'll have to lie?

You will if you don't have something real wrong with you like flat feet or cancer. This is your life we're talking about, man. You do what you have to.

Isn't there an alternative?

You can go to Canada.

I have some family in Vancouver.

The peace gods must be with you, man. That's your ticket out of the draft.

But I belong here in my own country.

Listen to me, man. You do not want to die in a freaking rice paddy. You're a citizen of the world now, and peace is your passport.

You make it sound so easy.

Like I said, we do what works.

What was your lottery number?

I was two hundred fifty-three.

That would make it easy.

No, man, the peace gods were with me too. So now I use my good fortune to fight the warmongers.

What about being a conscientious objector? I heard they spend two years working in hospitals or helping poor people. Even though it's a year longer than getting drafted, I like the idea of serving my country and doing some good.

That's all just a bunch of propaganda, man. I know a guy that served as a C. O. and he's still bitter about it. He said community service sounds all noble and good but it's really just punishment for bucking the system. All he did for two years is clean toilets and mop floors.

It's risky to draw conclusions based on one example. Maybe it's not all like that.

Okay, say he's wrong. You still have to make your case to be granted a C. O. Trust me, it's not easy. You need to have people who are willing to put in writing that you have a moral objection to war and killing.

That shouldn't be hard. No sane person is for war and killing.

The statements can't come from just anyone, like your friends or your dentist. They have to be written by respected types that have known you for a long time, people like professors and judges and preachers, people not related to you.

I know some professors but we never talk about the war.

They're no use, then. What church do you go to?

My grandmother is the only one in our family who goes to church.

Then you're toast, man. You practically have to be related to the Pope to make it, and you're not even close. You might as well start packing.

That's my only option?

It beats a body bag, brother.

In the predawn light of late September, Chancer parked his car at the curb and climbed out, following a broad sidewalk toward an intersection of two main thoroughfares busy with traffic in spite of the early hour. As he reached the corner the Federal Courthouse came into view halfway down the block. Young men already crowded the limestone steps.

Restless and alert, the group milled about the steps noting every sound, every movement. Chancer surveyed the crowd, surprised at how different they seemed from one another in race, dress and hairstyle. Several of the men sported military-style crew cuts. He could almost hear Ben quoting Sun Tzu, 'To know your enemy, you must become your enemy'.

He turned as a VW Bug sped around the corner, screeching to a stop. An instant later the passenger door flew open and a man jumped out, hitting the pavement in mid-stride and hopping up the curb. The car raced on, speakers blaring. The man padded toward Chancer in tattered flip-flops, his blonde hair rising above his forehead like a rat's nest. Stopping inches away, he leaned in, his eyes dilated and glassy.

The bombers are coming and they're righteous and beautiful and unforgiving. I saw them on the way here. At

202

least, I think I saw them. We had Blind Faith on the eight-track and their music always has a weird effect on me.

-He pulled a handful of white pills from his pocket and held them in Chancer's face.

'Take this brother, may it serve you well'.

What?

The Beatles said that, so it must be true.

What are they?

Wisdom.

They look like pills.

Wisdom disguised as Vitamin C.

You get wisdom from vitamins?

-He held up his free hand, waving it before Chancer's face.

Did you know air molecules vibrate violet and orange? The atoms wrap around your fingers like baby eels. That's the wisdom that comes from Blue Sunshine. You should try it.

What's Blue Sunshine?

-He peered at Chancer, pity in his eyes.

I mourn for you, man. Everyone knows Blue Sunshine is acid.

Acid?

You know, LSD, lysergic acid diethylamide, the ultimate psychedelic. Wisdom in a pill is what I call it. I can tell you need some for sure.

But won't they find out when you see the doctor?

That's the whole point. They'll think I'm totally unfit, psychotic even. That would be choice. I could do some time in the state hospital, maybe snag some valium.

-A bus rumbled to the curb. Moments later, a man in uniform stepped out, his shaved head shining beneath the dim morning light. He surveyed the crowd before yelling over the engine roar.

If you are here for your physical get on the bus now. Do not have a last smoke. Do not go to the can. Do not get a drink of water. You do not want to make me wait!

-The group filed onto the bus under the glare of the soldier, saying little. Chancer steered clear of the man with the pills, instead taking a seat next to a clean cut draftee wearing a dress shirt and tie. A tattered leather Bible rested in his lap. Chancer motioned toward the book.

Are you a conscientious objector?

-The man squinted at him, his eyes far from friendly, his voice rising with every word.

God tells us we must smite the evil unbelievers as the Israelites smote the Philistines. Like He did King David, God will teach our hands to war and our fingers to fight. The godless Gooks will fall beneath Christ's burning sword of justice.

I thought the Bible preached against war.

-He shook the book in Chancer's face.

This is the only way to understand the right and might of Christ's warriors!

-Chancer jumped up, squeezing back through the crowd and finding an open spot behind the driver where a bird-like man sat hunched over a thick paperback. Hoping to avoid any further conversation, he eased onto the seat. The bus pulled into the street and he leaned back, staring through the windshield and trying to avoid wondering where fate would next take him.

Chapter Twenty-four

Cheering Sanders looked nothing like the sad girl I had met weeks earlier. The dark eyeliner and wardrobe had been replaced by violets and blues, and her fingernails now matched the subdued red of her lips. Having once again arrived for our meeting early, she looked up from her chair as I stepped through the doorway, flashing a beautiful but not quite right smile.

I paused, trying to collect my thoughts, a nagging doubt pulling at the back of my mind. Though her outward appearance and manner had improved along with her grades, my intuition told me it was all show. She knew what to do and say in order to seem better while avoiding the real issue, what had gotten her to me in the first place. I decided the time again had come to push her.

You look like you have not a care in the world, Cheering.

-She held out a folded sheet of paper.

I have a note for you from my English teacher.

-The note spoke of her in glowing terms, only underlining my concern.

So your teacher thinks you're doing well.

-She squinted at me.

You don't agree?

What is there to disagree with?

You have a funny tone in your voice.

Do you agree with your teacher?

My grades are good and I've stayed out of trouble in all my classes. Aren't you proud of me?

Why are you here, then?

What?

If your life is so rosy, why are you here?

-Her face went pale, the false confidence gone.

You don't want to meet with me anymore?

What's the point if everything in your world is so wonderful?

But everything isn't so wonderful.

Isn't it?

You know it isn't. Why are you talking to me like this, Tegan?

I'm a counselor, Cheering. My job is to help people work through difficulties, the unexpected things in life that come along.

But I have difficulties.

Do you? I don't remember you talking about them, not really.

Are you mad at me for some reason?

Maybe you should go back to class where you can do something productive and make good use of your time.

-A pleading note entered her voice.

No, Tegan, please let me stay. I'll talk to you. Tell me what to say.

-I leaned toward her, peering into her dark eyes.

You know it doesn't work that way, Cheering. You've been talking around the problem. It's time you faced it head on.

I don't know how, Tegan.

Don't play dumb, Cheering. You do know how.

Why are you doing this to me, Tegan? Why are you talking so hateful?

I'm trying to help you.

No, you only want to be rid of me, don't you? Please don't go away, Tegan. Please don't be like...

-Fear twisted her features.

Like who, Cheering?

-She faced the floor.

I don't know.

Yes you do. You can say it.

No, I can't.

You can, Cheering.

-She looked up and searched my face, a look of resignation slowly filling her eyes.

It's not fair, Tegan.

No, it isn't.

Life is never fair.

Tell me why, Cheering.

-She stared at her hands as if they held the answer, her eyes glistening.

They left me, Tegan, both of them. If they hadn't left it never would've happened, I would never have been alone with him.

They were supposed to protect you.

Parents are supposed to keep you safe.

Yes, they are.

-She faced me again, her voice a near-whisper.

She just left me there, Tegan. She left me there and he put his hands...

-She stopped, unable to finish.

It should never have happened, Cheering, but it did happen.

I feel so dirty, Tegan.

We'll find a way to...

-A brisk knock rattled the door. I turned to find Esther standing in the entrance, a look of shock on her face, an expression so unlike her it took my breath.

You'd better come next door, both of you.

-Dismayed at Esther's timing, I followed Cheering out the door and across the porch to the office, my mind racing with possible reasons for the interruption. Was Pen ill? Had something happened to Diego?

-The office door stood half-open. Inside, three television sets on moveable carts flickered with the image of a downtown skyline. Smoke drifted from twin skyscrapers. My co-workers stood before the screens, talking among themselves in low tones. Cheering moved close to me.

What's happening, Tegan?

-I glanced around the room for Esther, hoping she might explain, but found no sign of her.

There are two buildings on fire. Other than that I don't know.

-Esther appeared next to me.

The news people say there was a terrorist attack in New York. Two commercial jets, passenger planes, have crashed into those buildings.

-She disappeared again as Cheering took my hand in hers, her eyes fixed to the screen. I studied her profile, wondering what must be going through her mind. A moment later a collective gasp erupted across the room and I turned back to the television, watching in horror as one of the buildings began collapsing in on itself. The other soon followed in shocking detail, surreal and beyond belief. Putting her hand to her mouth, Cheering stifled a scream.

Oh, Tegan, what is happening to those poor people?

-A tiny figure, arms and legs splayed, fell from one of the towers. Others soon followed. I pulled Cheering onto the porch, away from the gruesome images. She stared into my face, tears welling in her dark eyes.

Oh, Tegan, they're just people, people like you and me. What did they do to deserve that?

-I took her by the shoulders.

They didn't do anything, sweetheart.

-She leaned into me, weeping for all innocent victims including herself. The world was splitting at the seams, or so it felt at that moment. I thought again of my father and I blinked back tears of my own, knowing what fate lay in wait for him.

A gurney swept past Chancer as he knelt on the tile floor and scrubbed a blood-stained bed frame with a damp rag, turning the pan of disinfectant next to him a dull red. He had lost count of the stabbing and gunshot victims that had moved through the ward during the past weeks. The list seemed endless. Time had slowed to a blur of mayhem and death, the nightmarish images creeping into his dreams, interfering with his class work. He slept little.

He hurried to finish the bed, knowing another patient was soon to arrive. Down the row a group of interns had gathered around to watch a doctor tend a severely burned patient. Even from a distance, Chancer could smell the putrid odor of burnt flesh.

An instant later a metal tray crashed to the floor as the intern holding it collapsed to the floor, overcome by the grisly procedure. Nurse Berry strode past, paused and backtracked to where Chancer knelt. She wiped sweat from her forehead despite the ward's chill air.

Lord, what will become of us? Our chief of staff just told me we have set a record for shootings this month. Thank you for pulling a second shift, Mister Wylls. How are you holding up?

We're all a little tired, I think. How about you, Nurse Berry?

I keep reminding myself to follow the example of Job. He had his trials yet he kept his faith.

-She glanced at her watch.

I believe your shift ended a half hour ago. You best go home and get yourself some rest. There are only twenty-four hours in the day and you've just worked sixteen of them.

-She moved off down the aisle. As he watched her vanish into the surgical ward, a voice sounded behind him. An instant later, Raz appeared by his side, breathless and agitated, his eyes darting about the room. Chancer stood, puzzled by his presence.

Raz, what are you doing here? Have they sent us reinforcements?

-Raz grabbed him by the shoulders.

No, my god, Chancer, my uncle has been stabbed.

Your uncle Talin, the gambler?

Yes, he is to be here somewhere.

-Chancer followed as Raz hurried down the rows, checking from bed to bed. In the far corner he stopped before the prostrate figure of Talin. A tangle of tubes and wires crisscrossed his chest. Though his eyes were open, it was clear he saw nothing. Raz leaned toward him.

Uncle, do you hear me? It is Raz talking to you. Please say something.

-Chancer moved nearby, speaking to him in hushed tones.

Raz, he's in a sort of coma.

But his eyes are open.

They have him sedated.

-Raz shook his head.

I knew this would happen. I have told him so many times before.

Was it Ling?

-Raz pulled Chancer back toward the doorway.

I fear so. If only uncle had stopped the betting when we told him he must. But there is never enough winning to satisfy him. And now look what he must endure.

What about your parents' money?

I do not know. I fear Ling is not yet finished with him and perhaps us as well.

You think he'll come after you and me?

Ling knows you, and no doubt me also.

At this point I don't care. I've worked a double shift and I'm exhausted. I'm going home.

-Raz turned back to the bed, his face grim.

You will help me with him, will you not, Chancer?

-Chancer nodded as he turned toward the doorway, wishing he might soon find sleep.

A brisk wind moved through the damp night, coursing down the alleyway and whipping the black-limbed oaks behind Chancer's apartment. He willed his tired legs up the stairs, hoping Turley was asleep or off at some bar. He had been a polite and friendly houseguest but Chancer was in no mood to talk.

As he pushed through the door, a rhythmic wheeze greeted him, stopping him at the threshold. He flipped on the light. Turley's form lay sprawled across the floor, a small cut etched below his left eye. Chancer rushed to his side and knelt, relieved to find a pulse. He grabbed for the phone just as Turley stirred, opening his eyes.

Ben, is that you?

-Chancer leaned toward him.

It's me, Turley. It's Chancer. What happened?

I knew the bastard would return, Ben. I could feel him.

You're going to be alright. Just take it easy and I'll get some help.

No, don't leave me! Is that you, Wylls?

It's me. You need a doctor, Turley.

Screw the doctors. Listen to me, Wylls.

I'm listening.

Don't forget the little things.

What do you mean?

Don't forget to notice what's around you, the sunrise, the way clouds rise up and fall, the feel of a woman's hand on your face. Promise me you won't forget, Chancer.

I promise, Turley.

-He closed his eyes. Chancer phoned for an ambulance. He knelt as Turley stirred again, his breath shallow and rasping.

'The way of war is a way of deception', Ben.

-Chancer leaned close to his face.

That was Sun Tzu.

-Turley peered at him through half-closed eyes.

Sun Tzu was right, Ben. The damn yellow rain fooled us. The bastard came back for me.

-He stared into Chancer's face, seeing nothing. An instant later his eyes rolled back.

Chancer raced along the wet streets. Ahead of him the flashing lights of the ambulance vanished and reappeared between homes and buildings like Morse code. The damp, exhaust-filled night air streamed through his car windows, leaving him lightheaded and nauseous. For a moment he thought he might pass out. Then Turley's pale face appeared before him covered by a yellow veil, urging him on.

Minutes later he burst into the emergency room. Ben appeared in the opposite doorway, looking about until spotting him. Chancer watched him cross the room, studying his face for sign of Turley's fate. Busy with their own concerns, the crowd moved around them, surreal, dancelike. Ben stopped in front of him, clasping his shoulder.

You called the ambulance?

I found him at my place, on the floor.

Good man, Wylls.

-Chancer locked eyes with him.

He's gone, isn't he?

-Ben nodded.

I'm sorry, Chancer. He never regained consciousness.

-Chancer sat, the reality of Turley's death settling around him.

I can't believe it, Ben.

These things can be sudden.

But what happened to him? He seemed so much better.

The chemo can sometimes wreak havoc with your blood, even long afterwards. He developed a pulmonary embolism that went to his brain. The stroke is what killed him. Was he conscious when you found him?

He thought I was you. He quoted Sun Tzu, something about deception and the yellow rain.

He never stopped believing it was the Agent Orange that made him sick. In a way, he never left 'Nam and it never left him.

Whatever he was trying to say, he wanted you to know.

Turley was an angry man, and with good reason if you ask me, and he had a lot to say but few chances to say it. We were his only friends, Chancer.

-He peered at Ben.

He told me I should go to Canada.

Why would he say that?

I'm getting drafted, Ben. My number is thirteen so there's no doubt.

The lottery was weeks ago. Why didn't you say something?

I didn't know how to tell you. I'm not going to Vietnam, Ben.

-Ben took him by the shoulders.

Listen to me, Chancer. I'm proud to have served my country. I was honored to fight alongside Turley and the other guys in my unit. They did the best they could in a bad situation. We all did. Those soldiers, all soldiers, deserve the country's respect and appreciation.

But after I came home I realized we should've never been there in the first place. It's all wrong. Those people need to fight their own war and sort it out for themselves. I don't blame you for resisting that.

I still don't know what I'll do.

You're a good man, Chancer. You'll find your way.

-Chancer nodded toward the doorway.

Can I see him, Ben?

Are you sure you want to?

-Chancer nodded and moments later they stood before a sheet-draped gurney. Ben pulled back the cover. Chancer leaned toward Turley's pale face, his voice a near-whisper.

So long, Turley. Be at peace now.

-Ben made a fist and held it to Turley's chest.

'Know Heaven,
Know Earth,
And your victory
Is complete.'

Your victory is complete, Turley. They can't touch you now.

Chapter Twenty-five

Chancer struggled to keep his eyes open on the drive back to his apartment. The dim light of morning flickered through the overhanging trees, dappling the street in gold. In his exhausted state, he imagined Byes as he'd first seen her, red hair flowing to one side, her intense gaze locked on him. Flecks of sunlight warmed her pale cheeks.

Chancer blinked away the memory, parking in the alley behind his apartment and climbing out. As he rounded the corner, she stood waiting at the foot of the stairs, her arms folded across her chest, a bag at her feet. She squinted at him.

Her face had grown so round he scarcely recognized her yet he still found her beautiful. In her lapis-hued eyes he saw not warmth but a cool disdain. Turley's last words again filled his ears as he imagined his deceit finally at an end. He stopped feet away, waiting for her to speak.

Been out all night partying again, Chancer? Or maybe you've been sucking up to the college higher-ups. I hear there's lots of perks in that line of work.

-He could do nothing but try to continue the deception.

Byes, what's wrong?

Don't play dumb with me, Chancer.

What do you mean?

I saw Henry today.

He's back in town?

He's not giving up on the protest work, and I'm going to do more than just help him.

You're doing what? But, Byes...

-She interrupted.

He knows you turned him in, Chancer. A skinny policeman with big ears told him.

But I was...

The cop knew all the details, everything you said.
There's no point in denying it.

-In his shame, Chancer seemed to shrink into himself.
He could feel it. Still, he would not relent.

They were about to charge me with vandalism, Byes.
They would've thrown me in jail. What was I supposed to
do?

-She pointed a finger in his face.

What Henry did was a non-violent protest, not
vandalism.

The police called it that, not me.

Do you even know what they painted, the words?

-He lied.

I don't remember.

Your so-called vandalism said 'war criminals'. Does
that sound like a crime, Chancer?

I don't know.

Well, I do. The real crime is the immoral war this
country is waging halfway around the world. That and the
way you squealed on Henry. It's shameful, Chancer.

Was I supposed to go to jail for what he did?

Don't make excuses. You were jealous of him and
when you saw your chance to get rid of him, you went for
it.

-He started to speak but the truth of her words caught
in his throat. She lifted the bag.

I got my things out of your apartment. I'm moving out
of the dorm so don't try to find me.

Where are you going to live?

You don't need to know, Chancer. I don't want to
ever see you again.

-He stood watching as she vanished down the alley.
The world seemed to close in on him, bleak and
impersonal. Images of Turley, Raz's uncle, the shootings,
the murders, and now Byes leaving crowded his thoughts.
He dragged himself up the stairs, no longer expecting
sleep.

216

The next morning Chancer followed a winding street through rows of abandoned warehouses and empty storefronts, trying to recall the route without checking his map. The damp warmth of the last week had given way to a hint of autumn, though the sun still promised afternoon heat. He breathed in the cool air, trying to forget the previous day. After a fitful night, he needed someone to talk to, someone who knew nothing of his troubles, someone who would not judge him.

Passing a limestone gate overgrown with honeysuckle, he entered a neighborhood crowded with frame homes of varying shapes and sizes. Shotgun houses, some the width a single room, lined the curving street like outstretched fingers. Thick-trunked pecan trees, the remains of a long abandoned grove, towered overhead. He peered through the windshield at the small homes.

Moments later, he parked in front of a well-kept bungalow slightly larger than the surrounding homes and painted forest green. Crimson trim outlined the door and windows. A short set of stairs flanked by square columns led to a shallow porch cast deep in shadow. White lace curtains peeked from the porch windows.

A man kneeling over a flowerbed at the house next door a stood and watched as Chancer climbed out of the car. A gray beard framed his plum-colored face. He squinted at Chancer, studying him a moment before ambling over.

What'd you want 'round here, boy?
-His gruff tone took Chancer by surprise.
I, uh... I don't want anything.
Someone like you don't have business being here. You looking to cause some trouble?
No, I don't want any trouble.
You another one of them after the estate?
What estate? I'm here to see Beulah King.

What do you want with Miss King?

She gave me a book.

-Chancer held up *A Tale of Two Cities*.

Why are you bringing that book back? You don't like it?

She asked me to come talk with her about it.

Who wrote the book?

It's by Charles Dickens.

-A hint of recognition shone in his eyes.

Yes, I recall her saying there is no one like Mister Charles Dickens. He cared about the poor people of his time.

That sounds like her.

-The old man peered at Chancer.

You been here before, haven't you?

-Chancer glanced at the house.

I've come by a couple of times to talk about the book. We talk about other things too.

-A grimace passed across the man's face.

You don't know.

What don't I know? Has something happened?

-He nodded his round head.

Miss King died last Friday, son.

-Chancer stared at him, unbelieving.

But I just... how could... I was hoping she...

-His voice dropped to a whisper, words failing him. The ground seemed to tilt beneath him. The old man hobbled over and grabbed his elbow, leading him to the porch and easing him onto the steps.

You're not looking so good, son. You best sit a minute.

It's just that I was counting on seeing her. I wanted to ask...

-He stopped, again at a loss for words. The old man nodded and sat next to him.

You're troubled over something, aren't you, son? You needed Miss King's counsel, didn't you?

-Chancer faced him, puzzled by his guess.

How did you know?

Miss King had a special way with young people. She was willing to hear them out. Not many folks are willing to just listen these days. They're too busy caught up in their own concerns to care about someone else's troubles. But Miss King, she was different.

-Chancer stared at the ground, a deep sadness filling his throat.

I can't believe she's gone.

It's a hard thing to have a friend pass, son. But Miss King went in her sleep and she's at peace now. She lived a long, good life and had young people like you to take interest in her, to keep her mind sharp.

-He pointed toward the back of the house.

Truth is there's one of those young people here now. She's going through some of Miss King's belongings. You go on and talk to her. She was a special friend of Miss King. Just follow the driveway to the garage.

-The old man stood and ambled back toward his house without another word. Chancer grabbed the porch rail and pulled himself up, relieved to find the ground had stopped moving. Moments later he stepped into the garage. A figure in the far corner was bent over an open box, crying silently. He stopped, unsure what to do. She turned to face him.

-Taken aback by her striking appearance, he stared at her. A tangle of black hair outlined her strawberry-hued face. She wiped the tears from her cheek with the back of her hand, peering at him through damp eyelashes. Even from a distance her gaze seemed direct and without guile. Setting down a sheaf of papers, she moved through the maze of boxes, stopping in front of him.

You're Chancer, aren't you?

How did you... ?

You're just as Beulah described, only more handsome.

-He felt himself blush.

I, uh…

I'm Fiona Bain.

I'm sorry… I didn't mean to intrude.

You just caught me at an awkward moment. I was going through her things to see what to keep and what can go to charity when I came across a photo of the two of us.

You knew her well?

Beulah was my tutor. She got me through college algebra. I don't know what I would've done without her.

-Chancer took a step toward her, surprised by the news.

I never knew she had a talent for math.

She was a wonderful teacher but we became friends was because we shared a love of books. Beulah was a sweet, giving woman. I'll miss her.

-He tried to hide the sadness again filling his throat.

Yes.

-Sensing his discomfort, she motioned to a nearby bench.

Beulah said you're majoring in physics.

-He sat next to her.

That's right.

I'm majoring in history with a minor in journalism.

I guess you have to like reading to study history.

-She glanced at her watch.

Speaking of school, I'm going to be late for class if I don't get moving.

-Wishing she would stay, he held up the *A Tale of Two Cities*.

I'm here because of this.

-Her smile held a sort of warmth he had not seen in some time.

I know, Chancer. She told me all about your visits. In a way, I feel like I already know you.

-He peered into her luminous gray eyes, unsure of her meaning.

What did she say?

Don't look so worried. I liked what I heard. You may be surprised at what we have in common.

I don't know much about books outside of math and science texts.

Well, I'm no expert but I know what I like, and I learned a lot from Beulah.

-All at once, he realized he wanted to see her again.

Fiona would you... I mean... I was wondering if you'd like to go out sometime. We could talk about books. Maybe you can recommend a novel or two, or even a history.

-She locked eyes with him, a trace of sadness in her gaze.

Oh, Chancer, it's nice of you to ask. Only, you see, I can't. What I'm trying to say is that I'm involved with someone.

-Chancer turned his eyes from her with difficulty.

Oh, I see.

Chancer, I'm flattered that you would...

-He waved off the comment, sensing pity behind her words.

No, I understand.

-She stood and lifted her purse from a nearby stool, motioning into the room.

Look around to see if there's anything of Beulah's you'd like. They're going to donate the lot tomorrow.

-He turned to the pile of boxes.

No one else wants them?

Beulah had no other family. It makes me sad to think how lonely she must've been.

-He stared at her, realizing with regret how little of Beulah's life he had understood.

I never thought of her as lonely.

-She started out the door, calling over her shoulder.

She hid it well. Sorry, I have to leave.

-He watched her walk down the driveway, the sadness again pulling at him. Turning back to the room, he wandered among the boxes, wondering if he would die alone. In the far corner a thick tome, the cover black with age and unreadable, poked from a box of keepsakes.

-He lifted out the book, opening it. Across the title page a note read 'To my good friend, Chancer Wylls' in Beulah's scrawled hand. She had left him Dickens' *Great Expectations*. On a torn scrap of paper wedged inside she had written 'first edition - worth something'. Touched by her gift, he started for the door, cradling the heavy book in his palm and hoping his luck was about to change.

Chapter Twenty-six

After the terrorist attacks Cheering seemed a different girl, one willing to face whatever the truth might hold. Somehow, the horrible death and mayhem of that day had freed her from her past, proving that some small good can come from even the worst of nightmares. I had little doubt her change would never have occurred if we had not been together on that day, at that very moment. All at once she had realized she was not alone in her suffering.

My mind kept returning to the odd and fortunate coincidences that crowded my past, putting them together into something more than coincidence, something more like fate. I was alive because Eloy followed me into a place he would not go. Celia was safe because I happened along at just the right moment. Chancer's life had changed because of a meeting with his professor, setting the stage for my mother to leave him.

On the other hand, I had learned that coincidences may be more common than they appear. I had been reading Chancer's old math texts and came across something called the birthday paradox. The gist of the paradox is that in a group of only twenty-three people there is a fifty percent chance two of them have the same birthday. When the number is seventy-five or more, smaller than most of my college classes, the chances rise to ninety-nine percent. If I shared a birthday with someone in most of my classes, a possibility I would never have believed, were all the so-called coincidences in my life fate or luck or just simple mathematics?

Unsure what to believe, I turned at the sound of three crisp knocks on the front door. I peered through the lace window curtains. A black sedan sat parked along the curb, a dark-suited figure standing next to it. The clipped knocks sounded again just as I reached the foyer. I swung open the door and the agent I'd met at Celia's trailer stood before me, the same unreadable expression behind his sunglasses.

Good afternoon, 'mam. I'm Agent Price, FBI.

-Suddenly, I found myself worried that Omar had escaped and gone after her.

Has something happened to Celia Rivera or her son?

No, 'mam, the family is safe.

Then why are you here?

We've come to present you with a commendation.

You're giving me a commendation? I didn't do anything but almost get killed. Eloy Fuego is the one who should be commended.

Mister Fuego has disappeared. If you know his whereabouts, we would like to speak with him.

When did he go missing?

He disappeared immediately after the incident according to Miss Rivera.

Is he in some sort of trouble?

No, 'mam, he is not in any trouble. We're talking to all the people who had contact with the suspect. Do you happen to know Mister Fuego's location?

The last time I saw him was that day.

-He handed me a sheet of blank letterhead. *Government of the United States of America* filled the top in ornate script. Below it read 'Official Commendation'.

The federal government appreciates your bravery in service to your country.

My bravery? I don't understand. How did I serve my country? What does this have to do with Omar's arrest?

That's classified information, 'mam.

Is that why you gave me a blank piece of paper, agent?

-He sounded like he was reading off a card.

We apologize, 'mam, but all information related to this case is highly confidential. Please consider the certificate in the spirit in which it is given.

But I don't even know what I'm being commended for. Isn't there anything you can tell me?

-He adjusted his collar, clearly uncomfortable with the questions.

We were directed to present you with the certificate, 'mam. That's all.

Omar wasn't smuggling drugs across the border, was he?

Like I said, 'mam, the information is…

-I interrupted, impatient with his manner.

Does the government always give commendations to citizens who turn in drug smugglers?

We're not at liberty to…

Of course it doesn't. And what does a commendation have to do with the blueprints and photos I stole, I mean borrowed, from Celia's place?

Please, 'mam, I'm going to have to…

-An explanation came to me all at once.

Omar isn't just some common criminal, is he? They were planning something, something big.

-When he blushed, I knew I was right.

Whatever they planned had to do with the state capitol and flying an airpl…

-I felt the blood rush from my head. When the room began to spin around me, I thought I might faint but he grabbed my arm, leading me to a chair. Then he sat across from me. After a moment, he took off his sunglasses. I could see he wanted to tell me what he could. I took a breath, trying to clear my head.

This has something to do with the terrorist attacks, doesn't it?

-He leaned toward me, his face grim.

I may lose my job for saying this but I think you have a right to know something. All I can tell you is that day would have been much worse if not for what you did, Miss Wylls. Many more people would have died. You deserve a real commendation and recognition but that's not going to happen now and maybe never. There's still too much out there, too much we don't know.

I can't tell you how important it is that you say nothing more about the incident than what you experienced in person, and even that is risky. Anything more could compromise the mission and spell trouble for you, big trouble. Am I making myself clear?

-Seeing how difficult it was for him, I nodded and sat back trying to understand what I'd just heard. He stood and turned toward the door, disappearing without another word.

After the shock had passed, I had an overwhelming urge to see Claude. He was the one person in the world who knew what I'd done, the one person I could talk to about it. That kinship erased the hard feelings I had harbored over our broken date, so I started for the door hoping to catch him at home.

A moment later I stepped onto his front porch. The door stood slightly ajar but I thought nothing of it, the day being unusually warm, so I pushed through as I had many times before. I stopped in the foyer, listening. At first, the house appeared to be empty.

More than a little disappointed, I stepped into the living room to be sure. A noise sounded toward the back of the house so I checked myself in the mirror. My unruly curls stuck out in every direction. Sighing in dismay, I smoothed my hair as best I could and turned back to the living room. Just as I was about to call out, Kat Gunter, Claude's internship partner, walked into the room wearing nothing. I gasped, staring at her in disbelief. She squinted back at me, disdain in her eyes, before calling over her shoulder.

Claude, you have a visitor.

-I pivoted, heading for the door. Claude's voice caught me just as I reached the foyer.

Tegan, wait!

-I turned back to face him.

What for, Claude? I'm not blind.

-He nodded toward the back of the house and Kat vanished down the hallway. Then he again faced me.

It's not how it looks, Tegan.

Is that right? How is it then, Claude?

Kat and I are just friends.

-I glared at him, barely able to contain my anger.

You must mean friends with benefits.

It's only sex, Tegan. It's just something people do when they feel like it.

Oh, you mean like playing tennis?

Kat's not from here. They look at sex differently in Europe. They're more open about it.

We're not in Europe, Claude.

Nothing has changed, Tegan. We can continue just as we were.

You'd like that, wouldn't you? Why not bed any skinny foreigner that comes along and still have me hanging around looking foolish? What possible harm could come from that?

-Kat reappeared, hands on her hips.

You American women here are so uptight. You should be open to new experiences.

That's right, Tegan. What's wrong with an open relationship?

-I blinked away my tears.

How could you, Claude? How could you be so deceitful?

It's not like we've been spending time together lately, Tegan. We've hardly seen each other. Whose fault is that?

-I felt the blood rush to my face as the truth of his words sunk in. Anger and disappointment swept over me and I rushed out the door, determined to hide my tears from them both. Beyond the porch, the low autumn sun slanted through the trees, blinding me.

The terrorist attacks had changed the world forever and my life with it. Old landmarks I once counted on had vanished. I stumbled toward home feeling humiliated. At

227

that moment I wished more than anything to feel in control of my life again. Instead, I only felt sorry for myself.

I recalled that wish the next day as I stepped onto the sidewalk leading to Trewin's home. A compact, stone one-story with a sloping roof, the house reminded me of a Swiss chalet. His ancient but freshly washed Saab sat in the driveway. I glanced down the wooded street. October had arrived a week earlier yet the air was warm and damp, smelling of earth and wood smoke. Yellow leaves drifted past the porch, littering the lawn.

I had tried to check on Trewin twice before but he had politely refused to see me, so I'd waited a couple of weeks before trying again, and then again. Not long after, according to Pen and Beetie, he was back to his old self, as frank and ornery as ever. He had asked me to join him for a drink and to talk over something. Although I tried, I'd gotten little more about it out of him.

He opened the door as I stepped onto the porch, ushering me inside the living room with a broad wave of his arm. Our hug lingered and the thought occurred to me that he feared letting go. Then he disappeared into the kitchen without a word. Surveying the room, I tried to remember the last time I had been in his house though it had been years, I was certain of that. Little had changed.

Books crowded shelves lining the far wall, spilling out onto the rug in places. Scattered about the room, black and white photographs held broad mesas, saw-tooth horizons and rivers cutting through the rock-strewn earth like jagged wounds. Taken during his work as an oil company land man, the stark images had a rugged appeal that reminded me of Trewin himself.

Moments later he reappeared with two glasses of wine. I tried to hide my surprise as I accepted a glass. I had never seen him drink anything other than beer or Scotch. He settled into the chair opposite me and held his glass up to the light, studying the ruby-tinted liquid. Then he turned his intense gaze to me.

Go on and ask it then, Tegan. I know the question that's burning on those beautiful lips.

-I hesitated, unsure what he had in mind.

You mean the reason you asked me here?

Lord no, girl. Didn't you notice that we're drinking red wine? When was the last time you saw me drink wine?

I never have, unless maybe in church on Christmas Eve when I was too young to remember much.

Too young to remember is right. I don't partake in that particular ritual.

So, it would have to be never then.

There's the point exactly, isn't it, niece? I've decided to broaden my horizons, to taste more of what the world has to offer.

-He drank half his glass in one swallow. I frowned at him.

Wine is not beer, Trewin. To really taste it you need to let it stay in your mouth for awhile.

Now you're talking, niece. Whether wine or life, we must savor every drop.

-I was running out of patience.

Does that have anything to do with me coming here?

-He nearly choked on his wine.

Good gods, you do have a one-track mind, Tegan Wylls. You must learn to enjoy the moment and whatever comes with it.

Okay, I'll try. But in the meantime will you tell me why you asked me here?

-His eyes lost their usual mirth.

The truth is I went through a depression of sorts. The pall stayed on me long enough your grandparents got concerned.

I know. They were so worried they came to me about you.

Well, perhaps they had reason enough. I admit I was a sad sight, a mess in fact.

Did something happen? Pen mentioned a girlfriend of yours leaving.

I enjoyed her voluptuous company but, in truth, her leaving had little to do with it. I was feeling sorry for myself, you see.

-I thought with shame of my own self-pity.

But why, Trewin?

A couple of months back I was looking a bit peaked so I went to the doctor. The next thing I knew they were telling me I had some terrible illness, a death sentence more or less.

-I stifled a gasp at the unexpected news.

Oh, Trewin, I'm so sorry.

Hold on girl, I'm not under the ground just yet. Now while I was going through one test after the other and the doctors were probing this and sticking that, I thought to myself that though I'm not young, I still have a lot of living left to do, the problem being I have no time left to do it. I began thinking this, that and the other, imagining all the beautiful women - old to you, perhaps, but still beautiful to me - that I'd never meet and maybe have a fling with. And then I thought of all the good ale I'd never get to drink, and all the sights I'd never get to see. The world became a dark place indeed.

First I was angry and then I could hardly raise myself from bed, not because I felt ill but because I saw no point to it anymore. That's when the depression took hold of me like a black whirlpool, sucking me down and down. I had plenty of time to take a hard look at life and what I always thought I wanted out of it.

And it was not a pretty picture, I'll tell you. I even thought I might return to the kneeling and the praying and the confessing of you know where. Fortunately, I laid myself down and that harebrained idea passed out of my head.

-He stopped, lost in thought. I stared at his profile, feeling the tears filling my eyes. I had always imagined Pen would be the first to die. Trewin glanced at me and then jumped from his chair, taking my hand.

Good god, child, there's no reason to start crying now.

-I choked back the tears long enough to speak.

How can you be so cheerful knowing you're going to…

-My voice trailed to a whisper. To my surprise, he started laughing.

No, no, you've got it all wrong, Tegan. The fool doctors made a mistake, something to do with a defective lab or some such nonsense. They ran the tests over and said I'll last another twenty years or more, long as I stay well-pickled.

-With that I went from crying to sobbing. The tears ran down my cheeks in thin, mascara-streaked streams. All that had happened, all the disappointment, all the frustration, all the anger at the unfairness of the world came flooding back. Trewin pulled a handkerchief from his pocket, handing it to me.

Of course, that last bit about the pickling I added myself. Now you don't have reason worry, Tegan. Do you understand what I'm telling you?

-I managed a nod as I wiped my face and he thrust a wine glass at me. By the time I had downed most of it, I felt my composure returning. He patted my hand and leaned in close.

After all that, the honest truth is I asked you here because I'm making a visit to the gravesite of my late-wife and I wanted your company. You see, in all my thinking about what matters to a dying man, I realized my debt to Genevieve still remains.

She was my first true love and to this day I still miss her, truly. She taught me that love can be generous and unselfish. I'm ashamed to say I have been remiss in paying

231

her my usual visits, but I intend to remedy that from here on.

-I took a breath, grateful someone wanted my company.

I'd love to go with you, Trewin.

-He let go of my hand and pushed himself up.

I'm glad to hear it. And I have another reason for asking you here, Tegan. Thirty years ago, your father and I made a pilgrimage to Genevieve's birth place. The trip was a disaster of grand proportions, but unforgettable.

When I thought my time was up, I realized I could've passed from this world without ever telling you of our great misadventure. But the story will have to wait. The light fades early this time of year so we best be on our way.

-As we stepped out the door, an image of Chancer trekking along the coast filled my mind, and I again puzzled over him and my mother and how easily love is lost.

Chapter Twenty-seven

Chancer hunched over a sheet of Franklin's equations, punching numbers into his calculator and working out the likely positions of stars based on Bayesian probability. The project had proved more difficult than he had imagined and they were beginning to run short of time. After all that had happened between him and Byes, the thought of another failure terrified him.

Franklin had mentioned the possibility of a new grant and hinted that it might include funds to pay for his work, but Chancer knew he would be unlikely to keep him on if they lost the project. He tried to avoid thinking about it. With the draft hanging over him, he could count on nothing.

He had nearly finished the calculations when a car door slammed downstairs. Closing his eyes, he managed to keep the equation fixed in his mind only for an instant before footsteps sounded on the stairs. Trewin's cap passed beneath the window. Moments later the door rattled with his usual pounding knock. Chancer sighed and dropped his pencil on the table.

It's open Uncle Trewin.

-The door swung wide and Trewin stepped in, squinting at him as he smoothed back his dark hair.

A beautiful autumn day, the sun shining, a chill in the air, and I find you here hunched over a book, bags big as footballs under your eyes.

Finals are only eight days away and I have a project to finish.

-Trewin sighed, tossing his hat onto the table.

Don't you know it's a Saturday morning, man? And a fine day it is too, a bit windy but still fine. The winter solstice will be here soon. You can see it in the tilt of sunlight, feel it in the chill air.

-Chancer rolled his eyes.

I've been too busy to notice.

-Trewin leaned in close, sniffing through his bent nose.

You can *smell* it.

-Chancer moved away, frowning.

What are you doing here, Trewin?

I've come to take you on a pilgrimage to my late wife's family home. I believe you're old enough to appreciate a visit to your Aunt Genevieve's hometown. At least I hope you are. Besides, your place is on the way and I could use a cheerful companion for the somber occasion that it is. You can be cheerful if you try, now can't you?

-Chancer jutted out his chin, feeling defensive.

I'm cheerful.

-Trewin grabbed him by the cheeks.

Is that what you call this face? How must you look when dour, then? It startles the imagination to think of it.

-Chancer pushed away his hands.

Be nice if you want me to go.

-Trewin stepped back.

Right you are nephew.

-Chancer glanced at his calculations, part of him thinking he should stay and continue working, the other part longing to be free from the humiliation of Byes' leaving, the death and suffering of hospital work, the loss of Turley and Beulah, the uncertainty of his pending draft. The last weeks had left him depressed and listless. He wanted escape and here was his chance. He looked up at his uncle.

Alright, Trewin, I'll go.

-Trewin grabbed his hat and turned for the door.

And you'll be the better for it, too, my boy. Get whatever you need and we'll be off.

An hour later Trewin turned his car onto Rosenberg Avenue, trading the live oaks of Broadway for a row of thick palms that stretched to the seawall. Chancer leaned toward the windshield, watching for the glint of sunlight on seawater but the climbing road blocked all but a cloud-scrubbed sky. The Doors' *Morrison Hotel* blared from a passing car, reminding him of his uncertain fate. Banishing the thought, he focused on the road ahead.

Moments later they crested the rise and the ocean spread before them in a broad arc. Bisected by a wide pier and hotel perched above the water on cement pilings, the horizon stood featureless and razor-straight. White foam drifted on the olive-green sea. Chancer squinted down the seawall at a series of granite fingers jutting into the gulf at even intervals. Fishermen and sightseers moved along the furthest jetty like ants on a twig.

Trewin followed the seawall for a short way before turning onto a side street and then turning again, pulling to a stop halfway down the block. He leaned toward the passenger window and nodded at a columned two-story house surrounded by massive live oaks, their black branches stretching nearly to the ground. Framed by oleanders and hibiscus, a deep porch stretched the length of the home. A balcony of equal size sat perched above it. Trewin pointed through the window.

That's the house where Genevieve grew up. Her mother, Christine Thibodaux, still lives there. Time to go pay our respects.

-Moments later, they stood before a heavy walnut door, listening to the thump of approaching footsteps. Then a voice called from inside.

Trewin Wylls, what are you doing on my porch?

-The door opened to a short, birdlike woman wearing a flowered apron. She seemed to be looking past them to the street.

Otis and I don't usually expect to see you until sometime around Christmas or thereabouts.

-Chancer turned, wondering what she saw behind them. Trewin took her hand.

235

You know I can't stay away for long, Christine. And this time I've brought along my nephew, Chancer.

-She smiled and stepped aside.

Please come in, Chancer. You men take a seat anywhere you like while I get you something cold to drink.

-She vanished into the house. Chancer followed Trewin to a pair of overstuffed chairs. With no lights on and the curtains drawn, the high-ceilinged room stood nearly dark. Trewin rose as she appeared out of the darkness with two bottles of beer, taking them from her and handing one to Chancer. She sat across from them and Trewin leaned toward her.

How did you know it was me, Christine?

Oh, Trewin, don't you know your footsteps are as recognizable as an old song?

-Chancer chuckled.

My mother says she can recognize him by his walk long before she can see his face.

-Trewin snorted.

Genevieve used to give me hell about that.

She always said that lopsided gait of yours is hard to miss.

-Trewin shook his head.

But how do *you* do it, Christine?

I just listen.

-Chancer peered at her beneath the dim light, sensing he was missing something.

Your hearing must be better than mine, Mrs. Thibodaux.

I doubt that, Chancer, as old as I am. But when you have no sight you find other ways of seeing the world.

-He peered into her face.

Mrs. Thibodaux, you're blind?

I was born blind, Chancer.

I didn't realize.

-She snapped her fingers and a black mongrel ambled into the room, lying down next to her. She reached down and ran her fingers along his neck.

This is Otis. He helps me get around town when I need to.

I'm sorry, I...

Don't make the mistake of having pity on me, Chancer. Being born without sight was my fate. But instead of letting it rule my life, I've done most of what I wanted to. I believe I've had a wonderful life.

-Listening to her, Chancer felt a tinge of regret for his shameful self-pity. Trewin swept his hand through the air.

Christine has traveled more than most people I know. These shelves are covered with mementos from all over the world. That is if we could see them.

-Christine jumped from her chair, hurrying to the wall and switching on the lights.

Lord, where are my manners? Why didn't you men say something instead of sitting here in the dark?

-Trewin leaned back, drinking half his beer in one swallow. He motioned Chancer to do the same.

I like the mood lighting concept, Christine. By the way, we can't stay for long. Chancer has to get back to his work.

-She turned to face him, her eyes a milky blue.

I seem to remember Trewin saying you are in college.

That's right, Mrs. Thibodaux. I'm studying astronomy.

Tell me about the stars, Chancer. Through a telescope they're a beautiful sight to see, aren't they?

The Orion nebula is like a cloud of violet and blue. It has a mass two thousand times the greater than the Sun and is a place stars are born.

-She grew pensive, tapping her finger on the arm of the chair.

The birth of a star; what a beautiful thought. When I was a young girl growing up in Louisiana, my father made his living as a shrimper. Some summer nights he would take me out onto the bay where it seemed we were surrounded by the stars to hear him tell it. You may think it odd since in a way it's always night to me, but hearing him talk of the clear night sky over our heads and the reflection of it across the calm water made it as real as if I could see it for myself.

Or so I believed, anyway. But instead of just describing the constellations themselves, he told me of all the myths and tales behind them, making them more than just patterns of stars. They became exciting stories that captured my imagination in their own right.

When Genevieve was old enough to understand the constellations, I would take her out on the jetties away from the street lights and I'd describe the stars and tell her the same stories my father told me. There is something magical about the sea at night, Chancer, with the breakers exploding so close and the sea mist drifting past your face all full of salt and life. I believe those memories helped during her dark times.

-Trewin nodded.

She often talked of those nights. After we married, she gave me the same tour of the heavens along our favorite stretch of beach.

-Christine raised her hand, pointing a finger at Chancer.

You were telling me of Orion. You've seen this nebula yourself?

The physics department has a telescope students can use. I've been up there all night more than once. It's one reason I chose the university.

Well, I hope that's right where you stay. I do so hate to see these young men going off to war and coming back in coffins. Back in your father's day, the world was so much simpler. Men fought to keep the Nazis from taking over Europe and destroying England. The reasons for this war are far from clear. That is, except to the politicians, and we know how honest they are.

-Trewin stood, draining his beer.

Now, Christine, I'm sure Chancer will do his duty when the time comes. We'd better be on our way.

-She slapped the arm of her chair.

Oh, I should know better that to bring up politics with Trewin in the room. Do you really have to leave so soon?

-He patted her hand.

You know I must complete my pilgrimage, Christine.

Yes, I suppose you must.

We still have a ways to go yet. I'll be back for a longer visit in a couple of weeks, and then we can argue all we like.

Returning to the seawall, they followed the broad boulevard west before angling in front of a narrow blue building that stood facing the ocean. A giant crab sat atop the roof, its orange-tinted claws raised into the air. They found a booth along a row of windows looking out onto the water. Seagulls floated past, their muffled calls like mocking laughter.

Trewin ordered beer for them both and two platters of fried shrimp. As he chatted with the waitress, Chancer stared out the window at the rolling sea. The wind had died and the glassy surface held a reverse image of the sky and clouds, similar to but different from reality, reminding him of the lie he had lived before Byes discovered his deceit. His throat tightened, some part of him still hoping they might one day reconcile. Trewin tapped the tabletop.

This is the table where Genevieve and I always sat. We would wait for it to open up if there was a crowd. The manager always found a way to fit us in.

-Chancer thought again of Byes.

How long were you and Genevieve married?

Well, I came to marriage late, you know. To be honest, I never saw myself as the type to settle down. But we were together eighteen years. Genevieve was different from the other women I'd known, as willful and hot-tempered as a wild pony. We had our fair share of arguments.

But you were able to stay together?

Oh, those times didn't tear us apart, son, they made us stronger. We even argued on her last day.

What about?

-His eyes clouded with the memory.

She was determined that I would go on living a full, lusty life after she was gone. Of course, I didn't want to think of such a thing right then much less agree to it. She was that selfless, see. That's what real love is, Chancer. After I got through all my grieving, I realized the truth of her request. I had to do the living she'd never be able to.

From what Gammie says, you've done a good job at it.

Your grandmother will only be happy if I marry at fat old spinster or enter the priesthood. No, I'll not please her at the rate I'm going but I have no thought of settling down just now. There's a whole world to experience. Take Genevieve's words to heart, Chancer. Don't mess about feeling sorry for yourself when there's so much of life to live.

-The waitress set down a bowl of water and two damp washcloths before taking away their empty plates. Trewin watched after her as she walked away.

There's a good looking part of the wide world for you, son. She must be new here. I've not seen her before.

-Chancer pointed to the bowl and towels.

What are these for?

They're meant for cleaning up after your meal.

-They dunked their fingers into the soapy mixture, drying them with the towels. Then Trewin lifted the bowl, pouring the water into his empty glass and giving Chancer a quick wink. Just before the waitress reached the table, he lifted the bowl to his lips. She stared at him, her mouth open, her eyes wide. Trewin set down the bowl, sighing with satisfaction.

That was excellent. Can I have some more, please?

-She rushed off without a word. Chancer squinted at him.

You've done that before.

Of course I have, son. You must enjoy the chances life throws your way.

She looked horrified.

But she'll remember me the next time I'm here, won't she?

Chapter Twenty-eight

An hour later they pulled to a stop beside a deserted beach that curved away from them in a broad arc, disappearing beneath the yellow haze of early afternoon. White pelicans circled the shallows, now and then diving for fish. The autumn sun glittered among the breakers. A distant anvil-shaped thunderhead drifted over the water, the only blemish to the razor-like horizon.

Trewin climbed out of the sedan and set off for the water's edge. Chancer followed, wondering why he had come to this place. Trewin had said little since lunch, seeming lost to his thoughts. Chancer let him walk on. He paused to survey the empty shoreline. Massive piles of driftwood littered the high water mark, their bare trunks glowing white beneath the sunlight like giant bones. Down the beach a lone fisherman waded through the surf.

Trewin called out to him, pointing overhead where a flock of geese were silhouetted by the azure sky. Their high-pitched calls drifted along the shore. Chancer watched as they vanished into the south-tilting sun. All at once he was aware of time passing just as Trewin had said, of the holidays fast approaching, of the year end, of the mistakes he had made. Trewin appeared beside him.

Don't look so dour, my boy. I've brought you to a beautiful spot, one of Genevieve's favorites, and you look as if you've lost your dog. What's bothering you, then?

There was a girl...

I knew it! There's always a girl. Is she pretty?

-Chancer nodded, imagining Byes as he had first seen her.

I did something wrong, a mistake but more than that, a moment of selfishness I wish I could undo. She left me because of it.

Ah, well, we all make mistakes now and again, don't we? What's important is what you do to make up for it.

I don't know how.

You go and seek her out and you speak to her not proud but all humble and the like. You explain how you're not perfect, and you tell her you made a mistake that you regret but you're willing to do whatever it takes to make it right. That should do it, then.

And I *would* do whatever it takes, Trewin.

I know you would, son. But remember, you can never know the mind of a woman. Still, it's worth a try. I went to Genevieve with my hat in my hand many times.

-Chancer peered down the coastline.

You came here often?

She claimed this place had restorative properties.

Why did she think that?

She said she could feel it. I believed her too. Very unscientific to a physics major maybe but it seemed to help, especially toward the end.

And you still believe her?

I have to, Chancer.

But how can you believe in something you can't see or prove?

-Trewin squinted at him for a moment then swept his arm in a wide arc.

Look around you. What colors do you see?

What?

Come on, nephew, take a look.

Well, I see the blue of the sky and the green of the ocean and...

And how would a scientist explain what makes those colors?

They're the visible part of the electromagnetic spectrum.

And what percentage of the entire spectrum is that, mister physics major?

Visible light makes up less than three percent.

So, you look around you and see less than three percent of the world yet you know all there is to know?

I wouldn't quite put it that way…

Chancer, we live our lives thinking we know what's what. But we don't really, now do we?

We have science. Without scientists we never would have discovered the electromagnetic spectrum.

Sure, science is all fine and good as far as it goes. But what about all we can't see with our eyes, all we have yet to discover and, more important, understand? Think of it, Chancer. Bees can see ultraviolet light. What can other creatures see? If only we could ask them.

That would be difficult.

Don't be so literal. Use your imagination, boy. What might we discover if our eyes could see the entire spectrum? What lurks on the outer fringes of light that we have yet to find? It boggles the mind. Do you hear what I'm saying?

I suppose I do.

So, you see, believing Genevieve isn't so hard when you look at it that way. If only she were here, she could explain how it all…

-Trewin's voice trailed to a whisper.

You still love her, don't you?

Of course I do, son. The reason I come down here is to feel close to her. And I'll never stop loving her, no matter how many pretty ladies I meet.

You can love her and still have girlfriends?

-Trewin cocked his head, the hint of a grin crossing his lips.

They're hardly girls, Chancer.

Do they include Welsh witches?

Well, why on earth would I want to leave them out? That's just the point, you see. Genevieve wanted me to experience the world, to feel it on my skin, to taste it on my tongue. I aim to honor her wish.

By having women friends?

By living life. With that in mind, I know a nice little bar off the beaten path, a place I'll bet you've never seen the likes of.

Minutes later Trewin pulled to a stop in front of a wooden building set on short piers and surrounded by a reed-choked island backwater. A sign above the door read 'Duffy's'. Faded to a dull red, the windowless exterior held a single door covered by iron bars. Two cars sat next to the entrance. A quarter mile beyond, the bay stretched beneath an approaching cloudbank.

Trewin pushed through the door and into the dark interior, Chancer following close behind, and they sat at the bar before ordering beer from the gap-toothed bartender. A newly broken mirror filled the wall opposite them, its shards still littering the grimy floor. Cigarette burns dotted the bar. Two men huddling at the far end talked in low tones, their voices occasionally rising in argument. A sense of unease settled over Chancer as Trewin raised his bottle.

Now, here's to finding adventure wherever it hides.

-Glancing around the room, Chancer managed a half-hearted toast.

But this is a grimy bar in the middle of nowhere, Trewin.

Adventure isn't always nice and pretty, son. You must embrace the experience not fear it.

I'm not afraid of adventure.

Well, I'm glad to hear it. Your father and I used to come here when we were scouting the area for oil lease property.

Did the place look this decrepit?

-Trewin pointed around the room as he spoke.

This is a palace in comparison. Back in those days one wall and half the roof was missing, taken off by hurricane

Carla. After the storm passed, they stretched a big tarp over the rafters and it stayed like that for three years.

On a summer night somebody nearly stepped on a rattlesnake in that far corner. And once when your father and I were sitting right here, some hombre with a pistol shot a hole right through the jukebox. He said the tune reminded him of his ex-wife. They took the gun from him but the song played right on. Take a look, the hole is still there.

-Chancer walked to the jukebox for a look and slipped in a quarter while he was there, selecting the Doors' *Roadhouse Blues*. He leaned his elbows on the glass cover listening to the lyrics.

'Well, I woke up this morning and I got myself a beer
Well, I woke up this morning and I got myself a beer
The future's uncertain and the end is always near.'

-He watched until the spinning black vinyl came to a stop, the playing needle rising as a mechanical arm lifted the record, returning it to an empty slot. When he turned to leave, one of the men at the bar looked his direction. He thought nothing of it. Moments later, Ling stood before him.

-Chancer glanced toward Trewin's chair, dismayed to find it empty. Fear grabbed his chest but Trewin's words again came to him and he took a breath, refusing to live in fear. He met Ling's glare, trying to work out how he had followed him there and why. Before he had a chance to ask, Ling spoke.

Do you follow me, mathematician?

What? No, I'm not following you. Are you following me?

-Ling ignored the question.

If you think I am involved in your fat friend's unfortunate accident, you are mistaken.

Are you telling me he fell on the knife?

246

Do not misunderstand me. I arrange what is necessary for my employer to conduct business. But I do not work for the men who did this. Your friend won much thanks to you and paid what he owed my employer. My employer has decided his luck did not involve actual cheating.

Unfortunately for him, he intruded on another man's business when he somehow won in the fourth race. It is quite curious how he departed from his usual low odds bet and instead picked a horse that should have lost. This was not a very mathematical decision, I think.

He had a feeling the horse would win.

-He looked at Chancer askance.

His intuition may have been correct, if that is truly what guided him, but he paid a quite high price for his winning, did he not? Now, I will tell you he must leave this country before these men finish what they started. Why I tell you this I do not know. Perhaps I also have a taste for the mathematics. Tell your young friend to take his uncle home. And do not return to the races. If he or you try to bet again there will be consequences.

-Before Chancer had a chance to respond Ling turned and disappeared through the doorway. Moments later Trewin appeared next to him.

You look like you've seen the ghost of Bloody Mary herself, son. What's ailing you?

I have to get back home right away.

But why, son? What's happened?

I've heard some bad news about a friend.

What? Here in this place?

I ran into someone just now.

-Trewin looked around the room.

Where is this someone?

He left.

You ran into a friend at a bar in the middle of nowhere, as you like to call it? Now there's a twist of fate for you.

-An image of Talin came to him, his open eyes seeing nothing.

Can we leave now, Trewin?

Is the news very bad then?

Yes, Trewin, it's very bad.

Chapter Twenty-nine

Chancer tried to shake Talin's staring face from his thoughts as he followed Trewin through the barroom door and onto the stairway landing. Before them a cloud-strewn sky scudded over the featureless horizon in ragged lines. The air smelled of rain.

Trewin started down the stairs then stopped in mid-step, looking to his right and left. Chancer followed his gaze. The parking lot stood empty. Rushing down the steps, Trewin disappeared around the corner, emerging on the other side moments later. Keys in hand, he stood in front of the building, a stunned look on his face. Chancer peered down at him.

Where's your car?

-He slammed his keys into the dirt.

Damn it to hell, somebody stole her! She's a classic. I've had her since I was your age. There's no telling what the thieving bastards will do to her.

What should we do now?

-He hurried up the stairs, vanishing inside without a word. A moment later he reappeared cursing under his breath, his face red with anger.

What is it now, Trewin?

We can send a man to the moon, we can transplant a heart but we can't find a damn phone when we need one. The bartender says the cheapskate owner sees no need for one. I suppose if I keeled over in there they'd just toss me out the back and let the coyotes have my carcass.

I saw a town on the map not too far from here.

I know the place. Not far but too far to walk.

Why can't we hitchhike, Trewin?

No, we can't hitch...

-He looked up at Chancer, his eyes dancing.

Why can't we hitchhike indeed, nephew? I haven't thumbed a ride since I was a young lad. What a great excuse to try my hand, or in this case my thumb, again.

-The roar of an approaching car rolled across the parking lot as they hurried to the roadside. With elaborate gesture, Trewin stuck out his thumb. Moments later a black sedan rounded the curve and slowed, pulling alongside them. Two men in sunglasses peered at them through the grimy windshield.

-Chancer opened the rear door, sliding in before realizing the floor overflowed with empty beer bottles. Before he could say anything, Trewin slid in next to him and the car lurched onto the highway in a spray of gravel. Chancer fell against the seatback with his knees to his chest, his feet resting on the bottles.

-He watched as the man in the passenger seat turned to the driver, his profile revealing two black eyes hidden behind his sunglasses. He glanced at Trewin, giving his head a slight shake toward the man. Nodding in understanding, Trewin reached beneath his feet, grabbing the neck of a bottle and motioning Chancer to do the same. A moment later the man turned toward them, his face far from friendly.

Whereabouts you boys hail from? I don't reckon it's around here or we would've seen you at Duffy's place. We're regulars. I'm willing to bet you're city folk, dressed like you are, and probably have some spare gas money. Ain't that right, man?

-Trewin stared at him, his eyes expressionless.

I don't bet.

You don't bet, huh? Then what's a couple of straight-looking guys doing out thumbing a ride? You don't look like the hitching type.

Looks aren't always what they seem.

Is that so? You're not too friendly considering you're begging a ride, man.

You didn't have to stop.

You hear that, Cid?

-The driver stared into the rear view mirror.

I heard it, Willy.

-Trewin leaned forward, his face inches from Willy.

But we appreciate the lift.

-Willy moved away from him.

Well, alright then. Where're you headed?

We need to get to Swisher.

-Cid nearly jumped out his seat.

Why, Swisher's only a few miles from here. You mean we stopped just to cart your ass a few measly miles? You hear that, Willy?

I heard it. I say we take them for a good long ride, Cid, maybe all the way to Wharton. What'd you think?

-The man started to answer but the sound of breaking glass stopped him. Trewin lifted a shattered bottle by the neck, twisting the jagged edge before Willy's face.

I have to apologize. I accidentally broke one of the bottles you're obviously planning to turn in for cash. It's so crowded in here I'm afraid I might do a lot more damage unless I...

-Trewin paused to finger the sharp edge. Willy pushed himself away from the seatback.

What, man? Unless what?

-Trewin locked eyes with him.

I believe we'll get out right here.

-Willy glanced at Cid.

We're not there yet, man. We're nowhere.

-He tapped the seatback with the jagged bottle.

Like I said, right here will do.

-Cid brought the car to a screeching halt. Chancer followed Trewin out the door. The two men gave him a nervous glance before speeding off in a cloud of exhaust. He surveyed the road in both directions. Flat fields stretched into the distance, broken here and there by wind-stunted trees. Chancer struggled to steady his frayed nerves as he faced his uncle.

251

Maybe we should walk the rest of the way, Trewin.

Nonsense, boy. When you get thrown from the horse you have to climb back on.

But those two could've been real trouble.

-He tossed the broken bottle into the roadside grass and pivoted in a wide arc, his arms outstretched.

Look around you, Chancer. This is what I call a true adventure, one to make the blood rise. I can't remember the last time I felt this alive.

But Trewin, what if…

-Chancer looked up as a light rain began to fall. Trewin leaned close to him.

Still want to walk?

-A car appeared in the distance. Moments later a rusted sedan pulled to a stop before them, its torn vinyl top flapping in the wind. Chancer was still having second thoughts about climbing into another strange car when the passenger door flew open. The driver leaned his meaty face toward the window.

You'll have to squeeze in the front. The back is full of samples.

-Frowning, Chancer turned to his uncle. Trewin pushed him into the car next to a man with a belly so large his short arms only just reached the steering wheel. A handkerchief sat draped across his middle, protecting a frayed vest. Trewin squeezed into the passenger seat. An instant later the man put the car into gear, talking from the side of his mouth as he sped onto the highway.

The name's Merlin Hanks. Where you gents headed?

-Trewin glanced at him, noting the tobacco stains on his shirt.

We need to make a phone call.

Phones aren't easy to come by out here.

That's an understatement. The bar where we just came from didn't have one.

-The man chuckled.

So you discovered Seamus Duff's hatred of phones.

252

He must be the owner.

And tight as an oyster they say. He has no head for finances but he knows how to go cheap, and he's a master at rigging what's broken to avoid replacing it. Duct tape is his answer for every problem and about the only thing he'll buy new.

-Trewin glanced behind the seat. Cardboard boxes filled with kitchen utensils and pots of various sizes crowded the back.

Are you in the restaurant business, Merlin?

-He patted his belly.

Can't you tell? I'm told I like my work a little too much. Truth is I supply all the fancy seafood restaurants down here with whatever the kitchen needs, from boiling pots as big as bathtubs to the crystal glasses used for shrimp cocktail. Business has picked up so much I can hardly keep up with it. In fact, I'm running late again.

-They fell silent as Merlin gunned the engine, squinting over the hood as if half-blind and occasionally spitting into a paper cup. The highway turned from the coast, following a zigzag course through a patchwork of fallow rice fields and irrigation canals, the rain-slick asphalt glistening like oil. Chancer tried to stay calm as he watched Merlin's stubby fingers shuffle the steering wheel across his stomach in short jerks, barely keeping the car on the road.

-Moments later they came upon a sudden turn, sliding one way then the other and almost clipping a roadside fencepost. Merlin pressed on, oblivious to the near miss, pushing the accelerator to the floor. Chancer glanced at where Trewin sat staring through the windshield, his white knuckled hand clutching the armrest. Chancer leaned toward the speedometer.

Merlin, aren't you going a bit fast for these wet roads?

Got to make time else I lose business, not to mention a free lunch.

-The car lurched onto the shoulder, sending up a spray of mud and grass behind them before sliding back onto the pavement. Merlin yelled over the engine's roar.

We're alright, we're alright! I have everything under control, gents!

-Moments later a white chapel came into view. Merlin slowed the car and eased up to a small clapboard building perched over a wooded inlet of tea-colored water. A sign above the door read 'Dry Goods'. Running the length of the store, a covered porch faced the chapel and a nearby abandoned schoolhouse weathered to a dull gray. Sprawling live oaks cast both sides of the road deep in shadow.

-Trewin threw open the door and jumped out, his normally ruddy cheeks now a pale mauve. He bent over, his elbows on his knees, looking like he might be sick. Chancer stumbled from the car, thrusting his hands in his pockets to keep them from shaking. He leaned toward the window.

We appreciate the ride, Merlin. I hope you make your lunch on time.

Oh, not to worry, son. I never miss a meal.

-He waved a thick arm out the window as the car jumped back onto the roadway in a spray of gravel. Chancer turned to face the store where Trewin sat on the steps, his head between his knees. Chancer took a seat next to him. Trewin let out a groan and raised his head.

I believe I saw my life pass before my eyes two or three times before we landed at this blessed oasis. I was reminded of my terrible sea-sickness during the war. More than once I thought dying would be an improvement. War will do that to you.

-He stared into the distance, lost in thought. Then he turned to face Chancer.

But those times were nothing like what we have now. The war was terrible but understandable, at least the reasons for it anyway. I can't make sense of this present one at all. What do you young people think of the thing?

-Chancer hesitated, trying to decide whether to tell him his thoughts, unsure how he would react, but his need to talk about his predicament finally won out. He locked eyes with him.

I'm not going to Vietnam, Trewin. I've decided I can't go kill people halfway across the world and not know why. I'm going to Canada instead.

-Trewin flinched, his voice rising with every word.

You're doing *what*?

I'm against the war. Lots of people my age are against it.

Fine, be against it all you like but do your duty anyhow. Besides which you have to answer when your country calls on you. It's the law.

I've made up my mind. I won't fight an unjust war just to satisfy some politician. You said it yourself, there's no sense to it.

-Trewin's face went red.

I said I couldn't make sense of the thing, not that it had none!

Well, it doesn't.

-He pounded his fist on the stairs.

It makes no difference, man! You *have* to go. I won't have any nephew of mine disgracing the family by dodging the draft. No, you have to grit your teeth and bear it like your father and I did.

I won't go!

-Trewin jumped up from the step, turning to face Chancer.

You will!

-Chancer tried to calm himself.

Uncle Trewin, listen to me. Didn't you just say those times were completely different from today?

Well, I...

And you're right. They were different.

255

Yes, but...

When you were my age students weren't protesting across the country like they are now, were they? In April, five hundred thousand people marched against the war, and a month later twelve thousand protesters were arrested.

-Trewin paced before the stairs.

Those protesters are a bunch of no-good hippies.

No, Trewin, they believe in what they're doing.

It makes no difference, boy. War is war and you have to serve when called to.

I won't, not for you, not for my parents, not for anyone.

-Trewin stopped and searched his face.

You mean what you say, don't you? You've made your decision. I can see that.

I'm glad to hear it.

Are you certain, son?

I am.

-Trewin took a breath, exhaling slowly.

I have to admit, it takes a brave man to honor his beliefs by going against his country and his family. There's nothing I can say that would change your mind?

No, Trewin, there isn't.

You're sure going to Canada is the right thing to do, son? A decision like that can follow you for the rest of your life.

I see no alternative other than going to prison.

Draft dodger sounds a bit better than ex-con, I suppose. What do your parents say about it, then?

They don't know.

-Trewin's eyes grew wide.

You've not told them yet?

The time never seems right.

And it never will be, son. Best to take your medicine straightaway and give them time to get used to the idea. But you told *me* of all people. Why?

You're nothing like them, Trewin. I've always been able to talk to you.

Somehow I never would've guessed. Still, I'm touched to hear you say so. You can talk to your parents as well, Chancer. They'll hear you out. Just remind me not to be there when it happens.

-He stood without another word, hurrying up the stairs and disappearing inside the store. Minutes later he reappeared, a beer in each hand. He thrust one at Chancer before guzzling half his bottle.

Your grandmother and Weesie are on the way so we'd best prepare for the grand inquisition. The beer will make the ride almost tolerable.

Chapter Thirty

A low December sun angled through the living room curtains, flecking the floor with sunlight and reminding me of the approaching holidays. That nearly a year had passed since Chancer's death seemed beyond belief. So much had changed in my world. Looking back at it all, I might have started feeling sorry for myself again but Trewin had cured me of that ugly habit. He meant to enjoy life, to take what comes and make the best of it no matter what. I intended to do the same.

An image of my mother came to me. Lately, I often had found myself thinking of her. Chancer's journal painted a less than flattering portrait yet he never said a word against her. He must have seen something in her, something good in spite of the anger she held towards him. At times I wondered what it would be like to meet her.

A light knock pulled me from my thoughts and I turned to find Vincent stepping through the doorway, Diego in tow. Vincent tilted his head from side to side, studying me within the tunnel of his diminishing vision. Weeks earlier he had met a blind but highly successful artist and had since regained his typical enthusiasm. He pushed Diego into the room.

Diego has something to tell you, Tegan.

-He glanced at me but kept his eyes to the floor, a sheepish look on his face.

Don't be mad or anything, Tegan.

Why would I be mad? You're doing great in school and at home.

Vincent said I should've told you already.

Should've told me what?

He said you won't like that I kept it from you.

Now I'm starting to worry. What did you keep from me, Diego?

I entered a big art contest, one that's for the whole country. Vincent helped me pick out the painting. We chose the one of my mom.

-I was relieved to know he wasn't in some sort of trouble.

I'm glad to hear it, Diego.

You're not mad?

No, but why didn't you say something?

I meant to tell you. But I was afraid I wouldn't get accepted. That would've been embarrassing.

So, you were accepted?

-He nodded. Vincent nudged him.

And what else, Diego?

I won.

-I looked at them in disbelief.

You mean you won for your age?

No, I placed first out of all the artists, even old people like Vincent.

-Vincent gave him a mock frown before turning to me, smiling.

The competition is very prestigious and open to all artists, amateur and professional. He beat them all, Tegan.

-I took Diego by the hand.

That's wonderful, Diego. Senor Fuego was right. You do have the soul of an artist.

-Diego turned his eyes to the floor, clearly embarrassed by the attention.

If not for you I never would have known, Tegan.

-I was touched by his words. In a sudden moment of clarity I dropped his hand, realizing I no longer had anything to offer him. The time had come for us to say goodbye. Tears filled my eyes and I let them, uncaring of my companions, letting the mix of joy and sadness pass over me like summer rain. Vincent hurried to me, taking my hand in his.

What's wrong, Tegan? We thought the news would make you happy. Diego's paintings have already sold enough to allow him and his mom to keep the trailer. That's something to be glad about, isn't it?

-I wiped my eyes and nodded. Diego moved next to me.

Are you okay, Tegan?

I'm alright, and I *am* glad to hear your news. It's just a lot to take in, all the change.

-Vincent squeezed my hand.

You mean those are tears of happiness?

Something like that.

The following day Cheering stepped through the door of our meeting place. Wearing jeans and a loose sweater, she looked like any other teenager. Yet her eyes held a hint of trouble. In the weeks since the terrorist attacks she had spoken less and less of the abuse and more of her future plans. I had found myself wondering if, like Diego, her time with me was growing short. Now I was less sure.

As usual, I waited for her to begin. She perched on the chair as if she might bolt any second, glancing at me and fidgeting with the hem of her sweater. I fought the urge to speak. Instead I took a breath and sat back as if I had nothing else to do. Just when I thought I might not be able to hold out any longer she finally spoke.

What's your father like, Tegan? Does he live around here?

-I hesitated, surprised by the question.

He died about a year ago, Cheering.

-She stifled a gasp.

Oh, Tegan, I'm so sorry. I didn't know.

How could you? But you have a reason for asking, don't you?

My father has contacted me.

Ah, I see... and what has that been like?

At first, I wouldn't answer. But his emails sounded nice, not pushy or anything, so I thought maybe I could trust him.

But you're still not sure?

He left me, Tegan. How can I forget that?

Do you want to forget it?

Part of me does but the other part thinks it's important to remember what happened to me.

But you also want to stay in touch with him?

It's not just keeping in touch. I could handle that. I've even talked to him on the phone. But he wants to come see me.

Do you want to see him?

I don't know.

What does your heart tell you, Cheering?

I want to see him but I'm afraid I'll get mad and say something I'll regret.

Would you rather lie to him?

I'm not going to act like what happened never did. I tried that and it doesn't work.

Then can you talk to him honestly?

I think I can.

But you think you can't control your anger?

I can. I know how to keep my temper.

Then if you want to see him, why can't you?

No reason, I guess.

You get to decide, Cheering. If you don't want to see him you don't have to.

But how will I ever know if it's the right decision, Tegan?

We never know if a decision we make is the right one. If it's what you want then you have to take a chance.

-A light knock sounded behind me and I turned to find Esther standing in the doorway.

Cheering has to leave early today. Her grandparents are outside waiting.

-She jumped up.

261

I forgot, Tegan.

-I leaned towards her, speaking under my breath.

Have you told them about your father?

-She gave her head a slight shake, mouthing the word 'no'.

Then it might be a good idea to figure out how you want to do that.

-She nodded her agreement before hurrying out the door. Looking like she had something on her mind, Esther sat next to me.

How is our beautiful girl?

I was thinking we might have done all we could but now I'm not so sure.

She is doing well by all reports. Has there been a change?

Something's come up. She's trying to figure out how to deal with it.

Something as in her father reappearing on the scene?

-I squinted at her.

And how do you know this?

Her grandparents are monitoring her emails.

-I shook my head in disapproval.

Esther, that's so deceitful. They should tell her.

I agree but after what happened earlier this year, you can hardly blame them.

Is that what you came to tell me?

-She sighed.

I wish it were. The truth is the terrorist attacks are having a ripple effect on our funding. Money that normally would come to us is being diverted to national security, especially along the border.

-My heart sank.

Am I being fired?

Nothing is certain yet but it looks like there could be cutbacks. I'd hate to lose you, Tegan. But if it happens I don't want it to come as a complete surprise. I'm only telling you so you can start looking for something else if you want to.

I love it here, Esther.

-She patted my knee and stood.

I have a meeting to go to. Let's try not to think about what might or might not happen. These kids are counting on us, Tegan. Concentrate on doing your job and the rest will take care of itself.

-I watched her leave, again thinking of my father and how the unexpected so often moves us about like pawns on a chessboard. Thirty years earlier Chancer was living in limbo, his fate lurking in a time beyond the reach even of mathematical probability. With a new year fast approaching, he had no idea of the changes soon to arrive.

Chapter Thirty-one

The holidays were less than a week away as Chancer stepped onto a broken sidewalk that curved away from him before disappearing behind an abandoned Victorian mansion. In the fading dusk, slivers of cloud and sky reflected off its shattered windows. He paused and pulled a slip of paper from his shirt pocket, checking the numbers against an address a classmate had given him for Byes' apartment. Henry had left her weeks earlier. Having convinced himself she would take him back, Chancer had finally summoned the courage to go see her.

He started again, following the walkway around a tall hedge to the porch of a tiny frame cottage, its shiplap siding yellowed with neglect. He had imagined the moment for so long he could scarcely breathe. Trewin's advice to make things right ricocheted through his thoughts. Taking a breath, he rapped his knuckles on the doorframe.

Moments later the door swung open. For an instant Chancer thought he had been made the butt of a cruel joke. A young woman stood before him, clearly pregnant and only slightly resembling Byes. He peered into her face. She glared back at him, holding tight to the door as if she might slam it in his face at any moment.

What do you want, Chancer?
-A mane of auburn hair framed her wide face. He leaned closer, squinting at her.
Byes?
Who were you expecting, Joan Baez?
-Beneath the added weight he finally recognized her, still beautiful, her pale skin flawless, her gaze intense. He stared at her bulging middle.
You're pregnant?
Why do you think I look like the Michelin Man?
But how did… who is…?
-She snorted.

Why is it smart people have no sense? A ten year old kid could've taken one look at me and known months ago but you had no clue.

How long have you...?

For a physics major, you're pretty slow, Chancer. The baby is due in two weeks.

-He ignored the jibe, his head spinning.

But I heard that Henry left. Why would he...?

The imp belongs to you, Chancer.

-He stepped back, feeling light-headed.

How can you be sure?

You're the numbers expert. Do the math.

Why didn't you tell me?

What I do is not your concern.

But it is, Byes. I mean, I'm responsible aren't I?

-She sneered at him, her eyes full of contempt.

You think I could do this by myself?

I should do my part then, shouldn't I?

You think you're ready to be a father?

Well, no. But shouldn't we be together?

-She threw up her hands.

Oh, no, that's not going to happen, Chancer.

-Thinking again of Trewin, he pressed on.

Why not, Byes? I'll do whatever it takes to make it right between us. Just tell me what to do.

It doesn't work like that, Chancer. I've moved on. I have a life to live and I'm going to go live it.

How can you? You're about to have a baby, Byes.

That's not your problem.

I can make amends, Byes. Just give me a chance.

Chancer, you don't get it.

-He paused, searching for the right words.

Byes, I didn't mean for Henry to get kicked out of school. I was just trying to...

That's ancient history, Chancer. This is not about that.

-He peered at her, trying to understand.

What is it about then?

Don't you get it, Chancer? I don't love you anymore. I did once, I suppose. But things change and people change with it. It's time to move on.

You don't have any feelings for me, Byes? I mean, there's a baby now.

You don't know the first thing about raising a kid, Chancer. Babies are not all neat and tidy like one of your math problems.

I could learn, Byes. We could learn together.

-She pointed a finger in his face.

Listen to me, Chancer. You have to get that idea out of your head. The imp is my problem and I'm going to take care of it. You have no say in my life, not now, not ever.

What are you going to do?

I'm going to say goodbye, Chancer.

-He moved onto the threshold, his voice pleading.

Just give me time, Byes.

Don't make me be cruel, Chancer.

I know we can work this out. I can do better.

You're not listening. I keep trying to tell you that I'm past all that.

We can take it slow, Byes. I'll do whatever it takes.

-She pushed him back onto the porch.

You need to leave, Chancer.

But Byes, I...

Don't come back here or I'll call your friends, the police.

-The door slammed shut, rattling the windows as her footsteps faded into silence. Not knowing what to do or where to go he stood there, his hopes for a second chance lost beneath all he had heard. A dull sadness surrounded him, filling his throat. In the distance a siren came to life. He cast a final glance toward the cottage, turned and started for home.

The familiar tree-lined street stretched before him, its shadows interrupted here and there by restless pools of

light. A chill wind coursed overhead. Though he savored
the time of year, the world seemed to have turned against
him, leaving in its place a bitter taste. Turley and Beulah
were gone from his life and now Byes as well. He
wondered with a shudder if his father would be next. The
mathematics of probability no longer seemed so intriguing.
He wanted no more change.

As he neared the main avenue a cold rain began to
fall. Deciding to wait it out, he headed for a nearby coffee
shop, ducking inside and nearly running into Fiona Bain.
She stepped aside to let him pass then stopped as she
recognized him. She held out her hand. Chancer was once
again taken with her tangle of black hair and strawberry
skin. Her smile seemed as warm as he remembered.

I see you're a book *and* coffee lover, Chancer Wylls.
-He shook her hand.
Actually, I don't know much about coffee. I was
trying to get out of the rain.
Do you remember me?
Of course I do. How could I forget? I mean, you're so,
uh… so…
-He stopped, unable to finish. She leaned toward him,
grinning.
What am I, then? I want to know.
-He felt the blood rush to his face.
It's hard to put into words.
But you can try, can't you?
Words aren't like numbers. They can only
approximate what needs to be said.
What needs to be said, Chancer?
-The words tumbled from his lips.
You're an attractive woman, Fiona, striking even.
Striking is it? No one has ever said that to me before.
It's true.
Even when I've been crying?

-An image of her surrounded by Beulah's belongings, tears staining her cheeks, came to him.

Especially then.

Then can I have my hand back?

What?

-He followed her gaze, realizing with a start he still had hold of her. She peered into his face.

You're a surprise, Chancer Wylls. Did you find anything of Beulah's you wanted?

I came across an copy of *Great Expectations* she intended to give me. A note in it said it's a first edition.

Is it really a first edition? I'd love to see it.

Well, I could bring it…

-He stopped as a man appeared at her side. A head taller than Chancer, he looked like he could be the captain of the football team. He draped a thick arm across her shoulders and whispered in her ear. Fiona glanced at him.

Chancer, this is Melvin.

-He nodded distractedly, urging her toward the exit. Fiona smiled apologetically.

Beulah didn't give her beloved books to just anyone, you know. You're the only other person I've met.

What did she give you?

-Melvin reached up and pinched her earlobe, giving it a hard twist as he nodded toward the door. Fiona grimaced, trying to ignore the pain.

Anna Karenina, also a first edition.

-Melvin scowled at her.

Enough of this geek talk, let's go.

-Chancer spotted a hint of worry cross her face. Not knowing what else to do, he continued.

Did you and Beulah talk about it, about the story?

-Melvin slipped a hand under her coat, pinching her hard. Fiona stifled a scream. Without thinking, Chancer grabbed his arm, yanking it away.

Don't touch her!

-He turned on Chancer, taking hold of his collar and shoving him into the counter.

The geek is as stupid as he looks. Listen, you little twerp, don't you ever, ever...

-A thick hand appeared out of nowhere, grabbing Melvin by the neck and pressing his face to the counter. Chancer slipped out of the way as a man in a grease-stained apron leaned over Melvin, growling into his ear.

I've had enough of you frat boys scaring our patrons. You leave here now and don't return, ever. Do you understand?

-He tensed his sausage-like fingers and Melvin let out a scream before giving his head an exaggerated nod. The man led him to the door, pushing him into the street. Fiona moved to where Chancer still stood.

I'm sorry but I have to leave.

You're going with him after the way he treated you?

He's not always like that, Chancer.

You don't have to put up with it, Fiona. You could be with anyone.

It's complicated and I don't have time to explain. It was nice seeing you, Chancer.

-He watched her pass through the doorway and vanish, feeling the empty sadness again fill his throat. Stepping into the rain, he turned for home.

The rain had stopped by the time he slipped between the tall hedges marking the university campus. He knew he must try to forget Byes. Yet as he walked down the portico and across the mall where they had first met, he realized he had no idea where to start. His empty apartment was the last place he wanted to be. He felt a sudden urge to be around people he knew, people who would be glad to see him.

Backtracking across campus, he headed for the second floor of the physics building only to find Franklin's office empty. As he pushed back through the doorway, he paused at the sight of the medical center rising above the treetops. In all his worry over seeing Byes, he had forgotten to tell Raz about seeing Ling and his warning that Talin must leave the country. Cursing beneath his breath, he hurried toward the hospital.

Minutes later he stepped off the second floor elevator. Ben stood midway down the hallway talking to a young blonde woman. She seemed vaguely familiar. As he approached her, Chancer studied her face, searching his memory for a connection. Ben glanced at her and nodded toward him.

Here's the man you've been looking for.
-Chancer peered at her.
Do I know you?
-She gave her head a slight shake.
Is there somewhere we can talk?
-He looked from her to Ben.
How about you take her to the break room, Chancer? There's no one in there right now. I'll check with you later.
-He disappeared down the hall before Chancer could speak. Not knowing what else to do, he led the woman into the small kitchen, searching his memory for who she might be. She set her purse on the table, pulling out *The Art of War* and handing it to him.
Do you recognize this?
-He sat cradling the book in his hands, recognizing it as Turley's.
You're Turley's sister, Tanya?
-She sat across from him.
Thanks to you I found him. We didn't have long, not nearly enough for me. Still, we got to know each other again. He let me see him in a way I never would have expected, and I feel like I have my bother back. It means more to me than I can say, Chancer.
-She paused, her gaze lost to the memory.

You see, we had a difficult time growing up, especially him. Being older, he tried to protect me from our father so he took the brunt of the abuse. You probably know better than me the toll it took on him.

I've always felt guilty about all that happened to him. But you gave me a chance to do something about it, to be with him at the time he needed me most. I'll always be grateful to you for that, Chancer.

I didn't do much, Tanya.

You did more than you know.

-Two nurses pushed through the door, laughing. Tanya stood and took Chancer's hand.

I'm sorry to rush off but I have an early meeting out of town and I haven't started packing for it.

-He held out the book.

Are you sure you don't want to keep this?

I want you to have it, Chancer. I hope it will remind you of the way you once helped a friend.

-She slipped out the doorway. Chancer wandered into the hall, his thoughts again turning to the past. Could his help really have made a difference for Turley and his sister? He wondered at all the fateful encounters over the last year. An instant later Ben appeared before him. His eyes held a restless energy.

I'm glad you're still here, Chancer. I have some news.

Is it about Turley's sister?

-Ben glanced toward the elevator.

What do you think of her? She's a fox, isn't she?

I suppose so.

What do you mean, Wylls? She's a honey. Not only that but we have a date next week.

-Chancer frowned at him.

You're going out with Turley's sister?

More than once, I hope. I'm not about to let her get away if I can help it.

-Chancer sighed, in no mood to hear about his love life.

Is that what you came to tell me, Ben?

Don't sound so bored, Chancer. I have some big news. I'm being transferred to the new cardiac ward at Memorial.

-Stunned, Chancer stared at him, barely able to speak.

You're leaving the hospital?

Nurse Berry recommended me for the move and I got it.

We won't be working together anymore?

I'm only moving across the street.

-Chancer's heart sank at the thought of no longer seeing him.

It's not here, Ben.

But think of it, Chancer. I'll be working alongside the best heart surgeons in the world. I'll get to meet them, learn from them and watch them operate. Plus, it'll help me get into medical school. This is my lucky break. Be happy for me.

-Chancer tried to shake off his disappointment, ashamed of his selfishness.

You're right, Ben. The move sounds like a great opportunity.

-Ben clasped him by the shoulder.

You and me, we've got to keep our eye on the future. This is a hard place, Chancer. Don't stay too long. In everything we do there comes a point when it's time to move on. Are you hearing me, Wylls?

-Chancer nodded, trying to sound confident.

I hear you, Ben.

Speaking of moving on, I'm going to see if I can catch Tanya before she leaves.

-Chancer watched him disappear into the stairwell, his words stirring in his chest. What fate did the future hold, Canada, Vietnam, prison? Should he continue at the hospital? Where else could he go? His head hurt trying to sort through it all.

-Then a familiar voice sounded behind him, pulling him back into the moment. At the far end of the hall he spotted Raz hurrying toward the ward. Chancer called out to him and he turned, shuffling over in his scrub-covered sneakers.

What is it, Chancer? I am off to see my uncle.

-Chancer leaned close, speaking under his breath.

I saw Ling.

-Raz gasped, his eyes darting around the hallway.

He is here in the hospital? I knew he would come for us! What do we do, Chancer?

Calm yourself, Raz. He's not here.

Then where is he? Where did you see him?

I ran into him at a bar in the middle of nowhere, down near the coast.

Good god, Chancer, what are the odds of such a happening?

Listen, Raz, you have to take your uncle home. Ling said they'll kill him if you don't.

You mean Ling will finish him? I knew this would happen.

He denies doing it. The men I overheard are the ones who stabbed Talin. Ling told me because he was trying to help. Your uncle needs to leave.

-Raz sighed, a look of resignation crossing his face.

I too had reached this unfortunate conclusion, I am sad to say. Uncle is now almost able to travel. I am already making preparations.

I'm sorry, Raz. I should never have told him to change his pick for the fourth race.

There is no need to apologize, Chancer. You are my friend. You were only trying to help me regain my college fund and this you managed to do. Perhaps someday I will return to university. Will you be here if I do?

I doubt it.

Why do human beings have to war, Chancer? As a physicist, I see no logic in such behavior, only insanity.

I know, Raz.

The draft for you, the gambling for me, they move us about like quantum particles with a future beyond predictability. I long for certainty, Chancer.

I hope you find it, Raz.

But for now the only certainty is that I must go to my uncle.

-He disappeared into the ward as Chancer once again started for home, wishing the odds might finally turn his way.

Chapter Thirty-two

From his kitchen table, Chancer watched as gray clouds scudded over nearby rooftops, their torn shapes stretching into the distance. Tree limbs tapped against the window in some indecipherable Morse code, rattled by a chill wind. The gloomy day seemed a fitting end to his year.

He collected a thick stack of calculations and stuffed them into his backpack. Though it was New Year's Eve, he had arranged to meet Franklin that afternoon and give him the papers, the deadline being the first of January. In spite of all that had happened he had somehow managed to complete the project on time.

He turned as footsteps started up the stairs. For a moment he wondered if Trewin had decided to pay him another visit. Then his mother called his name. When he opened the door his mother and father stood before him, their faces grim. Gammie and Weesie hovered behind them. Beetie frowned at him, shivering.

Hurry and let us in, Chancer. It's cold out!
-He ushered them through the door and they each took a chair at the table. Beetie pulled an envelope from her purse and set it on the table, sliding it toward him. The return address read Selective Service System.
This was sent to us, sweetheart, but it's for you.
-He reached for the letter, seeing it was open.
You know what it says, don't you?
-Beetie nodded.
You're our only child, Chancer. We just had to know.
-Gammie snorted, talking to no one in particular.
I would've never done such a thing to Pen.
-Chancer lifted out the letter, studying it as a feeling of unreality settled over him. Though he knew the notice would eventually arrive, some part of him had been unable

to face the meaning of it until that moment. He took a breath, reading the words aloud.

'You are hereby ordered for induction into the Armed Forces…'

-Weesie gasped.

Lord, help us.

-Chancer paused to gather himself before continuing.

… into the Armed Forces of the United States and to report at 1:00 p. m. on…'

-His voice trailed off as he looked up at his parents.

I'm not going to Vietnam.

-His mother nodded solemnly.

We guessed that's what you would say, Chancer. That's why we're here, to talk with you about it.

Trewin told you?

-Beetie's face went red.

You confided in that old scoundrel and not you mother and father? Chancer, what's come over you? Who else did you tell?

-She glanced around the table. Gammie shrugged, giving her head a shake.

Sister and I are always in the dark on these matters.

-Beetie turned back to Chancer and tapped her finger against the tabletop.

Even an old rake like Trewin must have tried to talk some sense into you. After all, he served his country just like your father. Why didn't you listen?

I did listen but it's not that simple, mom.

Listen to me, Chancer. You may not agree with this war but you can't bring shame on yourself and this family by refusing to be inducted. I just won't have it.

I've made up my mind, mom. I'm not going to Vietnam. I know you don't like it but I see no alternative.

I'll bet Vietnam beats the inside of a prison cell.

I'm going to Canada, mom.

What in heaven's name are you talking about now, Chancer?

276

I've cleared it with Aunt Megs and Uncle Will.

You've talked with them too? What do you mean about clearing something?

They're letting me live at their place, at least for awhile.

But why would you want to do that?

The draft can't reach me there, mom. They already have a room ready.

-Beetie turned to Pen.

Aren't you going to say something?

-He leaned his elbows on the table.

Son, I don't agree with this war anymore than you do. I've read everything I can get my hands on and the reasoning doesn't hold up. I only wish you were a couple of years younger because I don't think it will last beyond that. The north is just too...

-Beetie glared at him.

Pen, this is not the time for one of your history lessons.

-He ignored her and peered into Chancer's face.

Son, our only concern is your welfare and your future. With the sort of ability you have it's unlikely they'd actually send you to Vietnam. Lots of young men with special talents go into intelligence and other noncombat areas. That might happen in your case.

-Chancer felt a fierce determination rising in his chest.

I'm not willing to gamble on what might happen, dad. I'm past playing the odds. Besides, war is sometimes unavoidable but that doesn't make it right.

History has not been kind to draft resisters, Chancer.

History will prove Vietnam has little in common with previous wars other than young men dying in it. Like you said, the war lacks justification. There is no Hitler or Mussolini set on ruling the world. There is no enemy threatening our allies or border. There's only a tiny country locked in a civil war we have no business sticking our nose in.

-Pen slowly shook his head.

Are you sure, son? This is a decision that could haunt you for the rest of your life.

I realize how serious it is, dad. And I know you're telling me all this because you and mom love me. But it's a decision that only I can make.

-Gammie rapped her knuckles on the table.

You couldn't have said it any better yourself, Pen. I for one am glad my grandson is brave enough to stand up to all of us for what he believes. We could use more of that sort of honesty around here.

-She squinted at Beetie.

What do you say?

I say I'm in shock.

Well then you need a drink. We all do, and you most of all Chancer Wylls. I've got just the thing over in my kitchen cabinet. It is New Year's Eve, after all.

-Chancer glanced at the clock and stood.

I'm going to be late for a meeting.

-Grabbing his backpack, he rushed out the door.

Orange shafts of sunlight broke from beneath the low clouds, bathing the leafless trees in gold. To the west the crimson sunset stretched along a horizon crowded with the tiled roofs of the university. The clock tower chimes drifted overhead.

In spite of the beautiful evening, Chancer kept his eyes to the sidewalk, unable to enjoy the night. He dreaded having to tell Franklin of the letter and face the reality of leaving after all their hard work. Having to simply walk away irked him. The odds of coming across such an opportunity again were slim. Still, he was determined to face the inevitable.

A rectangle of yellow light spilled from Franklin's doorway as Chancer burst through stairwell exit and hurried down the polished hallway toward his office. He glanced at his watch, pausing to catch his breath. An instant later Franklin's voice echoed from inside the office.

Are you going to stand there panting or come in?

-Chancer heard something in his voice, an energy he'd not heard in some time. He wondered if it had to do with the project's end, the New Year or both. Franklin looked up from a stack of papers, waving him toward a chair.

Happy New Year, Chancer. What are your plans for the evening?

-Embarrassed to have none, Chancer held up the thick folder.

I've been too busy to make plans.

-Franklin peered over his glasses, a look of sympathy in his eyes.

I don't mean to intrude, Chancer. I know this has been a difficult year.

-He decided to no longer postpone telling him about the letter.

Franklin, I...

-Franklin raised his hand, stopping him.

Chancer, I have something important to ask you, something that will put everything in a new light.

But Franklin, I got a letter from...

Please hear me out. I've been approached by the federal government to head up a highly classified project, a project that has to do with national security, and I want you to be a part of the work. You'll be...

-Chancer jumped from the chair.

Franklin, listen to me! I've been drafted. I got my induction letter.

-Ignoring the news, Franklin pointed a finger at him.

And you'll be paid for your work. This will be more than fulltime so you'll have to quit your job at the hospital, but you'll be able to continue taking classes. I can't tell you what an opportunity this is for the university and for us, for you and me. But this is serious work, Chancer. You'll have to swear under penalty of law to keep the project secret.

-Listening to him only added to Chancer's disappointment.

Why are you wasting your time telling me this, Franklin? I can't stay here any longer. If I don't report for induction I'll be arrested, and if I resist I'll go to prison.

-Franklin locked eyes with him, unfazed by the news.

Can you answer me one thing, Chancer? Would you want to be part of the project if it wasn't for the draft?

Of course I would. Working with you has been a dream come true, Franklin. The thought of going on to something bigger and more important is beyond anything I could ever hope for. But how does any of that matter?

Sit down and I'll tell you.

-Chancer took a breath, swallowing his frustration as he eased back onto the chair. Franklin tapped the stack of papers.

This project comes out of the defense department. I picked you over graduate students and even some of the younger faculty because I want the best for this work, Chancer. And I've been assured by people very high up that you would be exempt from the draft in order to do this work.

I'm flattered but…

-Chancer stared at him, unable to continue, his mind unwilling to accept the words.

What did…? Would you…? Say it again, Franklin.

You'll have a draft exemption, Chancer. The government considers the work important enough to keep you here.

I can stay?

Not only can you stay, you can continue with your courses, get paid for your work and know that you're helping your country. What do you say?

-He blinked, overwhelmed by the news. Franklin stepped around his desk, sitting on the edge and leaning toward him.

The project has to do with developing satellite tracking systems to monitor terrorists. That's all I can say for the moment. Will you say yes to it, Chancer?

-He managed a nod. Franklin placed a hand on his shoulder.

I want you to go home, Chancer. You have a future now, a future here in the place you live. Take time to think about how you want to use that time, and I'm not talking about work. You owe yourself that much.

Chapter Thirty-three

Stars blinked through the trees as Chancer made his way back across campus. Orion's belt emerged above the rooftops for a split second before vanishing. He watched the passing clouds, wanting to believe his luck might finally have started to change. In the distance a fireworks show lit the sky, marking the start of New Year's Eve.

Several women appeared beneath a streetlight ahead of him, hurrying along in the chill air, their coat collars up. Their laughter echoed between the buildings. His thoughts consumed by Franklin's words, Chancer paid them little notice. An instant later Fiona Bain stood before him.

Chancer Wylls, it is you! Why didn't you say something?

-Her companions stood twenty yards away huddling together and watching. He peered into her dark eyes.

I'm sorry, Fiona. I didn't see you.

Yes, you were off in another world, poor boy.

Well, I... a lot has happened, Fiona.

Has it ever!

-She grabbed his hand, pulling him into the light.

Do you believe in fate, Chancer Wylls?

I don't know, maybe.

Oh, yes, you're a physics major after all. Why would you? Well, I do. Look at your palm. What does it tell you?

-Feeling the warmth of her touch he began to relax.

Why don't you tell me?

See this line here? It shows that you'll cross paths with someone important in your life. So, just now I'm walking along talking to my friends about you when suddenly you appear.

Are you saying it's more than a coincidence?

That's just it, Chancer. What are the odds of us running into each other just now?

I'd say they're not good.

But we did anyway, didn't we?

I guess I'm just lucky.

Oh, I'm the lucky one. Are you off to a party?

-He cringed at the question.

No, I'm on my way home.

Then you must come to ours. Please say you will.

I don't know, Fiona. A lot has…

I know. A lot has happened. Well, include me in on the lot, won't you?

But what about Melvin?

That's what I'm talking about, Chancer. Just by chance I run into you at the coffee shop and nothing is the same again.

What do you mean?

I didn't realize it at the time but watching you stand up to Melvin changed me, Chancer. Instead of a handsome athlete, I began to see him as the bully he truly is, a bully and a coward. Your bravery gave me the courage to leave him, so I did.

I don't think of myself as brave.

Well, you are.

-She pulled a ticket stub from her purse, scribbled on the back and handed it to him.

Here's my address. The girls and I are having a few friends over. They're all nice people and you'll fit right in, I promise. There's a violinist and even a math major. So, there you have it. We need to leave now but you will come, won't you?

-Squeezing the stub between his thumb and finger, he again heard Trewin's voice urging him to live life. He nodded and watched as she and her friends slipped back into the night.

Minutes later he paused at the foot of his stairs. He sensed a difference, a change in himself he had no words for, as if the night itself held the power to transform. Even in the darkness his apartment seemed somehow smaller and shabbier than when he had left, subtle but unmistakable. He started up the steps, ruminating over the change.

The stairway landing held a faint smell of perfume, familiar and evocative. Fumbling with his keys, he turned a slow circle, puzzling over the odor. No explanation came to mind. A vague feeling of apprehension drifted over him as he turned the key.

As the door swung open an envelope fluttered to the floor. Reaching for it, he pulled out a single page and held it to the light. Byes' scrawled handwriting stared up at him. He quickly scanned the letter once then twice before reading through it word by word, trying to move past his disbelief.

Chancer,

I've done something I hope one day you can forgive. I treated you badly the last time we spoke, and before then as well. My doctor blames my raging hormones but I won't make excuses. I was wrong. It's true that I hated you for turning in Henry. But now I understand you only did what you had to. You are a good man in spite of your mistakes.

I, on the other hand, am far from good. But I have dreams I can't let go of, Chancer. I have to pursue them no matter the cost. By the time you read this, I'll have already left town. I've been awarded a full scholarship to the viticulture program at the University of Adelaide in South Australia. Once I'm able to travel, I'll leave. It's my time to do what I have to.

I left the baby on the back steps of the hospital where someone should easily find her. She came just after midnight. I figured a hospital is the best place to leave her. They take care of people, after all.

You, no doubt, think me despicable. Still, I decided you had to know. I owe you that much. Take care, Chancer.

-Byes

He stared at the letter, unable to move, unable to
think. How could she simply walk away? Who would take
the baby? What could he, a young student not yet out of his
teens, do? Try as he might, he could find no answers.
Having only just reclaimed his future, he felt it again
fading from his grasp.

Then an image came to him of Byes setting a small
bundle on the loading dock steps, steps he knew so well,
the same steps he had climbed countless times. Tossing the
paper aside, he rushed to the phone. Moments later Ben's
voice sounded in the receiver.

Chancer, what's wrong? The nurse said it was urgent.
There's a baby on the loading dock, Ben.
Someone left a baby? How do you know?
Trust me, Ben.
Whose baby is it?
Never mind that, just get down there as quick as you
can. I'm on my way.

-Ben stood waiting on the stairs, his arms surrounding
a pink blanket. Chancer had never seen him so nervous.
Nurse Berry hovered nearby, now and then stealing a peek
over his shoulder. Chancer hurried up the driveway. The
instant Ben spotted him he thrust the bundle at him.

What took you so long, Chancer? I thought you'd
never get here.

-Frowning, Nurse Berry stepped in front of him,
taking the baby.

Mister Wylls, I find myself wondering how a young
man such as yourself might come to know we have an
orphan baby on our doorstep.

-Chancer looked from her to Ben and back.
I know the mother.

And you're sure this mother chooses to give her baby
up for adoption? We are a safe haven, you know. That is

hospital policy. We have an agreement with the county authorities that babies may be left to us, no questions asked, and the parents will not be held liable.

-She moved aside the blanket to show a baby's pale pink face surrounded by wisps of rose-colored hair. She seemed a tiny image of Byes. Chancer swallowed, knowing he could delay no longer. He had to decide whether to keep her or let her go. He could walk away like Byes had, have a life of his own, a future full of promise. Suddenly, he realized why he had been spared from the draft. He took a breath, locking eyes with Nurse Berry.

The baby is mine.

-She squinted at him.

Say again, Mister Wylls?

Her mother left a letter telling me where she had left her. I'm here to take her home.

-She clutched the baby.

Lord have mercy, Mister Wylls, you're barely a man yourself. How will care for this child?

I have family here and back home. I believe we can make it work.

Do they know of the child?

No, but they'll find out soon enough.

-Ben clasped his shoulder, peering into his eyes.

Are you sure about this, Chancer? Raising a kid is a big job.

-Chancer felt a surprising calm settle over him.

'Opportunities multiply as they are seized'.

That's Sun Tzu.

I'm sure about it, Ben.

He crept toward home, dodging bumps and potholes while the baby stirred in the seat beside him. He had no idea what he was going to do but cared little. Distant fireworks crackled out of the night as if celebrating her arrival. In a sudden moment, his future came to him as clear as the stars of Orion. After the initial shock, Gammie and Weesie would fall over themselves to help out. Franklin would make allowances as long as he did his part. And his parents would be so relieved he had avoided the draft without shaming the family, they would eventually warm up to the idea of him as a father.

He tried to imagine Byes at her parents' home, or perhaps with a grandmother, maybe an aunt, recuperating and preparing for the long flight into the Southern Hemisphere. In spite of all that had happened he wished her well. Neither of them was blameless. She had been right in saying the time had come to move on. He could almost hear Trewin's voice telling him to live life while he can. And so he would.

Chapter Thirty-four

The shock of learning I had been orphaned on a hospital doorstep had nearly worn off when Esther Schultz appeared at my kitchen window. She pointed toward the front door. A wave of anxiety passed over me. That she would seek me out when the office was closed for the holidays was more than enough reason for worry.

I set down a half-washed plate and headed for the door, trying to sort through possible explanations for her visit. She had just reached the top step when I stepped onto the porch. I motioned her to sit and took a chair opposite her.

I know we're supposed to be off work, Tegan. It's New Year's Eve, after all. But I do have good reason.

-Thinking the funds for my position had finally been cut, my heart sank.

I've lost my job, haven't I?

Lord, no. I wouldn't ruin your holiday with that sort of news. This is more of a request.

What sort of request?

Our beautiful girl wants to talk.

-That surprised me. Cheering had seemed alright the last time I had seen her.

What's it about, Esther? Has something happened?

I'd better let her tell you. She's waiting in my car now.

-Doubly surprised, I glanced toward the street.

She's here?

-Never one to waste time, she stood.

Should I send her in?

-I nodded and Esther disappeared down the steps. Moments later, Cheering stood before me, her face awash with emotion. She sat with her elbows on her knees, her eyes to the floor. After what seemed forever, she looked up at me.

I spent the last week visiting my father in Arizona.

-I tried to hide my surprise.

The last time we talked you weren't sure whether you wanted to see him.

He just showed up without telling anyone so I had to decide. My grandparents said okay and we flew back the next day.

How did it go?

Good, it went good. He asked me to come live with him, Tegan. I want to but…

-She stopped, unable to finish.

But something's keeping you from it?

-She nodded.

It's someone not something.

Have you told this person?

I'm afraid to.

Because…?

-She grabbed my hand, tears filling her eyes.

Because I'm afraid I'll be sad, Tegan. I'm afraid we'll both be. I don't want to never see you again.

-I peered into her face, fighting back tears of my own.

Partings are often sad, Cheering.

I'm tired of being sad.

Sadness is part of being human.

It is?

And it's part of saying goodbye to someone we care for.

Will you be sad too, Tegan?

I will.

I don't want you to be sad.

I won't be sad forever. We'll remember our time together and be glad for it.

-She wiped her eyes.

You won't forget me if I go live in Arizona, will you?

No, Cheering, I won't forget you.

-Glancing at her watch she jumped from the chair, her face changing as her thoughts turned to the future.

I have to go, Tegan. Dad is flying back this afternoon.

-I stood and she gave me a quick hug before rushing down the steps. As I watched her climb into Esther's car, my thoughts again turned to my own father. What I had learned from his almanac had forever changed my view of him, leaving me both humbled and proud. The picture of him I now held was less than pretty but it was real.

-That was Chancer's gift to me. Instead of a disheveled, absent-minded physicist, I found in his journal a complex man, flawed but essentially good. I would have never have known that part of him without it.

-I looked up as Pen and Beetie pulled to the curb. Behind them, Trewin had already climbed out of his ancient Saab and was ambling up the sidewalk. They had asked if I would join them in toasting Chancer, and they wanted to wish me a happy birthday.

-Beetie had made a fuss about it being New Year's Eve, promising they would stay only a short while, but I didn't mind. I had no plans. For some reason, I had never gotten around to making any even though I was about to turn thirty. Or perhaps I had avoided it. But now that the anniversary of my father's death had arrived, I wanted some company. Panting, my grandmother frowned as she reached the top step.

Tegan, did you ask Trewin to join us?

I assumed you told him.

No, I did not. As a matter of fact, I made a point of not inviting him.

But why do that, Beetie?

He has some harebrained scheme up his sleeve, I just know it. He gets all sweet and chatty when he's up to no good.

Maybe he's just enjoying life.

If you ask me, he manages to enjoy far too much, especially if it comes in a dress or a bottle.

-Trewin stepped onto the porch, lifting a bottle of wine from a paper bag.

Did someone say bottle? I just happen to have one here filled with nectar of the gods, otherwise known as zinfandel. That's Tegan's favorite if I'm not mistaken.

-Beetie squinted at him.

Do you see what I mean, Tegan? He's up to some no good thing, probably more of that pagan worship or whatever the devil it is.

The devil has nothing to do with the Four Directions. Have some respect for a man's spiritual life.

The only spirit you ever get near is eighty-proof.

-I stood between them, mocking my disapproval.

What were you saying about wine, Trewin?

Ah, yes, we have a toast to make then, don't we? Unless we want to pass it around, we'll need some glasses. Now, mind you, I'm not opposed to passing the bottle. There's a fine tradition of brown-bagging the rot gut. But a good wine deserves better, don't you think? We wouldn't want your neighbors deciding our family has no class.

-Beetie grumbled under her breath.

One of us already fits that description.

-Trewin held the wine up for me to see, bowing slightly.

No, no, don't get up Tegan. I'll do the honors.

-He disappeared into the house. Beetie snorted and turned to follow.

He probably thinks old jelly jars are just fine.

-I looked up at my grandfather.

Why does Beetie dislike him so much?

-He sat next to me.

Your grandmother loves Trewin.

She has a strange way of showing it.

Everyone has their own way of showing affection.

-I thought again of Chancer, never one to show his feelings.

I suppose that's true.

-Pen took my hand in his, blinking tears from his eyes.

And you know how much we love you?

Of course I do, Pen. What is it? Has something bad happened?

-He wiped them away with the back of his hand. I had never known another man as open with his feelings.

No, no, I was just thinking of your father. A parent should never outlive their child, Tegan.

I know it's been hard, Pen.

Hard for all of us, I'd say. Trewin says you've been asking about Chancer and your mother.

I just finished reading his journal and it's an eye-opener. Why did you never tell me my mother left me at a hospital?

Beetie would've told you. You know how black and white she can be. But I didn't want you to grow up hating your mother. We finally decided that knowing she left you was truth enough for a young girl. We trusted the rest to your father.

He never said a bad word about her.

He came to believe your mother truly loved you but was too restless and headstrong to raise a child properly, and to her credit knew it. He saw her decision to leave you as a brave act, and doubly brave because she took you to the hospital instead of dumping you on him.

Well, he knew her better than any of us. I'm surprised to say it, but I'd like to meet her someday. Of course, the odds against it ever happening are huge but still…

-I left it at that. Pen squeezed my hand.

You never know what the future might have in store. Perhaps you'll meet her after all.

-The screen door flew open and Trewin strode onto the porch, setting four glasses on a small stool and pouring the wine with great flair. He raised his glass, a solemn look on his face. We took our glasses and did the same.

Here's to the memory of our Chancer, truly one of a kind.

-Beetie chimed in before we had even lowered our glasses.

And to the happier days that lay ahead for our thirty year old granddaughter.

-Trewin nearly choked on his wine.

Good God, Beetie, can she be that old already? Are you sure? Your math skills have never been up to snuff.

Of course I'm sure. I was there the day Chancer brought her home. I remember it like yesterday, all of us in Gammie's kitchen taking turns holding her, Chancer looking proud but scared out of his wits, Weesie making some of her homemade baby formula.

-I jumped from my chair.

If you're going to start telling baby stories, I'm leaving.

But you were so…

I mean it, Beetie!

-Trewin took my arm and raised his glass.

If you'll come with me I have just the cure.

-We drained our glasses and he led me down the stairs and onto the lawn, moving beside me.

If I'm not mistaken, we're facing north.

That's right, Trewin.

-Beetie called to us from the porch.

You're not going to do that pagan ritual of yours again, are you? The neighbors really will think we've gone over the edge.

-Trewin spoke from the side of his mouth.

Pay her no mind, Tegan. Rituals have great power. Just do as I do and you'll soon feel transformed.

-We raised our arms over our heads as he turned each of the four directions, calling out a chant for each. Repeating the words to myself, I followed his lead.

North provides us with logic and reason, east gives us hope, and the south brings comfort. Most important of all, west is the home of those no longer with us.

-I stared at the western horizon, silently sending my love to Chancer. Though I missed him more than I could say, I sensed the pull of my current life even at that moment. A year had passed but there was no pause in the circle of time.

-Trewin faced me, pulling an envelope from his pocket and pressing it into my palm. I looked from him to my hand and on to the porch where Pen and Beetie stood watching us. She motioned me to open the letter so I opened the flap, lifting out a roundtrip ticket to Australia. Before my mind could accept what my eyes were seeing, Pen called out to me.

Your grandmother wants you to promise you'll come back to us, sweetheart.

-I managed a nod as I stared at them in disbelief.

But how can you… it must cost…

-He waved off my concern.

Nonsense, Tegan, we all pitched in.

-Beetie climbed halfway down the stairs, her face dark with worry.

Now, you don't have to go if you don't want to, sugar.

I do want to go, Beetie.

But what if she's as bad a person as I fear she is.

Then I'll know.

-Trewin took my hand.

That's the spirit, Tegan. It's high time you met your mother. She's looking forward to your visit.

-Shocked, I looked from him to my grandparents.

She knows? But how did you find her?

-Beetie pursed her lips.

As much as I hate to admit it, this is all Trewin's doing, the rascal. He found her and then convinced us you needed to go see her. I suppose even a rake like him can have a good idea every now and then.

-A wave of tears filled my eyes as I turned back to him. He pressed a handkerchief into my hand and leaned close, whispering into my ear.

You've honored your past, now it's time to meet your future.

-Half an hour later I stood on the sidewalk, watching as my grandparents' car and Trewin's creaking Saab pulled from the curb and disappeared around the corner. An instant later, Vincent's voice called from behind me, and I turned to find him ambling along in a pair of strange-looking sunglasses. He stopped and tapped them with his finger.

How do you like my new eyes, Tegan?

They're very stylish.

I've volunteered to test a new prototype for low vision glasses. They hope someday to develop an implant that teaches you to see using digital signals. It's very experimental so I'm afraid to hope for much.

Then I'll hope for you.

Actually, I didn't come over here to show them off. I came to invite you over for a glass of wine before you head out to wherever you're going tonight. Please say you'll stop by, Tegan. Celia will be there.

-I looked at him askance.

You mean Celia, as in Diego's mother?

Do you know many others?

Vincent, are you telling me you're dating her?

Don't act so surprised, Tegan. She's a beautiful woman and, thanks to you, we were thrown together. Now we've become close friends.

Close as in very close?

That's all you need to know, Tegan the Nosy. So, will you come?

Will Claude be there?

-I had gotten past my anger at Claude, unsure who was more to blame for our falling out, him or me. I found myself wishing we could be friends again. Vincent blinked through the thick lenses.

I'll tell him to leave.

Don't do that, Vincent. It's his home too. Besides, I wouldn't mind seeing him.

-He squinted at me as a smile moved across his lips.

Tegan, you do surprise me. Actually, he's been driving me crazy asking about you.

Has he? Well then, I guess I'll have to come.

***

A week later I stepped from my Adelaide hotel into the brilliant summer sunlight of South Australia. Red gum trees towered above me. Across the street a broad park bisected by a wide gravel path stretched into the distance. Couples strolled beneath a purple umbrella of flowering jacarandas.

Crossing the intersection, I made my way toward the walkway. I stopped to watch a flock of pink galahs circling overhead. Below them, midway along the path, a woman stood facing me, a windblown mane of auburn hair framing her pale face. Taking a breath, I started toward her.

www.ingramcontent.com/pod-product-compliance
Lightning Source LLC
Chambersburg PA
CBHW020234180626
46810CB00006B/2192